AIR WITCH

BOOK THREE OF THE FRONTIER WITCHES

ANNETTE GRANTHAM

RAVENOUS SQUIRRELS PRESS

For my daughter, Jennifer, and her dear cat, Juniper, who passed too young and had the spirit of a raccoon.

CHAPTER ONE

THE NOISES OF THE market surrounded fifteen-year-old Gemma like a crashing wave. Vendors yelled their offers, their rough voices blending into a loud, confusing noise. Laughter and shouts mixed with the bleating of animals as people moved through Manorhamilton's narrow streets. Different smells fought for her attention—the yeasty smell of fresh bread, the earthy scent of mud, and the musk of animal pens.

Gemma tightened her fingers around the tasseled edge of her shawl until her knuckles showed bone-white. Her chest had a tightness, as though an invisible hand was constricting the air from her lungs.

This place was unlike her serene valley and cave home, where she had lived for fourteen years. There, she could hear the softest murmur of the wind or the splash of water against the rocky lakeshore with pristine clarity. Here, a thousand overlapping sounds flooded her senses until her head spun.

She jumped when a heavy hand grabbed her shoulder. "I'm here, lamb," said her great-aunt Lillian. Gemma leaned gently into the older woman's calming presence.

As they hurried forward, the crowd flowed around them like water in a busy ocean. People moved past, bumping Gemma again and again. Elbows jabbed her with quick apologies before fading into the chaos. Even among so many, she felt alone. Eyes never rested on her. No warmth at all—just brief looks of confusion, fun, joy, or frustration.

Colorful tents hung above the market, casting lively patches of light on the crowded paths. One tent was bright red, changing to yellow, then deep purple. These palettes danced over rugs and patterned fabrics until Gemma felt lost in the swirling sea of colors.

Children ran through the crowd, their shrill cries carrying ahead of them. A young boy, all elbows and tousled hair, dodged around Gemma like a woodland creature before disappearing again. An older girl balanced a basket of fresh greens on her shoulder, her steady stride unbroken even as people jostled her. She looked content, her chin lifted in casual vigilance.

Despite the constant noise and movement, Gemma found herself drawn to the simple marvels unfolding around her. A butcher carved glistening cuts of meat with the confidence of a performer, each slice precise and fluid. A young wife inspected bolts of cloth, the weave's texture and colors speaking unspoken meaning that hinted at a rich tradition. Two farmers laughed over worn-out jokes as they exchanged coins for firkins of ale, their friendship needing no formal words.

The weft and warp of daily life for others appeared extraordinary to her. The beauty in their traditions, an elegant rhythm, reminded her of the dances of birds in flight or animals on the hunt.

Lillian moved through the throng like the bow of a stately ship cutting through turbulent waters. Her snow-white bun crowned her head, stray wisps escaping to frame her features.

"Keep close, Gemma." Lillian's whisper carried enough authority to slice through the surrounding racket.

Gemma tightened her grip on the soft linen of her skirts. The explosion of sights, sounds, and scents threatened to overwhelm her. Golden, honeyed crust loaves sat beside piles of ripe produce—cabbages, beets, carrots that gleamed like gemstones. The smells of anise and ginger mingled amongst the warm aroma of bread, fresh-turned soil, and the musky scent of livestock.

Gemma swayed, unable to focus on any one thing for more than a dizzying second. Her chest heavy, struggled to draw breath from the spice-laden air. Heat bloomed across her neck, and her palms grew slick beneath her shawl.

Lillian's arm wrapped around her shoulders, the comforting weight steadying her. The older woman's gaze softened as she found Gemma's panicked eyes.

"Breathe, child," Lillian said, her thumb tracing a gentle arc over Gemma's knuckles. "This is life—busy and loud and always changing. It's not like our quiet cave, but there's magick here too, if you know where to look."

Gemma closed her eyes, seeking refuge from the dizzying chaos. She listened, focusing on each noise until they made sense. The lowing of cattle from a nearby pen. A sharp clang of a tinker hammering a pot. The gentle lilt of a mother haggling over a bundle of carrots. She took each sound in, one by one, until they formed a melody.

A sudden blast of salty ocean air startled her. She traced the scent to a fishmonger loudly promoting his morning's catch; leathery sheets of kelp and fresh fish laid out on slabs. Behind him, a peddler shouted about his iron and copper wares, each clang of his hammer sending a shiver through Gemma's bones.

Amid the clamor, Gemma spotted a tiny herb stall untouched by the surrounding chaos. An old woman sat there, her wrinkled face calm, her hands moving tenderly over bundles of lavender, thyme, rosemary, and mint. The sight of the herbs pulled Gemma closer, the soothing scents helping her find her balance.

The shopkeeper looked up, her gaze sharp and knowing. Lillian spoke first. "Maeve, show Gemma your finest herbs. She has a talent for the craft."

Maeve's eyes widened, and her lips curved into a smile that deepened the lines on her face. She reached beneath the counter and brought out a sprig of thyme, holding it out to Gemma. Gemma took it, feeling a warmth from the herb, almost like it was alive.

"For protection," Maeve said, barely a whisper. "And maybe a bit of courage, too."

Gemma closed her fingers around the thyme, breathing in its scent. Simple, but powerful. Something shifted inside her.

They moved from the stall, and Lillian spoke again, softer. "To live fully, you need to engage with the world. Hiding away won't work—not for someone like you."

Gemma thought of her powers, the ones she had tried to suppress. She had always feared them, concerned by what they could do. But now, as the thyme's scent grounded her, she questioned the apprehension.

She nodded slowly. She glanced back at Maeve, who laughed with a young mother, the two of them sharing a simple joy. What if she could be part of that, too?

She looked at the sprig of thyme, its aroma still strong. Its understated fragrance eased her last doubts before it ignited her inner resilience.

Grounded.

Emboldened.

Resolved to live a normal life like the people in town. Another steadying breath filled her lungs to capacity. Gemma lifted her chin with renewed determination and forged ahead into the surging heart of the teeming marketplace.

Lillian and Gemma walked down the narrow winding path toward the secluded farm. The late afternoon sun bathed the landscape in soft, golden light, casting long shadows across the earth like gentle fingers. The farm looked modest and worn, but in this light, it was almost magical. To Gemma, it could be a place where new beginnings might grow, a stark contrast to the dark, confining cave she had known for so long.

As they got closer, they heard the sounds of life on the farm—chickens clucking in their coop, the distant mooing of a cow, and the occasional bark of a dog. The smell of freshly turned soil mixed with hay and the faint aroma of cooking food gave the place a sense of warmth and home. Despite its humble look, the farm appeared hopeful to Gemma.

The farmer and his wife stood at the gate. Years of hard work and surviving the famine years ago lined their faces, but their eyes held a spark of optimism. The farmer had broad shoulders, calloused hands, and a sun-weathered face. His wife had a gentle manner, her hair tied back in a simple kerchief. She held a quiet infant against her chest while a lively toddler bounced at her feet, full of energy and curiosity.

Lillian stepped forward first and introduced herself and Gemma. "This is my niece, Gemma," she said warmly, her tone steady. "We've come to see how she does with your little ones." She turned to Gemma. "This is Patrick and Johanna."

Gemma smiled and bowed her head. "Hello. Nice to meet you."

Johanna replied, "We are glad you came." She held her toddler's hand up. "This is Conner. And the babe is Sean."

Lillian's eyes met Gemma's, sending her a silent plea for understanding and encouragement. This visit was more than a test of Gemma's abilities—it was a chance for her to find a lifeline, a way to anchor herself to something real and far from the isolation that had shaped her life until now.

Gemma hesitated for a moment before kneeling beside John, who looked up at her, eyes wide and curious. The child was so full of life; she moved cautiously, unsure of how to interact. But when she reached out, Conner giggled, grabbing at her fingers with tiny, chubby hands. A smile tugged at Gemma's lips, and she relaxed. Her actions grew more natural and confident as she amused the child, whose laughter bridged the gap.

Encouraged by the toddler's response, Gemma turned her attention to the now fussy infant in the mother's arms. "Can I hold your baby?"

Johanna hesitated before handing the bundle to Gemma. As she cradled him, small, soft, and warm, a sense of peace washed over her. She hummed a lullaby—one Lillian had sung to her long ago. Sean, who had been fussing moments before, quieted under her care, his tiny fists unclenching as he settled into the comforting rhythm.

Gemma glanced at the farmer and his wife, noticing the way they exchanged a look. Patrick's furrowed brow eased, and the tension in Johanna's shoulders softened. Gemma heard their doubt fading, as if her caring for their children had shown them something they needed. She knew not to reveal her gift of reading thoughts and worried how long she could conceal her gifts.

Lillian broke the comfortable silence. "Your journey to America is a new start—not only for you, but for Gemma as well."

The couple nodded, the weight of their upcoming journey clear in their expressions. Patrick cleared his throat. "Yes, it's a big step... for all of us," he said, his gaze drifting from Gemma to his children and back again.

Lillian took a deep breath, steadying herself. "I'm not going to make it through the winter," she said, emotion threatening to break through. "And Gemma... she shouldn't be left alone. I fear she'd end up like her mother, caught in a cycle of despair. She deserves more. I want her to have a family, a chance to be part of something better."

Johanna glanced at Gemma. "She's good with the children," she said. "We can see that. And we do need the help, especially with the move. She could be part of our family, if she's willing. But you have to pay for her ticket and food. We can't afford another mouth to feed."

Lillian nodded. "Of course."

Gemma's fingers twisted in the fabric of her skirt, her breath shallow. She lifted her gaze to meet Lillian's, her throat tightening. The idea of leaving everything she had ever known—no matter how lonely—for a new life in a faraway place scared her. Yet, the warmth of the family in front of her and the possibility of belonging tugged at her heart.

Patrick stepped forward. "We'll take her," he said firmly. "She'll be a big sister to these two, and, God willing, we'll find our footing in a new land."

Tears welled in Lillian's eyes as she nodded. She reached out to Johanna, her hand trembling as she rested it on the woman's arm. "Thank you," she said, choking with emotion. "Thank you."

Johanna smiled, her eyes meeting Gemma's with a warmth that made Gemma's heart lift a little. "We'll take good care of you," she said. Gemma heard the sincerity in her words, as if this promise was more than just spoken—it was something the woman truly meant.

As the evening light faded, the small group lingered, exchanging last words and making tentative plans for the coming days. The promise of a new life in America loomed large—a challenge and opportunity rolled into one.

As they prepared to leave, Gemma turned to Lillian, her eyes searching the older woman's face. "Is this really what you want for me?" she said.

Lillian placed both hands on Gemma's shoulders, pulling her close until their foreheads almost touched. "I want you to live, Gemma," she said. "I want you to have a chance to be part of something bigger. To be happy. To be free."

Gemma swallowed hard, the lump in her throat making it hard to speak. "I'm scared," she said.

"I know," Lillian said, her tone softening. "But you're stronger than you think. And you won't be alone. These people, they'll be your family now. And you'll always carry a piece of me with you, no matter where you go."

Gemma's last bit of resistance crumbled. She leaned into Lillian's embrace, letting her great-aunt's warmth and comfort push away the fear that had taken root in her heart.

CHAPTER TWO

GEMMA'S HEART POUNDED AS she walked along the path, leaving behind the only home she had ever known. The cool morning air stung her skin, each gust reminding her of the journey ahead. Lillian walked beside her, steady and strong, but Gemma could sense the heaviness of the moment between them.

The couple taking Gemma to America hurried to finish their preparations, loading the last of their things onto the creaking cart. The wooden frame groaned under the weight of their belongings, echoing the heaviness in Gemma's heart.

Gemma climbed into the back of the wagon, holding Sean close to her chest. The baby's warmth seeped through the blankets, offering her a bit of comfort. Beside her, Conner clung to the edge of the cart, his small fingers tight, much like Gemma's grip on her own—resolve. Her stomach twisted, and her jaw clenched.

Lillian walked over, her footsteps slow and deliberate. She stopped by the wagon, her eyes meeting Gemma's, and the intensity of her gaze made Gemma's breath catch. Lillian's eyes held so much—sorrow, pride, and love. It all crashed over Gemma, threatening to overwhelm her.

"Gemma, my dear," Lillian said, choked with emotion. "You're about to start a journey that will change you in ways you can't understand yet. Be brave, be kind, and remember, you already have the strength you need."

Tears welled up in Gemma's eyes, and she nodded, trying to hold on to Lillian's words like a lifeline. "I won't let you down," she said, barely louder than the rustling breeze. It was a promise to herself as much as it was to Lillian.

Lillian reached out, her fingers gently brushing the infant's cheek, drawing a soft coo. She ruffled the toddler's hair, her touch full of warmth. "Take care of them, Gemma. They are yours now, and they are your companions in this new world."

The couple exchanged a glance, mirroring set jaws and pressed lips. The man climbed onto the wagon, taking the reins in his calloused hands, while his wife settled beside him. Lillian stepped back, her form growing smaller as the cart moved. Gemma watched her until the bend in the road swallowed her from view.

The journey to Liverpool stretched out before them, the landscape blurring as each mile took Gemma far from everything she knew. Sensing the change, Conner nestled closer to her. Gemma wrapped her arm around him, embracing the new sense of purpose.

When they reached Liverpool, the city overwhelmed Gemma. The port was a whirlwind of noise, smells, and people, unlike anything she had ever experienced. The stench of salt, fish, and unwashed bodies filled the air, and she fought the urge to gag.

The ship loomed ahead, its dark hull towering over them. The couple led the way up the gangplank, their steps sure. Gemma followed, her legs trembling, the weight of the infant grounding her.

Below deck, the cramped, dimly lit space smelled of despair mixed with hope. The bunks, nothing more than rough wooden planks, offered no privacy. Gemma found a small corner for herself and the children, carefully placing their few belongings around them like a nest in the chaos.

Life was raw. Families huddled close, holding on to each other for comfort. Old men shared stories, their voices blending with the creaks of the ship. Children laughed and played, their joy a bright contrast to the adults' somber mood. Gemma pleaded silently to Danu, the goddess of wisdom, to help her shut out all her shipmates' thoughts, to give her peace.

Gemma moved among the passengers, helping where she could. She played simple games with the children, their laughter lifting her spirits. She listened to the old men as they spoke of Ireland, their words painting pictures of places she had never seen. One evening, she helped a mother soothe her crying baby, rocking the child gently until he fell asleep. In these small acts, Gemma connected with the others, their shared struggles binding them together.

One day, Gemma slipped away onto the deck for a moment of quiet solitude. She gripped the railing, watching the horizon swallow her homeland. The sea stretched endlessly, both terrifying and beautiful. The wind tugged at her hair, and Lillian's words echoed in her mind, urging her to be brave.

Back below deck, the ship rocked steadily, and Gemma moved among the other passengers, building connections. They shared stories of their struggles, and she saw her own fears and hopes reflected in their eyes. Each day, as she cared for the children and faced the challenges of ship life, she noticed a change within herself. The timid girl who had once hid away now found her strength.

Gemma wove her own story—one of resilience and courage. The fear that once gripped her loosened its hold, replaced by a growing determination to not only survive, but to thrive in this new world.

As the ship sailed toward America, Gemma looked ahead, her heart filled with both fear and hope. She was no longer the frightened girl clinging to the past. She was becoming a young woman, finding her place in the world.

The ship rocked as another wave struck the hull, the sea's sound a constant murmur. Gemma kneeled on the hard wooden floor of the ship's hold, her knees aching. Sean lay on a bed made of blankets and coats, but it did little to soften the unforgiving surface. Gemma's worn leather satchel spread open beside her, its contents scattered around as she searched for anything that could help.

Sean let out a weak cry, and Gemma's heart clenched. She turned back to the bag, her hands trembling as she rummaged through it. Bottles clinked together, dried herbs crinkled under her touch, and small cloth packets slipped through her fingers. Lavender oil, chamomile—nothing had worked so far.

"Please, there must be something," she said, barely audible over the ship's creaks and the muffled sounds of other passengers. She pulled out a small envelope of crushed yarrow leaves, her last hope. Her breath shaky, she opened the packet and sprinkled the yarrow into a tin cup of lukewarm water. She stirred it, whispering a silent prayer, her chest tight.

Gemma leaned over the infant, lifting his head and helping him sip from the cup. Sean's lips parted, and he swallowed weakly. Behind her, Johanna stepped closer, her eyes fixed on every movement. Her face, showing signs of exhaustion, softened as she witnessed her baby's attempt to drink.

"Will that help him?" she asked, barely more than a whisper.

Gemma glanced up, her expression uncertain but determined. "I'm trying everything I know," she said, her heart pounding. She caught the unspoken fear radiating from Johanna's mind, the worry circling around her own safety and the possibility that Sean's ailment might spread to her. She couldn't bring herself to meet the mother's eyes. Instead, she directed her attention to Sean, looking for any sign of improvement.

Patrick hovered nearby, his hand resting on his wife's shoulder as they both looked on, waiting, hoping. His brow furrowed deeper with each passing moment, matching the growing dread in Gemma's chest.

The gathered crowd remained in a reverent silence, their breath held, as they witnessed the small, fragile form of the infant battling for every shallow breath in the ship's hold. The air was thick with anticipation and dread, every creak of the ship's timbers and slap of the waves against the hull punctuating the gravity of the moment.

Gemma, her hands trembling as they cradled Sean, felt each labored breath like a physical pain in her own chest. Her eyes, red from tears and fatigue, never left the tiny, pale face of the child, willing him with all her might to keep fighting. On the other end of the bunk, Johanna sat vigil; her face a mask of controlled despair.

Suddenly, there was a change. Sean's chest, which had been rising and falling with increasing difficulty, stilled. A soft gasp escaped

Gemma's lips, a sound so faint it was almost swallowed by the surrounding quiet.

The silence that followed was complete and devastating. It was as if the entire world had paused. The air in the hold carried the finality of the moment. Gemma's heart thudded painfully in her chest, her eyes fixed on the now-still infant, unable to believe that he was gone.

A stifled sob broke the silence, the sound raw and gut-wrenching. It came from Johanna, who allowed her grief to surface in a wave of suppressed sobs. Her body shook as she cradled her head in her hands, her whole being radiating profound loss.

Patrick, his face stoic throughout the ordeal, allowed a single tear to escape, tracing a slow path down his cheek. He reached out, his hand trembling as he placed it on Johanna's shoulder, a silent gesture of shared sorrow.

Around them, the crowd dispersed, their soft footsteps and whispered condolences a background murmur to the intimate tragedy unfolding. They left Gemma and the family alone with their grief, a respectful distance allowing them the space to mourn.

Gemma remained still, Sean's body light in her arms, a devastating weight on her soul. The eerie calm that had descended was broken only by the mother's quiet weeping and the distant, haunting sounds of the sea.

Gemma felt a profound loneliness, a sense of helplessness almost unbearable. She had wanted to save this child, to prove her worth and her skills, but in the end, it reminded her of the harsh limits of her abilities. The finality of death, so definitive and cruel, left her feeling empty and defeated, her spirit as dark and tumultuous as the ocean that carried them toward a new but uncertain future.

Gemma laid Sean on her bunk. Her hands shook as she reached for a piece of soft cloth—a shawl that had once kept her warm on chilly nights. She spread it open, her fingers pausing for a moment as she gathered her strength. Then, with a deep breath, she wrapped him. Each fold was tender, each movement a final goodbye.

Johanna, her eyes tearful, watched while Patrick stood beside her, his arm around her shoulders. The silence between them was heavy, filled with a sadness too deep for words.

Gemma whispered a lullaby, the same one she had sung to Sean in his first days on the ship. The melody was soft, mournful, echoing in the dim hold.

Gemma stepped back after she secured the final fold, her eyes lingering on the small, wrapped form. It looked peaceful, like he was only sleeping. She turned to the parents, whispering. "He's ready."

Patrick nodded, his face grim but grateful. He lifted the tiny bundle, his hands rough but gentle. Together, they moved toward the deck, their steps slow and heavy.

As they stepped onto the deck, the sun cast a golden light over them. The three of them stood in silence, the infant cradled in his father's arms. Johanna leaned into her husband, her hand resting on the tiny bundle, not wanting to let go.

The group gathered on the ship's deck, quiet under the weight of their grief. Soft sobs and whispered prayers mixed with the wind that swept over them. The ship rocked on the waves, insignificant and fragile against the vast, indifferent ocean.

Gemma stood a little away from the grieving parents, her eyes swollen from tears that still threatened to fall. Patrick held the small, wrapped body of their baby close to his chest, his face tight with pain. His arms shook, and beside him, Johanna clutched his arm; her knuckles white as she leaned on him for support. Her face looked pale, her eyes hollow with sorrow.

Patrick took a deep, shuddering breath before he stepped forward to the ship's railing, holding the baby above the dark water. The deck fell silent, even the usual creaks of the ship fading away, as if everything held its breath. He whispered something, his voice lost to the wind, then lowered the baby into the sea.

The bundle slipped from his hands, falling into the water. For a moment, the cloth fluttered like a white bird before the waves swallowed it. Johanna gasped, her hand covering her mouth as she watched it disappear. Her eyes stayed fixed on the spot, as if trying to hold on to her child. Patrick pulled her close, tears glistening in his eyes, though he refused to let them fall.

Around them, the crew and passengers stood in silence. Some crossed themselves, others bowed their heads. The sense of loss hung heavy, drawing them together, strangers now united in their shared sorrow.

Gemma stood by the railing, gazing at the horizon where the sea met the sky. The wind tugged at her hair, and salt stung her eyes, though she wasn't sure if it was the wind or more tears. A hollow ache settled in her chest, the pain of knowing she hadn't been able to save the baby. It was a weight she knew she would carry, no matter how far they traveled.

She turned away and saw Conner standing alone, a few steps away. His small face was full of confusion, his eyes wide as he looked for

Sean. He reached out, his tiny hand trembling as he tried to find his mother, who still stared at the sea. Gemma's heart twisted at the sight. His thoughts whispered of fear and isolation from his mother, a raw ache that intertwined with her own, pulling at the edges of her mind.

Gemma stepped forward, scooping Conner into her arms. He trembled against her, pressing his face into her shoulder, seeking the comfort he needed. She held him close, feeling his small heartbeat, a reminder of the life that still required her care.

She hugged Conner tighter, her resolve hardening. He needed her now. She leaned down, whispering in his ear. "We'll get through this, little one. Together."

Johanna turned, her eyes catching sight of Gemma holding her son. For a moment, a flicker of gratitude crossed Johanna's face—a small spark amid the sorrow, but beneath it, Gemma caught the sharp sting of buried blame. Johanna's thoughts churned, tangled between the grief of her loss and the unspoken accusation that Gemma's presence, her otherness, had somehow brought this tragedy upon them.

Gemma met Patrick's gaze over the boy's head. He gave her a small nod, but his thoughts pressed against her mind, raw and heavy—anger at the unfairness of it all and the quiet, gnawing guilt of failing to protect his son.

As the ship sailed toward their new life, Gemma stood by the railing, the toddler in her arms, watching the waves. The journey would be hard, and the memories of what they had lost would stay with them. But Gemma also knew that strength could come from pain—that they could still find hope, even in the darkest moments.

She thought of Sean, the brief life that had touched hers. She said, "I will protect your brother. I will be braver, kinder, and always hold on to hope."

CHAPTER THREE

As THE SHIP ROCKED into the busy docks of Ellis Island, Gemma gripped Conner's hand tighter, her heart pounding. The Statue of Liberty faded behind them, replaced by the noisy, crowded harbor. Voices in languages she didn't recognize—Italian, Russian, Polish—filled the air. It felt like being caught in a storm of sounds, and each unfamiliar word made her seem smaller, more lost.

The wooden planks of the dock creaked beneath hundreds of shuffling feet. Officials barked orders, herding the passengers like cattle. "Move along! Keep the line moving!" they shouted. Gemma flinched with each command, her anxiety growing.

Stepping onto solid ground made Gemma's legs shaky. Johanna, usually so composed, stopped and stared back at the statue. Her shoulders slumped, and her gaze fixed on the symbol of hope. She stood frozen, tears welling.

Patrick hurried to her side, touching her back. "Johanna, we need to keep moving, love. For Conner," he whispered. His eyes looked at Gemma, seeking her help.

Gemma stepped closer, Conner holding tight to her. "Johanna, we'll take care of each other now," she said, even though fear churned inside her. She touched Johanna's arm, hoping to break through the grief.

Johanna blinked, her distant gaze turning toward them. She looked at Conner, his small face searching for his mother's comfort. She took a deep breath, wiping her eyes, and nodded. Patrick took her hand, and they moved forward again, inching through the crowd.

Around them, parents called for missing children. Families searched for loved ones. The smell of salt and sweat filled Gemma's nose, a reminder of how different this place was.

The family shuffled towards the great hall of processing which swallowed them, people pressed close from every direction. Inside, officials called out names and numbers, directing people to different lines. One young man was separated from his family, and his mother's wails echoed through the crowded hall. Gemma's chest tightened, her own fears amplified by the scene.

When they cleared the last checkpoint, they stepped into New York City. The towering buildings leaned over them, making Gemma feel trapped all over again. She glanced at Patrick and Johanna, their faces tired but determined. They had made it this far, but it was only the beginning.

A train whistle blew in the distance, and Gemma followed Patrick as he led them towards the next step of their journey. Conner's tiny hand in hers gave her a purpose, a focus amid the chaos.

The train was packed with people, everyone trying to find seats. Patrick found a pair near the back, but there weren't enough for all of them to sit together. Johanna shook her head. "I'll sit alone," she said, low but firm.

Patrick's face tightened. "Johanna, please. We need to stay together. Conner needs you."

"I need space," Johanna whispered, her eyes distant.

Patrick sighed and nodded, leading her to a seat by the window. He touched her shoulder before walking back to Gemma. He tried to smile at Conner, but sadness weighed it down. "She just needs some time," he mumbled.

Gemma nodded, though worry gnawed at her. She watched Johanna stare out the window, her grief a wall separating her from them. Gemma looked at Conner, who clung to her, confused and scared. She smiled at him, hoping to ease his fears.

"Would you like to hear a story, Conner?" she asked.

Conner's eyes lit up, and he nodded. Gemma leaned in, dropping to a soft, storytelling tone. "Once, in a place called Ireland, there were fairies who danced in the moonlight..." She watched as Conner's eyes widened, his fear fading into curiosity.

Gemma pulled a small, worn cloth from her bag, showing him a simple drawing of a leprechaun. "These little ones hide their gold at the end of rainbows. You have to be clever to find it," she said, tapping his nose.

Conner giggled, his laughter lifting the heaviness. Gemma taught him a game—a series of claps and taps that went along with her story. As they played, the tension eased, their laughter blending with the rhythmic clacking of the train.

"More, Gemma, more!" Conner urged, his eyes bright.

Gemma laughed. "Alright, but only if you promise to help me find the leprechaun's gold," she teased.

They continued, and as the train rumbled west, something changed inside Gemma. Conner's laughter gave her strength. She wasn't just a passenger; she was his protector, his family.

Hours later, as the train neared Missoula, the passengers talked about life in the West. An old man across the aisle spoke of hard work and hope. "The land's tough," he said, "but it can be good if you're willing to work."

Gemma listened, her heart torn between fear and determination. Could they find their place here?

When they stepped off the train, the cool air of Montana wrapped around them. Conner looked at her, his small voice full of innocence. "Are we going to be alright, Gemma?"

She bent down, squeezing his hand. "Yes, Conner. We'll be alright," she promised, though uncertainty still twisted inside her.

Early in the morning, Gemma moved quietly through the small house in Missoula. The wooden floor creaked under her careful steps as she made her way to the kitchen, the soft light of dawn peeking through the old curtains. Beside her makeshift bed, Conner slept peacefully, curled up in his nest of blankets. Gemma paused for a moment, her heart swelling with a deep protectiveness as she watched him.

She turned back to the kitchen, gathering ingredients for a simple breakfast. Her hands moved quickly and skillfully. The stove hissed softly as she lit it, almost drowned out by Conner's gentle breathing.

She cracked eggs into a pan, and the yolks sizzled as they hit the hot surface, the smell filling the small room.

The door to the parents' room creaked open, and Patrick stepped out. His face looked tired, worn from yesterday's long hours. He gave Gemma a small smile, then walked over and rested a hand on her shoulder. "Morning, Gemma," he whispered, his voice rough.

Gemma smiled back, warmth spreading through her chest at his appreciation. But when Johanna entered the kitchen a moment later, the mood shifted. Johanna's eyes were red, shadowed by sadness that still hadn't lifted. She didn't say a word, just moved to pour herself a cup of coffee, her expression hardening as she glanced at Gemma.

Gemma felt Johanna's stony gaze like a slap, her unspoken thoughts cutting deeper—blame for what had happened and bitter regret for ever taking Gemma with them. She turned her focus back to the eggs, flipping them over with more force than needed. The room filled with the smells of cooking, but the silence between them felt thick and heavy.

Patrick lingered, shuffling his feet as if unsure of what to say. "I'll just grab some bread and head out," he finally muttered, breaking the quiet. His weary thoughts lingered in Gemma's mind, heavy with the grind of simply enduring—pushing through another day with Johanna's cold distance and the relentless toil waiting at the mine.

"Hope the mine treats you well today," Gemma said, trying to fill the silence.

"Thanks, Gemma. Take care of our boy," he replied, giving her a weak smile before stepping out into the cool morning mist.

As the door closed behind Patrick, Gemma glanced at Johanna, who had settled stiffly at the table, staring at the wall. The tension hung in the air, a reminder of everything left unsaid.

"Patrick works so hard for us," Gemma said, her voice gentle as she tried to connect. "He always has a smile for Conner, even after a long day."

Johanna didn't respond right away. Her eyes shifted slowly to Gemma, her gaze sharp. "We all do what we must," she said, her voice flat. "Some of us better than others."

The words stung, cutting deep. Gemma looked down at her hands, gripping the spatula tightly. She took a shaky breath, her voice barely above a whisper. "I'm trying my best."

Johanna snorted, turning away. She busied herself at the sink, her movements curt, ending the conversation. The rejection left Gemma feeling hollow, the space between them even wider.

Conner's laughter broke the silence, echoing from the other room. Gemma let out a sigh of relief, grateful for an excuse to leave. She walked to Conner and lifted him into her arms, his giggles like music to her ears. She spun him around once, his laughter bubbling, and for a moment, it felt like they were a real family—one held together by love, not just circumstance. But Johanna's coldness lingered, a shadow over the warmth of the moment.

Outside in the small backyard, enclosed by a shaky old fence, Gemma tried to create some happiness. She gathered stones and made a ring on the ground, her voice cheerful as she explained to Conner, "This is a fairy ring. Fairies come here to dance, but only if we make it just right." Conner's eyes widened with excitement, and he eagerly grabbed a stone, placing it in the circle.

"Very good!" Gemma clapped, smiling as Conner laughed. They hunted for leaves and sticks, adding them to the ring, each one a "treasure" Conner found. The game filled the morning with joy, and for a little while, Gemma forgot the sadness in the house.

"Now we need a leaf big enough to be a fairy's boat," Gemma said, crouching down and pretending to search carefully. Conner copied her, his face serious as he looked for the perfect leaf.

When they found one, they set it to float in a shallow pan of water. Conner clapped, his face lighting up with pure delight. Gemma scooped him into her arms, spinning around as his laughter filled the air. "You're my brave little explorer," she whispered, her heart full as she hugged him.

But as they headed back inside, Gemma felt the weight of her responsibilities settle on her shoulders again. The house waited—filled with Johanna's grief and cold distance. Still, the laughter and smiles from their morning play gave her strength. No matter how tough things got, she would be Conner's light.

In the kitchen, the atmosphere turned tense again as Johanna prepared for her shift at the restaurant. Gemma watched as Johanna gathered her things, and she took a deep breath, stepping forward. "Can I help you with anything before you leave?" she asked, her voice steady.

Johanna paused, her eyes flicking to Gemma's outstretched hand, holding her coat. "I can manage, thank you," she said, her tone clipped and eyes distant.

Gemma's arm fell slowly to her side, her offer hanging in the air, unaccepted. She forced herself not to react, just nodded and stepped back. Johanna's coldness was a wall Gemma couldn't climb, no matter how hard she tried.

"Hope your shift goes well," Gemma said quietly as Johanna put on her coat.

Johanna gave a small shrug, not meeting Gemma's eyes. She opened the door and stepped outside, letting it close behind her with a soft click that echoed too loudly. Gemma stood still for a moment, letting the rejection sink in, then turned back to Conner, who was watching her.

She gave him a smile, though her heart ached. "Let's find something fun to do, okay?" she said, her voice bright.

They moved into the living room, toys scattered across the floor, books open from their earlier playtime. Gemma picked up a colorful book and showed it to Conner. "Want to learn some letters today?" she asked.

Conner nodded eagerly, toddling over and plopping down beside her. Gemma opened the book, pointing to a big letter A. "This is an A. Can you say A?"

"A!" Conner repeated, his little finger tracing the shape.

"Great job!" Gemma praised, clapping her hands. They went through each letter, Gemma cheering for every attempt, no matter how clumsy. The lessons filled the afternoon, each letter a small victory, a step toward normalcy.

As the sun set, Gemma closed the book and smiled down at Conner, who rubbed his eyes sleepily. She picked him up, feeling his weight relax against her as she carried him to his bed. She stayed beside him until his breathing deepened; the house growing quiet as he drifted to sleep.

When Johanna returned, Gemma tried once more to bridge the gap. "How was your day?" she asked, her voice hopeful.

Johanna barely looked at her. "Fine," she said, her eyes scanning the room until they landed on Conner, asleep under his blanket. She moved past Gemma without another word, heading to the kitchen.

Gemma's heart sank, but she followed, determined not to give up. "Conner learned some of his letters today," she said. "He's picking it up really fast."

Johanna paused, her face showing no emotion. "That's good," she replied flatly before walking away, disappearing into Conner's room.

Gemma stood alone in the kitchen, frustration tightening in her chest. She wanted so badly to help heal this family, to belong. But Johanna's walls were impossible to break through. Taking a deep breath, she pushed away her doubts. Conner needed her—that was enough.

She walked back to her small room, the silence pressing in on her. Tomorrow, she would try again. She'd care for Conner, reach out to Johanna, and keep holding on to hope. Tonight, though, as she lay down on her bed, the emptiness of the house was a cold reminder of how far she still had to go.

CHAPTER FOUR

GEMMA WOKE WITH A start as Conner's loud cry shattered the quiet night. Her heart raced as she threw off the covers, the cold air biting at her skin. She crossed the short distance to Conner's bed, her bare feet skimming the chilly floorboards as she reached his side. The dim light from the moon coming in from a nearly window barely lit the space, but she saw his flushed face, his small body twisting under the blankets.

Gemma touched his forehead, her hand trembling as the burning heat seared her skin. Her stomach tightened with fear. The fever burned hot. Panic clawed at her, but she tried to stay calm.

"No, please, no," she whispered. She lifted Conner into her arms, holding him close as he cried. "Shh, it's alright, I've got you," she murmured, trying to soothe him and herself.

She carried him to the kitchen and laid him on the table. After she lit a lantern, she removed his nightshirt. Her breath caught when she saw the red rash across his inner thighs and chest. The sight confirmed her worst fear—scarlet fever.

A wave of dread washed over her. Scarlet fever was dangerous, especially for a child so young. Her mind raced, trying to remember everything her great-grandmother Lillian had taught her, but fear clouded her thoughts.

With shaky hands, Gemma rummaged through her collection of herbs and remedies. "Come on, think," she whispered, full of fear and frustration. She tossed aside jar after jar, each one useless for what she needed.

Conner's cries grew louder, each one tearing at her nerves. Gemma took a deep breath, forcing herself to stay calm. She filled a basin with lukewarm water, hoping it might help lower his fever. Carefully, she lowered Conner into the water, her hands steadying as she worked, though tears blurred her vision.

"Help me, Lillian," she whispered. She bathed Conner, trying to remember anything that would help, but the knowledge was out of her reach.

The minutes dragged by like hours as Gemma tried to comfort him. The weight of responsibility pressed on her, almost too much to bear.

Noise in the kitchen woke Patrick. He hurried in, his face shifting from confusion to horror as he saw his son in the bath, and Gemma, frantic and tearful.

"What's happening?" he demanded as he rushed to the table.

Johanna followed, her hand flying to her mouth. "Oh my God, what's wrong with him?" she cried. She hurried to Gemma's side, her usual coldness replaced by fear. Gemma caught Johanna's fleeting thought, sharp and unkind: not about Conner's feverish whimpers, but the fear twisting through her mind—*What if it spreads? What if I get it too?*

"He's very sick," Gemma said as she continued to sponge Conner's feverish body, shocked by Johanna's thoughts. "Its scarlet fever. I'm trying to bring down his fever, to make him comfortable."

Patrick kneeled beside the table, his face twisted with worry as he touched his son's burning skin. "What can we do? Should we get a doctor?" Patrick's thoughts surged through Gemma like a vow etched in iron—*I'd give anything, everything, to see him well.*

"We can't afford a doctor," Johanna said, her fists clenching at her sides as her words cut through the air. "We have to do what we can here."

Gemma nodded. "I know some herbal remedies. I'll do everything I can," she said, trying to sound confident, though fear gnawed at her.

Johanna watched her, her eyes doubtful. "You tried that on the ship, and it didn't work then," she muttered. "What makes you think it will work now?"

The weight of their eyes bore down on Gemma as she prepared an herbal tea, every movement slow and careful. She poured the mixture into a cup, her hands steadying as she focused. She coaxed Conner to take a few sips, her heart heavy with worry.

The kitchen became a tense, makeshift hospital. The parents hovered close, their faces tight with fear as they watched Gemma work. Despite her efforts, Conner's condition worsened. His cries grew weaker, his small body shivering with exhaustion.

"Why isn't this working?" Gemma murmured, wiping her forehead with the back of her hand. She stared at her herbs, frustration building inside her.

"Maybe you're making it worse," Johanna snapped, sharp with fear. *You're going to kill another of my babies.*

Gemma turned to her, hurt flashing in her eyes. "I'm doing everything I can," she said, pleading for understanding. "Please, give it time."

Patrick rubbed his chin, looking torn between his wife's doubt and Gemma's determination. "Shouldn't we at least try to get a doctor?"

"We can't afford it," Johanna said again.

Gemma turned back to Conner, her hands trembling as she adjusted the cool cloth on his forehead. The tension in the room made it hard to concentrate, but she wouldn't give up. She mixed elderberry and nettle, hoping it might help. She held the cup to Conner's lips, urging him to drink, her heart aching.

As the night dragged on, the kitchen became a place of despair. The hours passed, filled with Conner's labored breathing. Each breath pushed them closer to a truth Gemma wasn't ready to face.

As dawn broke, Gemma saw the change. Conner's breathing turned shallow, his chest barely moving. His clammy skin met her touch, and fear stabbed at her heart.

"Please, stay with me," Gemma whispered as she cradled him. But even as she pleaded, his strength slipped away, weakening in her arms.

Johanna rushed over, her eyes wide with fear. "What's happening?"

Gemma choked on her words. "He's getting worse... I don't know if I can..."

"No, no, no," Johanna cried, nearly touching her son's forehead before she pulled back. Her eyes met Gemma's, filled with pure terror.

Patrick moved closer, his face crumpling as he looked at his son. "We can't let this happen," he said.

Gemma searched her mind for a solution, but there was nothing left. She had tried everything, every remedy, but nothing was working. Despair clawed at her, dragging her down.

The room fell silent as Conner's chest, once struggling for each breath, went still. The quiet was crushing. Gemma stared at Conner, unable to believe it. Johanna let out a heart-wrenching wail, collapsing beside her son. "No, no, no," she sobbed.

Patrick kneeled beside her, wrapping his arms around his wife and son, his face twisted with pain.

Tears fell on Gemma's cheeks, blurring her vision. She had failed. The realization hit her like a blow, knocking the air from her lungs.

She stepped back as the family gathered around him. The room, once full of frantic energy, now echoed with their grief. Outside, the first light of dawn cast long shadows across the yard. Gemma was an intruder, a failure who had let them down when they needed her most.

Overwhelmed, she slipped out the back door, the cold air biting her skin. She walked into the yard, her feet crunching on the frost-covered ground. Her mind replayed every moment, every decision.

"I did everything I knew," she whispered to the sky. "Why wasn't it enough?"

The wind rustled through the trees, offering no answers. The weight of her failure suffocated her.

Gemma thought of Lillian, of everything she had learned in their quiet home, and wondered if she had ever been ready for this. The burden weighed on her like a crushing boulder; the pain cutting into her like a jagged knife.

But as she stood there, shivering, Gemma realized she had a choice. She could let this defeat her, or she could learn and keep going. Lillian told her to be brave.

Taking a deep breath, Gemma turned back toward the house. The faint glow of lamplight spilled out from the windows, a small beacon in the darkness.

Gemma paused at the doorway, chest tightening under the weight of the room's tension. She stepped inside; the floorboards groaned beneath her feet, amplifying the oppressive silence. The living room appeared darker than before, heavy with grief and something sharper—blame.

Patrick sat rigid on the worn sofa, his gaze cold and piercing. The warmth that had once greeted Gemma was gone, replaced by eyes that twisted her insides. Johanna, wrapped in a thin shawl, stared at Gemma, her expression filled with accusation and raw pain. Her presence was to be a wound that refused to heal.

Gemma swallowed, her throat dry. "I just wanted to check on you," she said, the words weak and hollow.

Johanna let out a harsh, bitter laugh. "How do you think we are?" she snapped. "You were supposed to protect him."

The words hit like a slap, and Gemma flinched. "I... I tried everything," she stammered, voice shaky. "I..."

"Everything?" Patrick interrupted, standing, his face darkening with anger. "Our boy is gone, and that's all you can say?"

The room closed in, the air thick and suffocating. Gemma stepped back, bumping into the door. Their stares pierced her, their thoughts slashed her, each glare seething with grief and fury. They blamed her, and she had no defense.

Johanna stood, movements jerky and unsteady. She crossed the room, eyes blazing. "You should have saved him!" she yelled, her hand striking Gemma's cheek. Pain flared, and shock froze Gemma in place.

Gemma stumbled back, her face stinging. She met Johanna's eyes—only pain and fury stared back. "I'm sorry," Gemma whispered. "I did everything I could."

"Sorry?" Johanna spat, her face twisted with grief. "Sorry won't bring him back!"

Patrick moved forward, pulling his wife away. His face sagged with exhaustion, eyes hollow. "That's enough," he murmured. He pulled Johanna tightly against him, his eyes locking onto Gemma's with a fury that burned through his grief, unspoken accusations weighing heavier than any words could.

Gemma, cheek burning, tears streaming, watched the scene unravel. The slap broke something inside her—her sense of belonging, her confidence in her own abilities.

As Johanna's sobs filled the room, Gemma backed away. Patrick's angry eyes met hers, and she knew there was nothing left to say. She turned and walked toward the door, feet heavy under the weight of failure. The cold Montana air struck her face as she stepped outside, offering no comfort.

The door closed with a dull thud. Gemma stood on the porch, lost. Moments later, Patrick opened the door, tossing her small bag onto the porch. Her few belongings spilled across the wooden boards.

Gemma slumped onto the steps, gathering her things, hands trembling. Tears fell, hot and bitter. The bag, once a symbol of hope, weighed her down.

The night pressed in around her, the nearby houses dark and indifferent. She wrapped her arms around herself, shivering as the cold seeped into her bones. "Why?" she said. "I tried so hard."

The empty street swallowed her words. Loneliness wrapped around her like a suffocating blanket, a reminder of her isolation. She had tried to help, but now she was nothing more than a scapegoat for grief too immense to bear.

Gemma's chest tightened, each breath harder to take. Conner's bright eyes flashed in her memory, his laughter echoing in her mind, now lost forever. She hugged her bag, wishing she could undo everything, bring him back, ease the parents' pain.

Hours passed as Gemma sat alone on the steps, heart heavy and broken. She knew she couldn't stay forever, that when morning came, she would need to stand and move on. But for now, all she could do was mourn—mourn for the child, for her lost place, and for the harsh turn her life had taken.

CHAPTER FIVE

THE SHED OFFERED LITTLE comfort during the harsh night, acting as nothing more than a temporary hiding place than a true refuge. Gemma lay on the unforgiving floor, the cold biting through the thin blanket she had found. She shifted, searching for a spot that felt less painful against her back, each movement setting off a chorus of creaks from the old boards beneath her.

The wind outside howled, whistling through the gaps in the shed's weathered walls, turning it into a haunting tune. Faint sounds from Missoula drifted in—a distant laugh, the clatter of a passing wagon, a dog's bark. They reminded Gemma of a life she no longer belonged to, transforming the shed into more of a cell than a sanctuary.

She pulled the blanket around, though it offered insufficient warmth. Her breath misted in the freezing air as she curled into a tighter ball, trying to conserve what little body heat she could. The wind found every crack, chilling her to the bone and mixing with the stale scent of decay that lingered in the corners of the shed.

Her wide eyes darted around the dim space, picking out shapes that loomed and shifted in the faint moonlight. Shadows twisted into grotesque figures, and Gemma's heart pounded with every gust that rattled the old structure. Each sound carried a sinister edge, as if someone—or something—lurked just beyond the walls.

"It's only the wind," she whispered, her voice shaky, trying to reassure herself. The words vanished into the dark, swallowed by the overwhelming sounds of the night. The shed's silence magnified each creak of wood, every rustle of leaves, leaving her with the oppressive reminder of how alone she truly was.

Loneliness pressed on her, heavy and suffocating. She longed for the simple comforts—a warm fire, a door she could lock, the reassuring presence of another person. But here, all she had was darkness and cold, wrapping around her like a relentless tide. She closed her eyes, desperate for sleep to carry her away, though the bitter isolation refused to release its hold on her mind.

Sleep came in fragments, dreams blurring the line between comfort and torment. She found herself back at the hidden cave by the lake where she and Lillian had lived. The warmth of a crackling fire filled the air, shadows danced across the stone walls, and the earthy scent of herbs drifted through the space. In her dreams, Lillian smiled at her, eyes sparkling as she spun stories of ancient magick. Gemma, a young girl once more, listened, safe and cherished.

But the dream shifted, twisting into something darker. The warmth faded, replaced by the cold grip of the shed. The crackling fire vanished, leaving only the harsh chill of reality. Gemma jerked awake, heart hammering, sweat cooling in the frigid air. She clung to the memory of her dream, the warmth of Lillian's smile, but the loneliness of the shed crushed any comfort it offered.

She hugged her knees to her chest, trying to steady her breathing, each breath a struggle. The joy of her dreams clashed with the bleakness of her waking world. Her loss rushed over her, a wave of grief for the life she'd once had—a life filled with love, guidance, and security, now nothing but a fading memory.

As dawn peeked through the cracks in the shed, Gemma uncurled herself, her body stiff from the cold and the unforgiving floor. She pushed open the door, stepping out into the pale light of morning. The air hit her face, crisp and indifferent. Gemma squinted against the brightness, her eyes adjusting, while the town of Missoula woke around her. The sounds of life returned, clashing against the silence she had left behind.

The streets bustled with activity. Shopkeepers swept the walks, setting out signs and goods, preparing for the day. Delivery wagons clattered by, street vendors called out, and laughter echoed from some far corner. Each sound reminded her of what she no longer had—a place where she belonged, people who saw her.

She moved through the crowd, unnoticed, her thin shawl barely warding off the chill. Her stomach ached, a constant reminder of her long night without food. She ducked down an alley, searching the ground and bins for anything that might ease her hunger. It was a cruel descent, scavenging for scraps in a town that bustled with the scent of fresh bread and roasting meat beyond reach for her.

The alley behind the restaurants carried a mix of smells—some pleasant, some rancid. Gemma approached the bins, lifting the lids, her nose wrinkling. Rotting vegetables, old grease, and spoiled meat filled her senses, making her gag. She clenched her jaw, determined. A half-eaten sandwich, stale but still edible, caught her eye. She pulled it from the trash, the bread soggy, the meat gray, but it would have to do. Gemma tucked it into her bag, her cheeks burning from the indignity.

The sounds of people at work—chefs barking orders, waiters bustling in and out—drifted from the nearby kitchens. They were oblivious to her presence, unaware of the young woman scavenging only steps away. A mix of anger and shame twisted inside her as she remembered she'd been a caregiver, someone needed and respected, and now she was this—digging through garbage to survive.

She moved to the next bin, her motions mechanical, trying to detach herself from the situation. She had to eat, had to keep going. Her hand brushed something firm beneath a pile of damp newspaper—a wrapped packet of bread. Her heart skipped at the small find. She pulled it free, examining it. The bread was misshapen, but not spoiled.

A sense of relief mingled with a sharp pang of humiliation. Triumph over discarded bread—was this what her life had come to? She wiped the packet against her dress, opening it to find bread that, though stale, was edible. Gemma tore off a piece, her first bite cautious. It scratched her throat, but she swallowed, feeling the dryness settle in her stomach, both a relief and a reminder of her desperation.

"I'm sorry, Lillian," she whispered to the empty alley, the words caught on the edge of a sob. She pictured Lillian's face, stern but kind. Her great-aunt had taught her to be strong, to carry herself with dignity. Now, here she was, far from that strength, ashamed of what she had become.

But Gemma refused to give up. This situation wouldn't be forever. She would survive, climb out of this darkness, and find her place again. She tucked the bread away, wiping her hands on her dress, and moved on to the next bin. Survival was all that mattered now.

The sun dipped lower as Gemma trudged to the shed, found food bulging in her pockets. Missoula had quieted as evening settled in, and the streets cleared. The warmth of families gathering indoors made her path back feel even colder.

She pushed open the door, stepping inside and closing it behind her. The small space felt darker, colder, the day's weariness pulling at her bones. With mechanical movements, she ate her stash of food, choking on some of the less desirable parts.

Gemma prepared for bed, removing her dress. She folded it neatly, changing into her nightgown, slow and deliberate. The shed's hard floor waited, and she spread her blanket out again, lying on the unforgiving wood.

Gemma hugged her knees close, the loneliness seeping in like the night air, pressing on her heart. "One more night," she whispered, trying to convince herself. She stared through the cracks in the walls, watching the light outside fade away, surrendering to darkness.

As she lay there, her thoughts circled around all she'd lost. The family she'd wanted to protect, the life she'd dreamed of—now gone, replaced by this empty existence. The cold deepened, and she pulled the blanket closer, her spirit dwindling but not extinguished.

In her heart, a spark of hope remained, a small flicker refusing to die. She would survive. She would live, not just exist. Morning would come, and she would try again, facing whatever challenges waited with the strength Lillian had always believed she had.

The first light of dawn peeked through the cracks, finding Gemma still curled up on the floor, her eyes red and tired, but determined. She pushed herself up, rubbing her face, the night behind her and a new day ahead. She had no clear path forward, but she wasn't done fighting. Not yet.

Gemma crept into the alley behind the bakery, her steps light and deliberate, every movement tuned to avoid drawing attention. The early morning chill lingered in the narrow passage, the occasional waft of warm air from the bakery door the only contrast to the biting cold. She scanned the refuse bins with sharp eyes, searching for anything that might quiet the hunger gnawing at her belly.

The scent of baked bread floated from the bakery, rich and tantalizing, a reminder of everything she didn't have. Gemma approached the first bin, her heart dipping as she uncovered empty wrappers and spoiled scraps. She moved on, her fingers shaking from the cold as they sifted through the refuse, hoping against hope for something edible.

Her fingers brushed against something solid. Gemma held her breath, pulling at it until she unearthed a stale breadstick. Relief bubbled up—a rare emotion these days. She turned the breadstick over in her hands, inspecting it. Hard and cold, but intact. It would keep her going for a little while longer.

"At least there's this," she whispered. She slipped the breadstick into the pocket of her worn coat, glancing around. She'd learned the hard way that it was better to stay hidden while scavenging; hunger made people unpredictable.

As Gemma stepped away, footsteps echoed from the far end of the alley. Her pulse quickened. She slipped behind a stack of crates, her breath catching in her throat. Two men appeared, their faces hard, their eyes searching. A chill unrelated to the morning air crawled down her spine—they were looking for something, or someone.

Gemma watched them, her body tense, every instinct screaming for her to stay hidden. But the larger man's eyes swept her direction, and they locked onto hers. He nudged his companion, and they moved towards her, their pace quickening. Panic surged through Gemma, her mind racing as she backed away. She needed to escape, but the alley offered no exits, just looming walls and approaching danger.

Her heel caught on a loose stone, the sharp clatter echoing down the alley. The larger man lunged, grabbing her arm with a grip like iron. Fear surged, and Gemma twisted, trying to break free, her other hand clawing at his fingers.

"Let me go!" she screamed, the sound ricocheting off the alley walls. She struggled, but the man's grip tightened, his face twisting with annoyance.

The alley held its breath for one tense moment. Then, from the shadows, a raccoon launched itself at the man's leg, teeth sinking into his calf. He bellowed in pain, letting go of Gemma to swat at the animal. The raccoon held on, its growl a fierce, unexpected defense.

"Get it off me!" the man yelled, stumbling backward. His companion hesitated, unsure of how to help without getting bitten himself.

Gemma seized the chance. She pulled free, adrenaline propelling her as she sprinted towards the street. Her feet pounded the cobblestones, heart hammering in her chest as she pushed herself to run faster, farther—away from the men, away from the danger.

Behind her, the sounds of chaos faded, the man's curses and the raccoon's growls becoming muffled echoes. She dared a glance back and saw the men retreating, one of them clutching his leg, limping. The raccoon, her unlikely savior, had chased them off.

Gemma slowed, her breath coming in ragged gasps, and turned her gaze back down the alley. The raccoon sat in the center, watching her with bright, curious eyes. It took a step, then another, hopping side to side, like it was celebrating.

A laugh, unexpected and light, escaped Gemma. She watched the raccoon's strange little dance, a smile spreading across her face despite the fear that still coiled tight in her chest. "Thanks," she said. "I owe you one."

The raccoon paused, twitching its ears as if it understood, then continued its antics. For a moment, the harshness of the morning faded, replaced by the absurdity of a raccoon performing a victory dance in the alley. Gemma wiped her eyes, laughter mingling with tears as the tension of the morning ebbed away.

The raccoon scampered off, disappearing around a corner, but something had shifted in Gemma. She straightened, took a deep breath, and whispered, "Guess the goddesses are watching out for me after all."

As she left the alley, she heard a soft rustling behind her. The raccoon had returned, trailing her steps, its compact form blending with the shadows. Gemma looked down, her smile widening. "You're sticking around, huh?"

The raccoon tilted its head, eyes glinting, as if to say it was exactly where it was supposed to be. Gemma nodded, a sense of companionship easing the cold ache of loneliness. "Alright then. Come on, Shadow."

Together, they stepped out of the alley, into the bustling streets of Missoula. The weight of isolation lifted, leaving her grounded and whole, as though the missing pieces of herself had finally fallen into place. Shadow trotted beside her, a small but fierce presence, and with each step, she was a little braver—a little more ready to face whatever came next.

CHAPTER SIX

THE BOARDWALK BUZZED WITH life. People bustled from vendor to vendor, the wooden planks creaking under the steady traffic of feet. Gemma moved through the crowd, her shoulders hunched, trying to stay unseen. She kept her head down, her eyes flicking from face to face. Every jostle or brush against a stranger made her breath catch, and she had to force herself to keep walking. Voices, laughter, and the shouts of vendors selling their goods blurred together into a wall of sound that made her head spin.

She wrapped her shawl tighter around herself, as though the thin fabric could shield her from the chaos. A couple, deep in their own conversation, bumped into her without even noticing. Gemma stumbled, muttering a soft, "Sorry," though they were already gone. Her heart pounded, her chest tightening with each shallow breath. She was an intruder here, an outsider in a joyful, noisy place.

Gemma pressed forward, trying to find a pocket of space, but the crowd was relentless. The aroma of fried dough and grilled meats wafted through the air. Her stomach twisted, half from hunger, half from the overwhelming crush of people. She needed to get out of the crowd, to find somewhere quiet where she could breathe.

She stepped back to avoid a cluster of children chasing each other and collided with someone. Gemma stumbled, nearly falling. Panic surged through her, and she spun around, her hands shaking as she tried to steady herself. "I—I'm so sorry," she stammered, tears springing to her eyes before she could stop them.

The woman she'd bumped into turned, her eyes widening in surprise. She wore elegant clothing, a white, flowy feather in her hat, and her dark hair pulled back neatly. Her expression softened. "Hey, it's alright," the woman said, placing a steadying hand on Gemma's shoulder. "No harm done. Are you okay?"

Gemma shook her head, her breath hitching as she tried to hold back her tears. "I—it's … it's all too much," she whispered. The crowd, the noise, the endless press of people—it had all become too much to bear.

"Come on," she said. "Let's get you out of the chaos for a minute." She guided Gemma away from the crowd, steering her toward a quieter corner of the boardwalk.

Once they reached a quieter spot near the edge of the boardwalk, Marisol turned to face her. "My name's Marisol," she said, smiling. "What's yours?"

"Gemma," she mumbled, wiping her eyes with the back of her hand. She sniffled, trying to pull herself together. Marisol's kindness made her vulnerable, but also a little less alone.

"Nice to meet you, Gemma," Marisol said. "Are you here with anyone?"

Gemma shook her head, her eyes stinging with fresh tears. "No," she managed. "I... I don't have anyone."

Marisol's gaze softened even more, her eyes sympathetic. "Oh, sweetheart," she said. She squeezed Gemma's shoulder. "You're not alone now."

Gemma's tear-streaked face searched for any hint of insincerity. All she saw was genuine care. She nodded. "Thank you," she whispered. This woman's thoughts radiated compassion and a shared understanding that wrapped around Gemma like a protective shield, dissolving her defenses and inviting an immediate trust.

Marisol smiled. "Let's get you something warm to eat, and then we'll talk about a more permanent plan. How does that sound?"

Gemma clasped her hands under her chin. She nodded again. "That sounds... really nice." A shy smile broke through her tears.

The hotel lobby offered a stark contrast to the clamor of the noisy boardwalk. Polished marble floors gleamed under the glow of soft chandeliers, their grandeur making Gemma acutely aware of her own smallness. Marisol guided her through the lavish space, her hand steady on Gemma's shoulder. Despite the imposing elegance, the lobby exuded a warmth that wrapped around them like a rare embrace.

Upstairs, Marisol opened the door to her room and guided Gemma to a seat by the window. The view stretched out over the city, and the soft lighting made the room cozy and safe. Marisol disappeared for a moment, then returned carrying a small basin of water and a washcloth.

"Here, let's freshen you up a bit," Marisol said. She dipped the cloth into the water, wrung it out, and stepped closer to Gemma. Gemma lifted her head, unsure but trusting. Marisol dabbed at her face, the cloth wiping away grime and tension. The soft touch was like a luxury—something Gemma had almost forgotten existed.

Marisol continued, her hand moving with care. "How long has it been since someone looked after you like this?" she asked.

Gemma closed her eyes, a tear escaping. "Since I saw my great aunt in Ireland," she whispered. "It's been such a long time since anyone showed concern."

Marisol paused, then lifted Gemma's chin so their eyes met. "Well, you're not alone now," she said. "You deserve to be cared for, Gemma. We all do."

Gemma's heart tightened, and the shell around it cracked. She nodded, pressing her fingers to her smiling lips.

"There, that's better," Marisol said, folding the washcloth, smiling. "Now, let's get some food. You need something hearty."

Gemma stood, a sense of herself returning that she hadn't experienced in days. As they left the room for the hotel dining room, a small spark of hope ignited inside her.

In the dining room, Marisol led Gemma to a table near the window. The elegant space buzzed with the quiet clinks of silverware and low conversations. Gemma glanced around, out of place in her worn clothes. Her shoulders hunched as people's curious glances made her want to shrink away.

Marisol leaned closer. "Gemma, look at me."

Gemma raised her eyes, her gaze meeting Marisol's steady one. "You are my guest, and you belong here as much as anyone else. Let them stare if they want to. We have nothing to be ashamed of."

Gemma swallowed and nodded, reassured by Marisol's words. Though her discomfort didn't vanish, it eased enough for her to sit straighter.

Marisol smiled and shifted the conversation. "What do you like to eat? Today, you can pick anything you want."

When the waiter arrived, Marisol ordered for them both, adding a hot chocolate for Gemma. The waiter smiled, his demeanor softening, causing a tiny warmth to spread in her chest.

As they waited for their food, Marisol talked about the hotel, the city, and pointed out landmarks visible through the window. Her stories and laughter drew Gemma in, helping her forget the other diners' looks and the strangeness of her surroundings.

When the food came, Gemma took a deep breath and tasted the hot chocolate. The warmth filled her, soothing something deep inside. Each bite of food was a reminder of what it was like to be cared for—to be seen.

"See?" Marisol said, smiling at her. "No worries here. Enjoy the meal. Let the rest of the world disappear for a while."

The small bell above the door chimed as Gemma and Marisol stepped into the dress shop. The room buzzed with the low hum of sewing machines. Dresses of every color and design filled the racks, their soft fabrics rustling as a seamstress walked by. Marisol led Gemma to a section where several beautiful dresses hung, picking out a soft green one that was perfect.

"Try this on," Marisol said, handing Gemma the dress with an encouraging smile.

Gemma's hands trembled as she took the garment. The fabric was soft, luxurious—so different from her worn clothes. She stepped behind the folding screen to change, her heart pounding as she slipped out of her ragged dress and into the new one. The smooth fabric hugged her, reminding her of what it was like to be comfortable, to be cared for.

When she stepped out from behind the screen, a quiet settled over the shop. The seamstresses paused in their work, casting curious glances her way. Gemma took a deep breath and moved toward the full-length mirror, her heart thudding in her chest. She barely recognized the girl looking back at her. The green dress made her eyes seem brighter, and the way it fit gave her an elegance she hadn't seen in herself for a long time.

Tears welled in her eyes as she turned, examining herself from different angles. Marisol came up behind her, their reflections side by side. "You look beautiful, Gemma," Marisol said.

Gemma said, "I hardly recognize myself. It's like... I'm seeing who I could be, not who I've become." Her tears flowed, a mix of awe and sadness.

Marisol placed a gentle hand on her shoulder. "This is who you've always been," she said. "Sometimes we need a little help to see it again."

Gemma met Marisol's eyes in the mirror, her heart full, her knees weak. The seamstresses returned to their work, sensing the importance of the moment. Gemma took a deep breath, her gaze locked on her reflection—not only a girl in a dress, but someone with the chance at a new beginning.

"I don't know how to thank you," she whispered, her eyes glistening.

Marisol smiled. "No thanks needed. Just promise me you'll think about coming with me when I go home. You don't have to decide now, but consider it."

Gemma nodded, the idea already forming in her heart. The dress was a sign of something better, a reminder that there could be more to her story than surviving. The tears that slipped over her cheeks now carried hope.

"Gemma," Marisol said, "I know you deserve more than what you've been given. Would you come home with me?"

Gemma turned, tears spilling over as she nodded. "Yes," she said, shaky but sure. "I would love that. More than anything."

She glanced down at her side, where Shadow sat, watching as if he understood the weight of the moment. Gemma reached out and stroked his head, then looked back at Marisol. "Can Shadow come, too?"

Marisol looked at the raccoon, her brow furrowing. After a moment, she met Gemma's eyes again and smiled. "Of course, Shadow can come. He's part of your journey, too."

Gemma's smile brightened, a rare expression of pure joy. She kneeled to bring her face close to Shadow's, whispering, "Hear that? We're going home, both of us."

Shadow patted his cheeks with his tiny paws, making Gemma laugh—a sound that carried a sense of hope she hadn't known in a long time.

Standing, she faced Marisol, her eyes shining. "Thank you, Marisol. For everything. This means... it means the world to me."

Marisol reached out, pulling Gemma into a warm hug, a promise of a new start wrapped within her arms. "Then let's go home," she said. Together, they walked out of the shop—a girl, a woman, and a raccoon—ready to begin the next chapter of their lives, filled with hope, healing, and the promise of belonging.

CHAPTER SEVEN

GEMMA HESITATED ENTERING THE Tin Creek Boarding House. The wooden sign above the door swayed in the breeze, its faded letters barely readable as they creaked with each gust of wind. The sturdy two-story structure painted in a worn blue had seen better days under the Montana sun. Taking a deep breath, she stepped inside, her heart caught between hope and unease.

Inside, dim light filtered through dusty curtains, and the air held the smell of wood smoke mixed with something old, like fabric that had seen decades of use. Marisol led her along a narrow hallway decorated with faded photographs of mountain views and Tin Creek landmarks. The floorboards groaned beneath their feet, adding to the sense of age and charm. Halfway down the hall, Marisol stopped and pushed open a door. "This is your room, Gemma," she said, smiling.

Gemma stepped inside. Her eyes moved across the modest space: a small bed covered in a patchwork quilt, a wooden chair by the window, and a dresser with chipped paint. Each piece had its own story, worn by the many people who had used them before. She approached the bed, her fingers brushing over the quilt, feeling the raised stitching and softness of the fabric. Despite the simplicity, it was clean, and that alone gave her a sense of security.

She moved to the window, pushing aside a thin curtain to look out at the street below. Tin Creek was alive in its own way. As people strolled on the hard-packed dirt road, the vibrant sounds of the nearby saloon, including piano music, laughter, and cheerful chatter, seeped through the window. The noise felt strange, almost comforting in its own way, so different from the quiet loneliness she had left behind.

Marisol waved her arm out in a sweep motion. "Will it do?" she asked.

Gemma turned back, swallowing against the tightness in her throat. "Yes, thank you," she said. "It's... it's very nice."

Marisol's warm smile eased the knot inside her chest. "Good. The boarding house is quiet most of the time. Mrs. Langley, the owner, is kind and knows about your little friend." She nodded toward Shadow, who had followed them inside and was busy sniffing every corner of the room.

Gemma glanced at the raccoon, her lips lifting in a small smile as he investigated. Gratitude bubbled inside her, but beneath that, there was still an edge of worry. It was a fresh start—one more beginning, carrying more uncertainties.

When Marisol brought Gemma to the Sapphire Saloon, Gemma clutched the frame as she peered in. The noisy saloon buzzed in color, a stark contrast to anything she had ever known. Laughter rose above the sound of piano keys, and the air held aromas of tobacco smoke and the rich, spiced scent of whiskey. Oil lamps glowed, casting a warm light over bright tapestries on the walls.

Gemma took a deep breath, stepping inside. Her heart pounded as she weaved through the crowd, her senses overwhelmed by the clinking of glasses and shouts from card players. The sensation of being watched washed over her, making her cheeks burn.

"Hey there, you must be Gemma!" someone called above the din. A red-headed woman flashed a wide grin while approaching her. "I'm Sally. Marisol told us to expect you. Come on, I'll show you around."

Gemma gave a timid smile, grateful for the friendly welcome, and followed Sally through the crowded room. The other girls glanced at her as they passed, expressions curious but kind. Their colorful gowns sparkled in the lamplight, and their laughter came easy. Gemma shifted in her plain dress, eyes darting around as she struggled to find her place in this vibrant setting.

"This is the bar, and that's Mr. Jacobs—best bartender in all of Montana," Sally said, pointing to a burly man who tossed a bottle in the air, catching it with practiced ease. "And over there's the stage. We get local musicians, sometimes even traveling acts."

Gemma's eyes widened at the sight of a small band setting up, the fiddler adjusting his strings while others tuned their instruments. It was a lot—too much, maybe—but it was also alive. A different world than what she had known, one filled with noise and laughter she had never experienced.

"Looks like a lot, huh?" Sally chuckled. "You'll get used to it. It takes time. Everyone here is nice, and you've got your...ah...coon, too."

Gemma looked at her raccoon, who stayed close by her side, his nose twitching at all the fresh smells. He didn't seem bothered by the noise; if anything, his bright eyes curious.

"Yeah," Gemma said. "It's so different."

"I get that," Sally said, giving her a reassuring pat on the shoulder. "Why don't you help me with the tables tonight? You can meet some of the regulars. They're a harmless bunch, mostly. Marisol keeps them that way."

Gemma nodded, her anxiety easing. She followed Sally to a nearby table, carrying a stack of clean glasses. She moved amongst the patrons; her steps uncertain but steady. For the first time in a long while, Gemma allowed herself a bit of hope. Maybe there was a place for her in this world of music and laughter where her quiet presence might fit in after all.

Later that evening, Gemma sat at a long wooden table in the back of the saloon, surrounded by the girls who worked there. They passed around plates of food with roast beef, fresh bread, and vegetables. Her stomach growled, drawing a laugh from Jess, a girl with sparkling blue eyes and a tumble of curly brown hair.

"Don't be shy. Eat up," Jess said, sliding a plate toward her. "You'll need the energy to keep up."

As they ate, the girls shared stories—tales of demanding customers, funny moments from the day, gossip about the townsfolk. Gemma listened, her eyes wide, nodding, a small smile tugging at her lips. Their laughter filled the space, warm and full of life.

After a while, Gemma worked up the courage to share a story of her own. "Shadow can be a real rascal," she said, growing more confident. "He'll do tricks if he thinks there's a treat involved."

As if on cue, Shadow jumped onto the bench, stood on his hind legs, and twirled around. The girls burst into laughter, clapping as the raccoon looked expectantly at them.

"Well, he knows how to work a crowd," Sally laughed, tossing a scrap of meat to him.

Gemma's smile widened, warmth spreading in her chest. "He's been my friend when I had no one else," she said, stroking Shadow's fur. "He found me when I was in trouble, and he's stayed ever since."

The other girls grew quiet, their expressions softening. Jess leaned in. "He's not just a pet, is he? Sounds like he's family."

"Yeah," Gemma agreed, her eyes glistening. "He really is."

Gemma hurried down the dim hallway of the boarding house, her heart hammering as the man's heavy footsteps followed her. The familiar unease that lingered since her arrival grew sharper, sending shivers down her spine. The narrow corridor closed in on her, the peeling wallpaper and creaking floorboards only amplifying her rising panic.

"Hey there, Gemma," the man slurred, his breath reeking of whiskey. He blocked her path with a crooked grin that made her stomach turn. "Why don't you keep me company tonight?"

Gemma's breath caught, her chest tightening. She tried to slip past him, but he mirrored her move, his fingers reaching out to brush her hair away from her face. "Please, I want to go to my room," she stammered, her eyes darted for an escape.

He chuckled, his grip closing around her wrist, rough and unyielding. "Don't be like that," he said, pulling her closer. "You'll like it, I promise."

Terror surged through Gemma, her pulse pounding in her ears. "No!" she cried, struggling to yank her arm free, but his hold only tightened, his breath hot and foul against her cheek.

A blur of gray fur shot between them. Shadow lunged at the man with a fierce growl, his sharp teeth sinking into the man's leg. The man howled in pain, stumbling back as his grip on Gemma loosened.

"Get it off! Get it off!" he bellowed, trying to shake the raccoon loose. Shadow clung on, growling with determination, protecting Gemma with everything he had.

Gemma didn't waste a second. She tore free from the man's grasp and sprinted down the hallway, her heart pounding as she ran for the door. "Shadow, come!" she called. Shadow released the man and dashed after her, his fur bristling.

They burst out into the cool night, the man's curses fading behind them. Gemma kept running until she reached the end of the street, leaning against a building, gasping for breath. Shadow pressed close to her leg, his eyes scanning the darkness, ready to defend her again if needed.

Tears stung Gemma's eyes, a mix of fear and heartbreak. The boarding house had been her refuge, and now it had turned into a place of danger. She wiped her face, her gaze dropping to Shadow. He stared up at her, his small body still tense, and she kneeled down, wrapping her arms around him. "Thank you," she whispered. Shadow saved her again. He was her guardian as much as she was his.

Gemma stumbled down the street, her vision blurred, her breaths ragged. She didn't stop until the Sapphire Saloon's warm glow came into view, spilling light into the night like a beacon. She pushed through the swinging doors, her sudden entrance halting the lively chatter and clinking glasses inside.

The saloon girls, who saw Gemma as a little sister, stood open mouth as she staggered in. Their laughter faded, replaced by concern as they rushed to her side.

"What happened, sweetheart?" Marianne, one of the older girls, asked, pulling Gemma into a comforting hug.

Gemma choked back a sob, her words tumbling out in a rush. "He...he grabbed me. I had to get away."

The girls exchanged glances, concern turning to anger. "Who did this?" Jess demanded, sharp with protective fury.

Before Gemma could answer, Shadow appeared at her feet, his fur still bristling from the encounter. He nuzzled against her leg, grounding her in the chaos.

Marisol, alerted by the commotion, joined them, her expression hardening as she took in the scene. "You're safe here," she said, cupping Gemma's face so their eyes met. "Tell me everything."

Surrounded by the saloon girls, Gemma recounted what had happened. Their presence, their care, soothed her frayed nerves. Though fear still clung to her, the saloon became her sanctuary—a place where she was not alone.

The next morning, Marisol accompanied Gemma back to the boarding house to confront the manager. Gemma stood beside her, her heart pounding as Marisol said, "That man attacked her last night. Shadow defended her. Are we really going to punish a girl for protecting herself?"

The manager shook her head, her expression indifferent. "I've had complaints about that animal. We can't have vicious pets attacking guests, no matter the reason. She has to leave."

Gemma's stomach dropped, the word "vicious" echoing in her mind. She looked at Shadow, who had only tried to protect her, then at the boarding house that had turned its back on her. The betrayal cut deep.

"But where will I go?" Gemma whispered. "He attacked me, and now I'm the one being thrown out?"

The manager didn't meet her eyes. "My hands are tied."

Outside, Marisol wrapped an arm around Gemma's shoulders. "You'll come to the saloon," she said. "It's not ideal, but you'll be safe, and I'll take care of you."

Gemma nodded, the weight of her situation sinking in. The boarding house, which she had thought could be a home, was lost to her. But Marisol's promise gave her a sliver of hope. She wasn't alone. Not entirely.

Gemma's first few days at the saloon were tough, but she worked hard, determined to prove herself. She scrubbed tables, organized supplies, anything to repay Marisol's kindness.

One afternoon, Marisol handed her a stack of ledgers. "I've been struggling with these numbers," she admitted. "Can you take a look?"

Gemma took the ledgers to a quiet corner and studied the numbers. It didn't take her long to spot the mistake—a simple error of a transposed number that threw everything off.

"Marisol," Gemma said. "I found the mistake. It's here."

Marisol came over, listening as Gemma explained. A smile spread across her face. "You've got a sharp eye, Gemma. Would you like to handle the books from now on?"

Gemma hesitated, pride swelling in her chest. "I'd like that. Thank you."

Marisol nodded. "Good. They're yours."

Gemma set up her workspace, the saloon's noise fading into the background as she focused on the ledgers. The job was more than numbers; it was a sign of trust, an anchor in her new life.

As the night wore on and the last patrons left, Gemma reflected on how far she had come. From the fear at the boarding house to the safety of the saloon, she had found strength she never knew she had. Marisol gave her a home, the saloon girls became her family, and Shadow, her loyal companion, protected her through it all.

Gemma looked around the quiet saloon, a sense of peace settling over her. She wasn't just a scared girl with a raccoon—she was part of a community, ready to face whatever came next, surrounded by the people who cared for her.

With a small smile, she leaned back in her chair, allowing herself to relax. The future still held uncertainties, but Gemma knew she was ready, and that made all the difference.

CHAPTER EIGHT

WHEN MARISOL LED GEMMA into the bustling dry goods store, she smelled fresh coffee beans, dried herbs, and oiled wood that overwhelmed her senses. Shelves stretched high, crammed with jars of preserves, tins of lard, coils of rope, and boxes of nails. Barrels of grain lined the walls, their lids askew, while bolts of fabric in every color imaginable filled one corner. The soft flicker of kerosene lamps overhead cast a warm glow on sacks of flour and sugar piled in another corner. The shop was alive with activity as a mother negotiated a price, her children running around and hiding between barrels. Isobel, managing everything on her own, called out to other customers. It was chaotic, messy, and different from anything Gemma had known.

Gemma hesitated, her eyes darting around the crowded room, taking in the chaos. She had seen nothing quite like this—everything was loud, bustling, and full of energy. She clenched her hands at her sides, her chest tightening as she tried to steady her breathing. Marisol gave her a reassuring pat on the back, tucking a loose strand of hair behind Gemma's ear. The touch grounded her, even if it made her cheeks flush in embarrassment.

"Relax, dear. Everyone here is getting on with their day," Marisol whispered, guiding her toward the counter where Isobel stood.

Isobel looked up, her eyes softening as she caught sight of them. "Welcome, Gemma," she said, extending her hand. "Marisol has told me so much about you. I'm glad you're here. I need someone to help me."

Marisol nudged Gemma forward. "Gemma, this is Isobel. She runs this place and keeps it all running. Better than her father," she said with pride.

Gemma swallowed hard, extending her hand to meet Isobel's. As soon as their fingers touched, something shifted deep inside her. Her vision blurred, and out of nowhere she saw green fields, stone walls, and waves crashing against jagged cliffs—the wild, untamed landscapes of Ireland. It was so vivid, so real, that her knees nearly gave out beneath her.

She stumbled, pulling back, and Marisol caught her by the shoulders, concern flashing across her face. "Easy, sweetheart. You alright?" Marisol asked, her eyes searching Gemma's face.

"I'm... fine," Gemma whispered, shaking her head as if to clear it. "Just... felt strange for a second." Her gaze flickered to Isobel, hoping for some sign that she understood. She realized Isobel's thoughts were blank, nothing to read like it was with Lillian.

Isobel's smile turned thoughtful, her brow furrowing. "It's okay, Gemma. Take your time," she said. She let her hand drop, which gave Gemma space to orient herself.

Marisol's arm stayed firm around Gemma's shoulders, a steadying presence. "It's a lot at once," she said, her eyes still on Gemma. "New places, new people."

Gemma nodded, her face growing warm under their gazes. She forced a smile, though it wavered. "I'm happy to be here. Thank you for giving me this opportunity," she said.

Isobel's face brightened again, her tone warm. "We're happy to have you, Gemma. You'll fit right in." She gestured toward the shelves. "Why don't you take a look around? Get a feel for things."

Gemma gave a hesitant nod and stepped away, her eyes moving over the shelves packed with goods. She touched the fabric rolls, the rough burlap of potato sacks, the cool glass of jars filled with pickled vegetables. The sheer amount of stuff made her head spin, but she focused on one detail at a time, trying to ground herself.

As she approached the back of the store, Isobel led Gemma to a counter where a thick ledger lay open. "This is where we track our inventory," she said. "It's important work. Every item that comes in or leaves, we write it here."

Gemma leaned over, looking at the careful lines of ink. It was a puzzle she needed to solve, a key to understanding this new place. She nodded. "I understand," she said.

Isobel smiled at her. "You'll catch on quick, I can tell," she said, turning to a fresh page. "Help me log today's shipments. It'll be a good start."

Marisol said, "I'll check in later to see how you two are doing. Bye." A quick wave and she was out the door, her heels clacking on the boardwalk.

After Gemma waved, she took the pen, her fingers trembling as she held it. She focused on the numbers, each careful stroke of ink a small but meaningful step toward belonging. As the afternoon wore on, the work took on a soothing rhythm—writing, counting, following Isobel's gentle guidance. For the first time since arriving, a sense of calm settled over her.

Isobel asked, "Ready for a look upstairs?"

Gemma set the pen down, smoothing her apron. "Yes, thank you," she said. She was ready to see more, to take another step into this strange, daunting world.

As Gemma followed Isobel up the narrow staircase to the apartment above the store, a strange unease settled over her. Each step creaked underfoot, echoing the uncertainty that churned within her. The bustling warmth of the store below faded, replaced by a cool stillness that enveloped the upper floor.

Isobel pushed open the door at the top of the stairs, revealing a cozy kitchen bathed in soft, filtered light of a window. The scent of dried herbs lingered, mingling with the faint aroma of something baked earlier that morning. Pots and pans hung on the walls, and a small table near the window framed with lace curtains completed the homely scene. Yet despite its charm, a chill had settled in her bones, a feeling that didn't belong to the early spring air.

"This will be your home instead of the saloon. You're too young for that," Isobel said, her words warm and encouraging. She gestured for Gemma to step inside. "You can live here with me."

Gemma nodded, but her response was automatic, her thoughts elsewhere as she stepped into the room. The chill intensified, creeping up her spine and prickling at her senses. The kitchen appeared normal—everything in its place. Still, beneath the surface, she sensed something darker, an unseen presence lingering.

Her hand brushed over the cool surface of the wooden countertop, and a shiver ran through her, though she wasn't sure if it was from the cold or something else. The room held memories that weren't her own—memories that whispered of pain and loss, of someone struggling to breathe, to live. Gemma's gaze drifted toward the window, where she saw a healthy, vibrant willow tree swaying outside. She frowned. Something didn't add up.

Isobel led her through the kitchen, chatting about the apartment, but Gemma's attention drifted, her senses attuned to the silent echoes of the past that clung to the walls. When they reached the bedroom, Gemma hesitated at the doorway, a deep unease settling in her chest.

The room was empty, like a blank canvas. Gemma entered, feeling an urge to disrupt the vast, almost suffocating emptiness pressing down on her.

She spun, her skirt billowing around her, trying to shake off the strange sensation. But as quickly as the lightness came, it was swallowed by a darker presence that filled the room. The thick and oppressive air came with an overwhelming sense of despair.

"Illness. Cursed," Gemma whispered, the words slipping out before she could stop them. They barely broke the silence, but the impact lingered, heavy and ominous.

Isobel's steps faltered, her brow furrowing. "Cursed?" she repeated, her eyes narrowing in concern. "What do you mean?"

Gemma's heart pounded in her chest as she realized what she had said. Panic surged within her—she had revealed too much, too soon.

She bit her lip, searching for a way to backtrack, to downplay the words that had escaped.

"I'm sorry," Gemma stammered, her cheeks flushing. "I just... sensed something. It's probably nothing, just my imagination."

Isobel studied her for a moment, her eyes softening. "It's alright, Gemma," she said. "Sometimes places carry memories, feelings. You're sensitive to that, aren't you?"

Gemma nodded, surprised by Isobel's acceptance. She had expected disbelief, maybe even ridicule, but Isobel's reaction was one of quiet empathy. The tension in her shoulders eased, though the heaviness of the room's history still pressed against her.

Isobel offered a small smile, stepping back to give Gemma space. "This place has been through a lot, but it's also a place of new beginnings. I hope you can find some peace here. I ordered a bed from a carpenter and I'll let him know we need it as soon as possible."

Gemma let out a shaky breath, the words offering her a fragile thread of hope. The fear of being rejected for her strangeness, for the things she sensed but not always understood, loosened its grip. Maybe in this shadowed apartment, she could discover not just a place to live but a place where she fit in, where she wouldn't need to conceal her true self.

"Thank you," Gemma murmured. "I'll do my best."

Isobel nodded, her smile widening a touch. "That's all I ask. Come, let's head back downstairs. There's still plenty to do today."

Chapter Nine

As dusk settled over the shop, casting long shadows across the floor, Gemma moved behind the counter, organizing jars of herbs and spices. The dim light brought a calmness to the store, and she listened to Isobel's rhythmic scooping of beans from an old burlap sack. The beans rustled like whispers from faraway lands as they poured into the bin.

Shadow, Gemma's raccoon familiar, perched on a nearby shelf, his dark eyes watching Isobel with curiosity. He flicked his tail as the sturdy cart squeaked when Isobel pushed it back into the storeroom. The sound made Gemma glance over her shoulder, a faint smile touching her lips as she remembered Isobel's story about the day the burlap sack had torn, spilling beans everywhere. Ben, the carpenter, had helped her gather them, slipping and sliding on the scattered beans, laughing all the while. He'd even built the cart for her, refusing any payment.

Gemma asked, "Can you put these boxes on the top shelf? I can't reach." She held a box filled with goods, looking at the top shelf. Isobel turned, her gaze assessing the ladder. "How's this? Try turning the ladder so the steps lead to the shelves," she suggested, moving to adjust it. Gemma nodded, climbing to place the box while Shadow hopped down to explore the counter.

The calm didn't last. A sudden, loud series of knocks—THWACK! THWACK! THWACK!—echoed through the store, shattering the peace. Gemma's heart leaped into her throat, her eyes darting to the back door. Shadow hissed, his fur bristling as he scrambled to hide beneath the counter.

Isobel's face tightened, her eyes narrowing. She ran past Gemma, her hand slipping under the counter to grab the pistol she kept there. Gemma felt her breath catch, fear coursing through her veins. The door shuddered as the blade of an ax bit into the wood, splintering it with each strike.

"Get help. Go next door," Isobel ordered. Gemma hesitated for only a moment, her eyes locking with Isobel's, before she turned and ran. Her feet pounded across the wooden floor, Shadow darting out to follow her. Together, they rushed out the front door, the cool evening air hitting her face as she sprinted next door to the hotel.

Gemma ran into the lobby, her breath coming in gasps. "Help! Isobel's in trouble! Someone is breaking in the back door!" she yelled.

Jane and John stood at the front desk, where Jane, the hotel owner, was handing John, a local rancher and Isobel's beau, his family's mail. The sight of Gemma rushing in, panic etched across her face, made Jane's eyes widen in alarm. She didn't hesitate. Snatching her shawl, she hurried around the desk and followed Gemma, John right on her heels. As they moved, Jane's voice rang out, sharp with certainty, "I'm sure it's Tom!"

Shadow led the way, his small form racing over the boardwalk, a silent guide.

Before they reached the door, a gunshot echoed through the small shop. Gemma winced at the sound, her hands covering her ears. A man let out a scream.

Gemma watched through the window as Tom, the saloon owner who harassed Isobel daily, stumbled backward, his hand clutching his foot. Blood pooled beneath him, staining the wooden floor a dark crimson. "My foot! You shot me in the foot, you damn—" he howled, his words cutting off as Isobel slapped him across the face, her palm stinging from the force of it.

Gemma's breath came in quick gasps as she opened the door while Isobel stepped back, her eyes wide with shock. Shadow peeked out from behind Gemma's skirt, his ears flat, sensing the tension.

Jane's face went pale at the sight of Tom on the ground, blood spreading around him. John's expression darkened, his eyes blazing with fury. "Isobel, are you alright?" he demanded, running to her side.

Isobel nodded as she leaned into John's embrace. Gemma watched, her own chest tightening at the sight of Isobel seeking comfort. How strange and unsettling to see Isobel, normally strong and independent, now vulnerable.

Eyes blazing in anger, Isobel pulled away from John. "You broke in! You deserve every bit of it," she snapped, her hands on her hips. Gemma saw the struggle in Isobel's eyes and sensed the darkness she was fighting to push away.

Jane stepped forward. "What happened?" she asked, her eyes shifting between Isobel and Tom.

With a deep breath, Isobel's voice trembled. "Tom broke in with an ax. He said he was taking me. When he grabbed me, I shot him...in self-defense."

Tom slammed his hand on the counter, his face flushed. "I'm the one bleeding here! When is someone going to get Doc?" he barked, his arrogance undiminished.

Jane laughed, the sound cutting through the tension. She nudged Tom's uninjured shin with her foot. "You still have another foot. Hop over to Doc's," she said, her eyes glinting with disdain.

A small giggle escaped from Gemma before she clamped her hand over her mouth. The image of Tom hopping down the boardwalk broke through the fear she grappled with. Now she wanted to hide from her inappropriate response.

Jane's tone grew stern. "Maybe if you stay away from Isobel, you won't get shot," she said, securing the pistol she took from Isobel's hand in her skirt's waistband.

Tom slid down to the floor, his head resting against the counter. "Not going anywhere," he muttered, his bravado fading.

John stepped forward, his eyes locked on Tom, his face hard. He lifted his boot, pressing it on Tom's injured foot. "Does it hurt?" he asked, low and threatening.

Tom winced, his eyes widening. "Yeah, that hurts! I didn't do anything to you," he protested as John applied pressure. John held his gaze for a long moment before stepping back, his eyes filled with contempt.

Gemma noticed the tension in Isobel's posture, the way her hands clenched and unclenched at her sides. She knew Isobel was struggling, caught between the desire for revenge and being a good and lawful person. Gemma's own heart ached.

Jane turned towards the door. "I'm going to get the sheriff. Paul needs to know Tom attacked a woman again." She shot Tom a glare. "You can nurse your foot in jail." With that, she stormed out.

Gemma hurried after Jane, her heart still racing, Shadow scurrying at her heels. She heard Tom groaning behind her, but she didn't look back.

Gemma raced ahead to the store, holding the door open. Paul, the Sheriff, strode inside, his boots heavy against the floorboards. Jane followed close behind, her expression tight as a bowstring. Gemma's breath caught as she entered and rushed to Isobel's side, her body tucked close to the counter as if she could disappear into its shadow.

Paul's gaze fixed on Isobel like iron to a magnet. "I have to place you under arrest." The words rang out cold and sharp, slicing through the room, leaving a silence that hung heavy, like the weight of an approaching storm.

Jane's voice cracked the quiet, her hands flying up as though to push back the chaos. "Wait! I told you—Tom attacked her!" She spun toward the splintered doorway, the jagged wood and shattered edges a silent witness to the violence. Her hand shot out, a blade of accusation, pointing at the ax laying on the floor. "Look at the door. The ax is right there!"

Gemma's stomach twisted as all eyes shifted to the weapon, but her voice broke through the thick air before anyone could speak. "It was scary. I ran to get help." She wrapped her arms around herself, the lingering tremor of fear making her voice smaller than she intended. The confession felt fragile in the room, lost amid the anger crackling between Paul and John.

Isobel stepped closer to John, her presence steady but fragile, her voice low and firm as she spoke. "He used an ax. I had to shoot him. It was self-defense."

The plea trembled at the edges, but Paul gave no sign of listening. He shook his head, his words a hammer striking cold iron. "I can't let people go around shooting in town."

"No!" Gemma lurched forward, her small hands clutching Paul's sleeve. "You can't take her!" The words tumbled out, desperate and pleading, but Paul's rough gesture sent her stumbling back, her feet tangling against the floor. She would have fallen if Jane hadn't caught her, pulling her upright with a firm hand.

"Did you shoot Tom?" Paul's voice cut through the chaos, hard and unrelenting as he turned to Isobel.

Gemma's gaze darted to Isobel, willing her to stay calm, to explain, to make them see. Isobel squared her shoulders, her voice burning like fire against the cold accusation. "I told him to stop! Tom grabbed me, threatened to kidnap me. What was I supposed to do?"

Tom's voice oozed through the space like poison, a cruel counterpoint to Isobel's defiance. "She didn't give me time to stop. She just shot me." His words hung in the air, dripping with deceit, twisting the truth into a weapon only he could wield.

Gemma's heart pounded in her chest as Paul stepped forward, his verdict ringing like the crash of an anvil. "Isobel, you need to come with me. I'm arresting you for attempted murder."

"What?" The word shot from Gemma's lips like a cannon blast, echoed by the stunned voices of Jane and John. The air seemed to shatter, disbelief and outrage raining down like shards of glass.

Paul ignored them all. "Isobel, are you going to come willingly?"

Gemma's hands balled into fists as she watched him grab Isobel's arm.

"This isn't right," Isobel said, her voice straining against the weight of injustice. Gemma could see it, the desperation, the pain, the unraveling of everything Isobel had fought for.

Tom's laughter crackled like a fire too close, cruel and jagged. "Now you're a murderer. Another title after whore."

Gemma flinched as if struck, but Jane's retort was a sharp lightning strike cutting through the dark. "You're not dead yet."

John towered over the chaos, his voice thundering through the room like a storm rolling in. "You can't be serious. You're going to arrest her for self-defense? Charge her with attempted murder for a flesh wound?" He turned on Tom, his gaze cutting like a blade, promising a reckoning.

Paul shoved him back, his authority cracking like a whip. "If you interfere, I can lock you up too."

Gemma's mind raced, the world tilting off its axis as Paul pulled Isobel toward the door. Her feet dragged across the worn floor-boards, her face pale but unbowed. The injustice of it twisted like a knife in Gemma's chest. She wanted to scream, to pull Isobel back, to stop it from happening, but she couldn't move, couldn't think past the pounding of her pulse.

Jane's voice, urgent and low, broke through Gemma's haze as she grabbed John's arm. "Wait. You can help her better outside a jail cell. We'll come up with something." She glanced at Gemma, then pressed a pistol into her shaking hands. "Put it back where it belongs."

Gemma gripped the cold steel, the weight of it sending a shiver up her spine.

John stepped forward, his voice a rock in the shifting storm. "Isobel, we'll get you out. I promise."

The promise rang clear and true, but it couldn't stop the scene unfolding before Gemma. Isobel stepped out into the growing night, Paul's grip firm, his presence a steel wall around her. Dust rose around her feet, caught in the slanted light from the lanterns—her figure stark against the dim glow, like a tragic painting.

Gemma stayed rooted to the spot, her breath shallow, the chill of the pistol still heavy in her hand. Through the haze of disbelief, her mind spiraled. How had it come to this? Tom's lies, Paul's blind justice, the cracks in their world widening with every step Isobel took into the dark.

Isobel, one of her truest anchors, dragged away under the weight of false judgment. The whispered echoes of dark spells, retribution, and despair swirled through Gemma's mind, clinging like smoke. She blinked hard, forcing her focus back as Jane moved to her side, her voice a quiet thread of determination.

"Come on," Jane murmured, tugging Gemma toward the door. "We're not done yet."

Gemma looked at the street where Isobel was disappearing, the town's silence stretching wide and hollow around her. A low, dark part of her stirred, a hunger for something she didn't understand, something sharp and dangerous. But she swallowed it back, forcing herself to breathe, to think of Isobel, to think of John's promise.

They weren't done yet. And neither was she.

Gemma's heart drummed in her ears as she crept toward Isobel's room. The dimly lit kitchen offered little comfort, shadows clinging to every corner like secrets waiting to be uncovered. Her fingers hovered above the cool brass doorknob, trembling as they touched the smooth metal. The chill against her skin did nothing to ease the growing tension in her chest.

What am I doing? Should I even be here? The questions buzzed through Gemma's mind, each one more insistent than the last. But her curiosity, like a siren's call, drowned out the whispers of doubt. She knew Isobel's kindness, her strength, but what hidden truths lay behind this door? Why couldn't she read Isobel's thoughts? What happened when they touched that first day?

With a gentle push, the door creaked open; the sound echoed through the silent apartment like a warning. Gemma hesitated, breath caught in her throat as she peered inside. The thrill of uncovering something unknown sent a shiver down her spine, mixing with the heavy sense of intrusion that weighed on her conscience.

She stepped into the room; the door clicking shut behind her, sealing her inside. The late afternoon light filtered through lace curtains, casting delicate patterns on the wooden floor. Her gaze landed on a small framed photograph on the nightstand, Isobel smiling beside a man Gemma didn't recognize, their happiness frozen in time.

Gemma moved deeper into the room, her eyes tracing over the intimate details that painted a picture of Isobel's life. A stack of well-worn books lay on a dresser, their spines creased from frequent use, while a vase of fresh wildflowers added a burst of color against the muted tones of the room. A shawl draped over the back of a chair, as if waiting for Isobel to return and wrap it around herself, exuded a sense of warmth that only heightened Gemma's unease. Shadow hopped on the chair, sniffing the air.

She reached out, fingers brushing the soft fabric of the shawl, and the weight of her intrusion became like a physical presence in the room. *It's like she's watching me, even when she's not here.* Her pulse quickened. She ran her hands along Shadow's body to calm herself.

The scent of lavender mingled with a faint trace of what was Isobel's favorite tea, creating an atmosphere that was inviting yet private. The warmth of the room clashed with Gemma's purpose for being there. She was an outsider, driven by a need for answers, but every object she touched reprimanded her for overstepping. The charm of the space, reflective of Isobel's vibrant spirit, only deepened Gemma's inner conflict. Each item held a story, a secret, and demanded the respect of being left undisturbed.

Her resolve wavered as she stood surrounded by Isobel's belongings. The line between seeking understanding and violating someone's personal space blurred, her heart racing with a mix of thrill and guilt. She took a deep breath, her curiosity battling with her conscience as she made her way toward the dresser.

The polished wood gleamed under her touch as she approached, the simple, elegant handles tempting her to explore further. Her hand hovered over the top drawer, the cool metal sending a shiver through her as she grasped it.

"What are your secrets, Isobel?" she whispered. With a gentle pull, she opened the drawer, the sound of wood sliding against wood loud in the quiet room.

At first, the drawer appeared empty, its stark interior deepening the mystery. Gemma furrowed her brow as she leaned closer, expecting to find something, anything, that might offer a clue. Nothing there, only shadows playing tricks on her eyes.

Driven by an inexplicable instinct, she ran her fingers across the bottom of the drawer. The surface felt smooth and cold, but as she touched it, her fingers brushed against something solid, yet invisible. Books. Her breath caught in her throat as the realization hit her like a physical blow. The books were there, concealed, their presence revealed only under her touch.

The tension in the room thickened, the air charged with the weight of the unseen. Gemma's heart pounded, the discovery both exhilarating and terrifying. She had stumbled upon secrets meant to remain hidden, delving into depths not meant to be explored.

She jerked her hand back as if burned, staring at the empty drawer. The gravity of what she had uncovered set her nerves on edge. Was Isobel a witch? The implications were vast, the danger palpable. Gemma knew all too well the risks and responsibilities that came with such power.

She closed the drawer, sealing her unspoken vow to tread carefully. The discovery had added to the complexity of her relationship with Isobel, binding them together by a shared thread of mystery and power.

Standing motionless beside the dresser, Gemma's mind raced. The room felt smaller, as if the walls were closing in, privy to her thoughts and fears. *Is Isobel like me?* The possibility that Isobel might understand Gemma's deepest secrets and fears, was both comforting and terrifying.

Gemma's fingers brushed against the wood of the dresser, grounding her as she pondered her next move. The invisible books were no accident; they were a sign, a nudge towards a truth she had suspected but never dared to confirm. The thought that she wasn't alone, that Isobel might be a kindred spirit, offered a sliver of hope.

But with that hope came the dangers Lillian had warned her about, the dark paths, the heavy prices. The cost of power was high, the line between protection and peril razor-thin.

Gemma caught sight of her reflection in the mirror, seeing not only herself, but the potential of what she might become. The fear of exposure, of vulnerability, loomed large, yet so did the possibility of finding someone who understood her.

The tension between these thoughts, finding a kindred spirit versus the fear of unknown dangers, tightened the knot in her stomach. She knew she had to be cautious, to protect both herself and Isobel from the potential consequences of their shared secrets.

With a deep breath, Gemma stepped away from the dresser. The connection between her and Isobel had deepened through the bond of a hidden world they both navigated.

"I'll be careful," she whispered to her reflection, a promise to herself and to the unseen forces that guided her.

CHAPTER TEN

A HEAVINESS WEIGHED IN Gemma's stomach as she crossed the street to Tin Creek Saloon, turned and passed the livery to arrive at the sheriff's office. The small building, usually a normal part of Tin Creek, now looked bigger and more threatening. This place kept Isobel from her, away from everything they shared. It festered into an ache like she never had before, like missing something she's only now found. Like losing a sister she never had.

She stood there, heart pounding, fingers itching to grab the handle and open the door, but it wasn't that easy. This wasn't about getting past a door. It was about the sheriff, the rules, and what everyone thought was right and wrong. And those lines were blurry.

Gemma turned the doorknob, but it didn't budge. Locked. She dropped her shoulders and huffed. She glanced through the window beside the door.

Isobel sat, shoulders slumped on a bench in the jail cell. Her face, tilted down, appeared tired. Gemma's heart ached seeing her like that. Isobel was so close, yet untouchable behind that glass. Gemma moved closer, pressing her hands against the window. She wanted Isobel to realize she was there.

Isobel's eyes, usually bright and full of warmth, looked worried and worn. Gemma's throat tightened. She had to do something, anything, to help. She kept her hands on the glass, wishing she could somehow reach through.

Gemma focused on her thoughts. Aunt Lillian had always warned her to keep her abilities hidden, to be careful. But Gemma wouldn't stand by now. She closed her eyes and whispered in her mind, "I'm here. You're not alone." She pushed the thought toward Isobel, hoping it would somehow reach her.

At first, nothing happened. Gemma waited until Isobel's eyes widened, a spark of recognition lighting them. Isobel heard her. They weren't alone, not really, even if it was dangerous. That old, hollow space inside her filled with a bond she'd only heard others talk about, a bond that feels like family. She had felt it when they first shook hands.

Seeing Isobel's eyes light up, even a little, made it worth it. It gave Gemma strength. She would help Isobel, no matter what.

Their eyes held for a moment, a silent promise passing between them. She wouldn't let Isobel stay trapped, not if she could help it.

The tension in Gemma's shoulders eased, but a fresh wave of concern replaced it. She had exposed a part of herself that had remained hidden, stepping into a realm of magical interaction that was fraught with peril. The connection they had shared also fortified her resolve. Now their paths aligned, a partnership forged not only in friendship but in the shared secrecy of extraordinary abilities.

Shadow tugged on her skirt, so she stooped, allowing him to jump into her arms. Gemma held up her familiar to the window. He scratched at the glass as if he could dig his way through, making Isobel smile.

Gemma stepped back from the window, opening her eyes and taking a deep breath to steady herself. Isobel needed her, and Gemma wasn't about to let fear stop her. The telepathic connection, risky as it was, had created a new link between them. Gemma was ready to use it, no matter what.

She lingered for a moment longer, looking from the locked door to the wide Montana sky. Everything was quiet, but inside, her thoughts swirled. Her family's legacy, the stories of power and danger, the warnings from Aunt Lillian, became more real. They were a part of her, and maybe a part of Isobel too.

Her family's history pressed on her, but it also gave her purpose. She could be part of something bigger now that might change everything in Tin Creek.

Inhaling deep, Gemma stepped away from the window "We'll find a way." She wasn't alone anymore. She was stronger, being part of a legacy, and now a partnership. Together, they would face whatever came next.

As she walked away from the sheriff's office, her gait was steady. The evening sun cast long shadows on the ground, mirroring the mix of hope and worry inside her. With each step, Gemma beamed, her chest expanded, about the connection to her family's legacy and to Isobel. Her magick wasn't the focus; it was about supporting each other through any challenge.

Morning light poured through the windows of Isobel's store, making everything glow, the shelves stocked and faced and the counter clean. So far, it had been a quiet morning, but the weight of all her extra responsibilities pressed on Gemma as it fell to her to manage the store. She stood alone by the counter, her body relaxed but her eyes alert, like she was guarding something precious.

Gemma scanned the shelves, making sure everything was in its place. Lillian's words echoed in her mind: be careful, use your gifts with care, and let no one know, ever. There was no room for errors, not now. Every action mattered.

The calm of the morning should have been comforting, but it did little to ease Gemma's worry. This was her test, her chance to prove herself. The pressure weighed on her, a reminder of the delicate balance she had to keep between the everyday world and the magick she carried.

To make the time go by quicker, Gemma entered the back room to review the order for the week. Tomorrow, it would go by stagecoach for that week's delivery.

The door creaked open, breaking the silence, and Gemma's heart jumped. She turned to see Sheriff Paul walking in, his steps heavy and sure. The air shifted, the earlier calm replaced by a tension that settled in the room.

Paul's eyes swept over the store before landing on Gemma.

"Hi, are you wanting to buy something?" Gemma flashed a smile at him, hoping he would turn around and leave. He was an impossible man, like Tom, across the street.

Paul walked to the counter, his gaze sharp. "No. I came for Isobel's pistol for evidence. Where is it?" He crossed his arms while tapping his foot.

Gemma's stomach tightened, fear rushing through her. She wouldn't let him take anything that might make things worse for

Isobel. Her hands clenched at her sides, her body stiffening. She had to protect Isobel and not let this spiral out of control.

She met Paul's gaze and shrugged. "I don't know where her gun is," she said. She needed a moment to figure out what to do. She spun around like a ballerina on her way behind the counter to distract him.

Gemma took a breath, thoughts racing. The shelf behind the counter, where the gun lay, became her focus. Action was necessary. Channeling energy, her eyes flicked toward the shelf, willing it to appear empty. To anyone watching, she appeared confused, masking the magick of creating an illusion.

Her hands moved in a pattern, hidden by the counter, as she focused on the shelf. The air shimmered for a second, and the gun disappeared from sight. Gemma kept her expression calm, her heart pounding as she waited for Paul's reaction.

Paul stepped around the counter.

Gemma raised her hand, blocking his way. "No customers behind the counter."

"I'm not a customer. I am here on official duty," he growled. He pushed forward, his eyes locked on the shelves, but stumbled as he tried to maneuver around the counter. Gemma stood her ground, her gaze unwavering as she watched his every move.

Shadow, sensing the tension, hopped off the shelf and slipped under the counter, his small body hidden from Paul's view. He moved with the precision of a predator, his eyes following Paul's feet, ready to act if needed.

Paul rifled through the shelves, his frown deepening as he found nothing. The silence stretched, broken only by the ticking of the clock and the muffled sounds from the street outside. "Why is there nothing here?"

"Because there is nothing there right now." Gemma stood still, her breath shallow as she held the illusion. Her hands trembled, still hidden from view. She smiled as she watched Paul's confusion grow, his frustration clear. He stepped back, jaw clenched, and his eyes narrowing as he looked at her.

After a moment, Paul let out a sigh, his face hardening. "Find that gun and bring it to me, or you'll find yourself in jail with your boss." He threw his hands up as he turned and walked out; the door swinging shut behind him with a loud thud.

Gemma noticed Paul's sudden flinch out front, his hand moving toward his pistol. Following his gaze, she spotted a hawk perched on the railing outside. The bird spread its wings wide, as if taunting Paul, before it took off, swooping low over the boardwalk and vanishing into the sky. Gemma smirked, seeing the unease in Paul's posture as he shook his head. Shadow peeked out from under the counter, his eyes meeting Gemma's as if sharing in her satisfaction at Paul's rattled demeanor.

Gemma let out the breath she'd been holding, her shoulders sagging as the tension eased. She'd done it, at least for now.

Gemma leaned against the counter, her body relaxing a bit more. But it wasn't over. She had protected Isobel's secret, but the close call was a stark reminder of how dangerous it was for someone to discover her special abilities.

"I did it," Gemma whispered. No longer just standing by, she had become part of the fight, a part of the hidden world of witches and secrets.

Gemma straightened, ready to get back to work. The fear of being discovered was still there, but it didn't paralyze her. Instead, it fueled her determination. She would protect Isobel, protect herself, and face whatever came next.

Gemma glanced around the store one last time. The shadows weren't as threatening, the light warmer. With a nod, she stepped away from the counter, ready to face whatever the day would bring, armed with her magick, her courage, and the bond she shared with Isobel.

Chapter Eleven

Gemma organized the herbal remedies behind the counter, concerned they would run out before Isobel got out of jail. She wasn't sure she could make them like Isobel. Maybe she should have Isobel write the recipes for her.

The front door flew open with a loud bang, shattering the morning silence like a sudden thunderclap. Her head snapped up, her hands still among the envelopes, as Jane rushed inside, her face pale and her eyes wide with fear.

"They took her, Tom and Paul! They took Isobel!" Jane gasped, her hands splayed on the counter. The words hit Gemma like a punch to the chest, making her shudder. The soft morning light felt wrong, too bright for such terrible news. She tried to blink it away.

Jane came around the counter and embraced her. "We'll figure this out. Don't worry. I have to get back to the hotel. I'll be back." Jane raced out, her footsteps loud.

Gemma's heart pounded, the calm of the store now out of place. The shelves blurred, her mind only on what Jane had said. Tom McCall and Paul Burke, names that always spelled trouble in Tin Creek, had gone too far. They had taken Isobel.

One moment, it was a normal morning; the next, everything had turned into a nightmare. Jane's words trapped Gemma in a panic. Fear for Isobel mixed with growing anxiety about what this meant for all of them. The usual noises from outside sounded louder, clashing with her racing thoughts.

Gemma's shock turned into a need to act. But what could she do? She wrung her hands and paced. Nothing came to her, as she was too wound up to be useful. She focused on her breathing to get it under control.

Hurried footsteps echoed outside. She looked to the door, her nerves on edge as John burst in, his face set with anger and determination. He scanned the room, his eyes meeting hers for a heartbeat, before turning back to the door. Behind him came Matt and Walter, their faces grim.

The three men paced as they moved through the store, their boots thudding against the wooden floor with purpose. Gemma watched, her anxiety matching the intensity on John's face, as they moved back out towards the livery where their horses were tied. She followed to the doorway, her heart pounding.

"We're getting her back, no matter what," John said, his voice rough with determination. He mounted his horse, his movements sharp and focused. Matt and Walter did the same, their faces set with the same fierce resolve.

The clatter of hooves as they rode away broke the usual calm of Tin Creek, sending a ripple of unease through the town.

Gemma stood in the doorway, watching as John and his group galloped away, dust swirling around them. Seeing them ride out with such purpose made her chest tighten. John's love for Isobel, his unwillingness to let anything happen to her, showed in every move he made. It was a moment of bravery that resonated with Gemma, reminding her of just how serious the situation was.

As the golden afternoon sun dipped below the rugged peaks west of Tin Creek, Gemma stood near the hotel with Jane, her heart still pounding in her chest. The stagecoach rumbled to a stop, dust swirling in its wake. The door swung open, and Marisol stepped out first, her presence a comforting sight. Gemma rushed forward, embracing Marisol, drawing strength from the familiar warmth. "Tom and Paul took Isobel!"

Marisol hugged her, then pulled back. "What! Oh, no! Good thing the US Marshal is on his way. He'll be here soon, and he'll get her back."

Behind Marisol, a tall man with a stern expression and gray streaks in his hair emerged. Marisol's smile conveyed something that Gemma wasn't sure how to decipher. "This is Henry, Isobel's uncle, who came all the way from Chicago. He helped free Jack and wants to set things right here."

Gemma offered a quick, polite curtsy, feeling the weight of his sharp gaze on her. Henry nodded in acknowledgment, his eyes softening only as he took in the young woman before him. "I'm sorry Isobel isn't here to greet you herself, sir."

Henry nodded in agreement. "I can only hope the Marshal will bring her home safely."

Jane stepped forward, her eyes still worried but hopeful. "Hello. I'm Jane, owner of the hotel," she introduced herself. "This is Gemma. She helps Isobel run the store."

Henry extended his hand. "Isobel's written about you both, Jane and Gemma. I feel like I know you already." He gave a small, reassuring smile. "Thank you for standing by her."

Jane swept her hand towards the door of her hotel. "Why don't we make ourselves comfortable in the dining room? Henry, I can get you checked in if you are staying."

At a table by the front window, they sat and watched. Jane and Fred brought coffee, tea, and pastries. The silence made Gemma uncomfortable, but she wasn't sure what to say. Isobel's absence created an ache in her heart, so she was sure Henry was beside himself.

The sun climbed higher, casting shadows across the streets. Dust rose again at the edge of town. This time, the US Marshals rode in, drawing a crowd as they stopped in front of the sheriff's office. The Marshal, a broad-shouldered man, jumped down from his horse, his steely eyes surveying the scene.

The crowd grew quiet, everyone watching the Marshal take charge. His deputy stood beside him, waiting. With a nod, the Marshal signaled for people to gather, his presence demanding attention.

"Listen up, everyone," the Marshal called out. "Tom McCall's wanted for murder, and Paul Burke has been impersonating a law officer."

Gasps rippled through the crowd, people exchanging shocked looks. The severity of the accusations sunk in, and the tension grew thicker. The townsfolk stood in stunned silence, the reality of the situation hitting them hard.

"We'll bring them in. Justice will be served," he said. His authority cut through the fear, shifting the mood towards action.

The Marshal scanned the crowd, pointing to a few men. "You. And you. Get your horses and meet me here. We're riding out right away." The men nodded, stepping forward without hesitation.

He turned to the others. "Tom and Paul won't get far. I figure they are heading east. Maybe to Virginia City. We'll split up." He turned to his deputy. "Ben, take the southern route, and I'll lead a group straight across the mountain pass. We'll cut them off."

Fred, Jane's husband, frowned, his brow furrowed. "What if they split up, Marshal?"

The Marshal looked up, eyes sharp. "That's why we'll spread out. Keep your eyes open and don't take any risks. These men are dangerous." His gaze shifted between the men, his tone firm. "We bring them in alive, but we don't let them get away."

Ben nodded, tightening his grip on his reins. "Understood, Marshal. We'll get 'em."

Henry pushed his way to the front of the crowd, his face filled with worry. "Marshal, please," he called out. "Tom McCall has taken my niece, Isobel. I'm begging you, bring her back to us."

The Marshal stepped closer to Henry, his eyes softening. He gave a firm nod. "We'll do everything we can, sir. I promise you, we won't stop until we bring her back safe."

Henry swallowed hard, his shoulders sagging. "Thank you." He extended his hand, and they shook.

"We'll get her," the Marshal assured him before turning back to his men. "Good. Saddle up, and let's move. We don't have time to waste. It's a kidnapping, too, so time is of the essence." The men moved with purpose, their steps quick and focused as they followed the Marshal's orders, ready for the mission.

Gemma stood among the crowd, hugging herself despite the warmth of the sun on her skin. A chill ran down her spine, a gnawing fear that wouldn't let go. What if they didn't find Isobel in time? The thought looped endlessly, each possibility worse than the last. Tom was far more dangerous than she had ever imagined. Dark scenarios twisted through her mind like writhing worms, eating away at her hope. Her chest tightened, each breath shallow as the minutes stretched into hours, her concern for Isobel growing with every heartbeat.

Gemma trailed behind Henry as he led the way to the bank, her stomach churning. Days had passed without a word about Isobel, and Gemma's fear only grew with every hour. She lingered outside the Sapphire Saloon, her eyes scanning the street, searching for any sign of hope. When Henry returned, her breath caught at the sight of Mr. Johnston, the banker, following him. The man looked nothing like his usual smug self, his face pale, his hands clenched around his hat. Something had shifted, and it gave Gemma a flicker of hope.

They moved to the hotel, where she sat alongside Jane, Henry, and the shaken Mr. Johnston. The sunny day was out-of-place amid the turmoil boiling inside her. The quiet town felt tense, as though holding its breath, waiting for something to snap. Gemma watched Mr. Johnston fidget, his eyes darting like a cornered animal. She sensed his fear, the way he avoided eye contact with everyone around him. He wasn't used to being on the receiving end of power.

Gemma's attention wavered when she saw a small group approaching the hotel. Her heart skipped a beat, her breath catching in her throat as she recognized the figures, John and Matt, with Isobel between them. Relief flooded through her like a wave, her shoulders sagging as the tightness in her chest eased. Isobel was safe. She looked exhausted; her steps slow, but she was here. She was alive.

Henry leaned closer to Gemma. "Keep an eye on Johnston. We can't let him slip away before the Marshal gets here." His eyes met hers, giving her a look that spoke of trust, of the importance of her role.

Gemma nodded, swallowing down her own worry. She had to focus, to stay strong. She turned to Mr. Johnston, her gaze steady despite her racing heart. "Let's get you inside, Mr. Johnston." The banker hesitated, his eyes flicking between her and Henry, but he knew he had no choice. With a sigh, he stood, and Gemma led him into the hotel.

The dining room was warm, the golden afternoon light streaming through the windows, casting a gentle glow over the tables. But Gemma held none of its comfort. She directed Mr. Johnston to a chair in the corner, away from the windows, where she could keep a close watch on him. He sank into the seat, fidgeting, his eyes avoiding hers.

"Sit tight," Gemma instructed, leaving no room for argument. She settled into the chair across from him, her body tense despite her attempt at a relaxed posture. Her eyes scanned the room, noting every detail, every person.

Across the room, Gemma saw Jane guiding Isobel to a seat. Jane spoke softly to Isobel, making it so Gemma couldn't make out the words. The way Jane cared for her, the tenderness in her movements, made Gemma's eyes sting. Despite everything, there was still kindness, still people who cared for one another. It was a reminder of what they were all fighting for.

Jane brought a spoonful of soup to Isobel's lips, and a rush of relief washed over Gemma. Isobel accepted it with a grateful nod,

her exhaustion clear but her spirit unbroken. It spoke of resilience, of the strength they all needed to hold on to.

Gemma's gaze lingered on Isobel, her heart swelling with both
admiration and gratitude. But she wouldn't allow herself to
relax, not yet. Her eyes returned to Mr. Johnston, who sat staring
at the table, his fingers twitching. He looked like a man who
wanted to vanish, and Gemma knew she couldn't let her guard
down for a second.

The room filled with an unspoken tension. The scene was
peaceful, but Gemma knew it was fragile. One wrong move, and
it would all come crashing down. She took a slow breath, trying
to steady herself, to focus on the task at hand.

Outside, the sun dipped lower, its light filtering through the
curtains, casting shadows that stretched across the room. Gemma clenched her jaw, refusing to let herself get distracted by the
calm exterior. She had to stay sharp, to stay ready.

Her thoughts flickered back to Isobel, who now rested her
head on Jane's shoulder, her eyes half-closed. Gemma's resolve
hardened. She would protect Isobel, protect everyone in Tin
Creek, no matter what. The challenges ahead were daunting, but
Gemma was ready.

Her eyes snapped back to Mr. Johnston. He hadn't moved,
but she sensed his unease, the tension that radiated from him.
Gemma leaned back, her gaze never wavering. She couldn't let
him slip away, not with everything at stake.

The minutes ticked by, and Gemma's responsibility pressed
on her. The town was waiting, holding its collective breath for
the Marshal's return. Gemma would stay here, at her post, a
silent guardian of this fragile peace.

Gemma watched as Jane helped Isobel up, guiding her toward the staircase. Each step creaked, and Gemma's heart tugged as she saw the exhaustion etched in her friend's face. She wanted to be there, to help Isobel herself, but she had a job to do.

Henry's voice broke through her thoughts. "I'll keep an eye on Johnston," he said, his gaze steady as he looked at the anxious banker. "Go be with Isobel."

Relief washed over Gemma, and she nodded, standing up. She followed Jane and Isobel up the stairs, her footsteps soft but quick. She reached the room just as Jane helped Isobel inside. Gemma paused by the ajar door, listening to Jane's quiet, soothing voice as she helped Isobel settle in.

Gemma hesitated for a moment, then stepped inside. Jane looked up, giving her a nod before slipping past her and out of the room, leaving the two of them alone. Gemma approached the bed, her eyes on Isobel's weary face. She pulled a chair close, sitting down, her heart aching at the sight of her friend so drained.

"Isobel," she whispered, "are you comfortable?"

Isobel's eyes fluttered open, and she nodded. "Just tired," she murmured. "It's good to have you here."

Gemma reached out, brushing a strand of hair from Isobel's forehead. "Rest now," she urged. She watched as Isobel's eyes drifted shut, her breathing evening out as she slipped into sleep.

For a long moment, Gemma sat there, letting the quiet of the room wash over her. The day's tension faded, leaving only the soft sound of Isobel's breathing. Gemma's gaze lingered on her friend's face, her heart full of both relief and determination.

Then something caught her eye, a glint of light below Isobel's collarbone. Gemma leaned in, her breath catching as she saw the necklace. The trinity of gemstones was unmistakable. It was the necklace Lillian had spoken of, the one Gemma had only heard about in hushed whispers. The necklace of power. *How is it on Isobel's neck?*

Her fingers hovered over the delicate chain, her thoughts swirling. The pull of her family's legacy was strong, the promise of power almost overwhelming. But would she take it? Would she betray Isobel's trust like that?

Gemma's hand reached out, her fingers brushing against the cool metal. Her heart pounded, the weight of her actions settling in her chest. She hesitated, her breath held, but the call of the necklace was too strong. With trembling fingers, she unclasped it, slipping it into her pocket.

Gemma stepped back, her gaze lingering on Isobel's peaceful face. *What have I done?* The question echoed in her mind as she turned, leaving the room with the necklace heavy against her side.

Outside, Gemma clutched the necklace through the fabric of her pocket, her thoughts in turmoil. She had taken a step there was no coming back from, and the consequences of her choice loomed over her like a dark shadow.

Chapter Twelve

Henry sat behind an oak desk before dawn, the ledger spread open before him. The pages contained neatly written figures detailing the bank's accounts. The room was quiet, save for the occasional creak of the building settling and the rustle of papers as Henry flipped through them.

Henry had taken over the bank only a few days earlier, after he exposed Mr. Johnston for extortion and other questionable practices. Now, he was determined to bring order to the chaos Johnston had left behind, and that started with a thorough audit of every account. His brow furrowed as he worked, his fingers tracing the columns of numbers, his mind sharp as he calculated and reconciled each figure. It was tedious work, but necessary. He needed to understand where the bank stood, both financially and ethically. But each account had money siphoned from every deposit made.

Hours passed, and Henry's concentration broke when his eyes landed on an unexpected entry, an account under his own name. His heart skipped a beat as confusion settled in, prompting him to double-check the ledger. Mary, Isobel's mother, must have opened the account fifteen years ago, not long before she died. The figures were clear: the account held a substantial amount of money.

"What the hell?" Henry muttered, pushing back from the desk, the chair's legs scraping across the floor. His thoughts whirled. He had never opened an account, and he did not have any idea how the money had ended up there. There was only one person in town who might know something—Marisol.

The sun had risen as Henry made his way to the Sapphire Saloon. The town hummed with activity as shopkeepers opened their doors. Henry barely noticed as he walked, his mind preoccupied. He approached the saloon, nodding to a few familiar faces, and stepped inside.

The saloon offered a welcome coolness, where the smoky aroma of whiskey mingled with the heady scent of perfume, clinging to the darkened corners like whispered secrets. He approached the bar, catching sight of one of Marisol's girls, and gestured to her. "Please fetch Marisol for me."

Within minutes, he heard her descending the staircase, her usual grace clear even in the hurried steps. Marisol's smile faltered when she saw Henry's grim expression. "Henry," she said. "What brings you here so early?"

Henry didn't waste time with pleasantries. "I found something strange while auditing the bank's accounts," he said. "There's an account under my name that I never opened. Mary opened it a year before she died. It holds quite a lot of money. Do you have any idea where it came from?"

Marisol's brow furrowed, her eyes searching his. "An account in your name?" she echoed. "That doesn't make any sense."

Henry followed her to a small sofa, and they both sat. He kept his eyes on her, searching for any glimmer of understanding. Marisol looked thoughtful, her gaze drifting.

"I remember…" She hesitated, then continued, "Peter opened an account for Mary around that time. Jack did the same for me, since women can't open bank accounts in their own names. But why would she use your name instead of Peter's?"

Henry leaned forward, elbows resting on his knees. "That's what I need to figure out. I'm going to ride out to the Carlyle ranch, see if Peter remembers anything about it."

Marisol nodded, worry in her eyes. "If Mary had it set up that way, she must've had a reason, Henry. But what that was, I can't guess."

Henry sighed, a weight pressing on his chest. "I'm going to change that, Marisol. At my bank, women will open accounts in their own names. It's ridiculous Mary had to jump through hoops to manage her own money."

Marisol reached over, giving his hand a squeeze. "That's a wonderful change, Henry. Mary would've appreciated that. I know I do."

Henry managed a small smile, though it didn't reach his eyes. "I wish I understood what she was doing, where the money came from," he murmured, feeling a pang deep in his heart as he thought of Mary. He looked at Marisol—something in her eyes reminded him of Mary. Her passion, her strength, stirred something in him that had lain dormant for far too long.

By the time Henry reached the Carlyle ranch, the sun hung low in the sky, the distant mountains casting shadows over the land. He rode up to the barn where Peter worked, repairing a fence. Peter looked up, surprise flashing across his face.

"Can I help you?" Peter called, wiping his hands on his pants. He approached, curiosity in his expression.

Henry dismounted, tying his horse to the nearby post. "My name is Henry. I'm Isobel's uncle. Uh, actually, father. Mary left me a letter with that surprise. But I came to ask you a few questions about Mary."

Peter's expression grew serious, and he nodded toward the house. "Good to meet ya. Come on in. My wife, Anna, will want to hear this too. Especially the part that you are Isobel's father instead of George."

Inside, the cozy warmth of the kitchen greeted Henry, the smell of fresh bread hanging in the air. Peter said, "Anna, this is Isobel's real father, Henry. He has some questions about Mary."

Anna offered a kind smile as she approached. "Well, that's a surprise. I'm sure it's a good one. Henry, it's lovely to meet you. We adore Isobel. She's a sweet young lady." Her gaze shifted between him and Peter, the concern in her eyes clear. "There's more? What's going on?"

Henry set the ledger he carried on the table, taking a deep breath. "I found something strange at the bank. There's an account under my name, opened before Mary died, and it holds a large amount of money. I don't know where it came from."

Peter exchanged a glance with Anna before nodding. "Mary asked me to help her set up an account," Peter said, pulling out a chair for Henry. He sat, his brow furrowed. "It was in your name, Henry. She insisted on it without explaining why, but she seemed... determined. She only deposited a few dollars at first, so I didn't think much of it. To be honest, it was strange she didn't put it in my name, seeing as she'd need your approval to do anything with it. But now I see there was something more."

Henry's heart pounded in his chest. "She was planning something," he muttered, trying to piece it together. "But what? And how did she save up so much?"

Anna shook her head, her face softening. "She never said anything to us, Henry. Whatever she was doing, she kept it close."

Henry ran a hand through his hair, frustration bubbling. "She kept it hidden, even from me," he said. "If I had known…"

Peter leaned back, crossing his arms. "Maybe she was saving it for Isobel," he suggested. "Or maybe she wanted to leave Tin Creek, start over. I wish I knew, but Mary… she was always private, even with those closest to her."

The weight of it all bore into Henry, his thoughts a tangled mess. He glanced at the ledger, then back at Peter and Anna. "I think the money should go to Isobel," he said. "It's hers by right."

Anna reached across the table, laying her hand on Henry's arm. "That's the right thing to do, Henry. Mary loved Isobel more than anything. She'd want her to have it."

Peter nodded. "It's her legacy," he said.

Henry swallowed hard, his throat tightening with emotion. "Thank you. Both of you. I wish I understood how Mary had this sum of money." He looked at the table, the mystery gnawing at him.

Anna squeezed his arm. "She had her reasons. Someday, you might find the answers. For now, you're doing the right thing, Henry. I'm so glad you're here for your daughter. It was nice to meet you."

Henry nodded, though the unanswered questions still lingered. As he rode back into Tin Creek, the town bathed in the soft glow of early evening, the streets quieting as the day wound down.

He dismounted in front of the bank, his gaze lingering on the small, quiet building. He hadn't expected to find such a secret hidden in its ledgers, a secret that changed everything he knew about Mary. What was she doing?

Henry rested his hands on the counter, his knuckles whitening as he leaned into the silence of the empty room. He scanned the rows of ledgers, the arranged stacks of coins, but the numbers only deepened the pit of uncertainty in his chest. The money would go to Isobel, he was sure of that. But the questions gnawed at him: Why had Mary saved it out of her reach? How had she gathered such a sum? The answers remained just out of reach, like shadows slipping through his grasp, and the unease gnawed at his insides.

He straightened, exhaling slowly, his breath echoing softly in the stillness. "I'll make sure she has the life Mary wanted for her," he muttered, the words catching in his throat.

Turning toward the door, Henry's boots scuffed the wooden floor, the sound swallowed by the weight of his thoughts. He pushed open the door, stepping out into the evening air, the chill biting at his face. The door clicked shut behind him, sealing the emptiness inside. Overhead, the stars emerged, their faint light a reminder that even in the darkness, hope was found. But Henry's jaw tightened, hope wouldn't be enough. He needed answers, and he would not rest until he had them.

Gemma tossed and turned, her sleep plagued by restless visions. Shadows danced across the walls, taking the shapes of a face she knew well, her grandmother, stern and cold, and other spectral figures whose names eluded her but whose presence was familiar. They crowded around her, their voices intertwining in a cacophony of beckoning and warning.

"Embrace your power," they whispered, their words heavy with both promise and peril. "It is your birthright, Gemma. Take your place among us."

But instead of filling her with resolve, the voices left her more lost than ever. She tried to elude them, to bury herself deeper into her blankets, but the chorus only grew louder, urging her towards a destiny she was not sure she wanted.

When the dawn broke, its light filtering through the curtains, Gemma opened her eyes to a world that was no more real than the dreams she had left behind. She lay still for a moment, her heart heavy, the remnants of the night's visions clinging to her thoughts.

With a sigh, she pushed herself up, her body aching as if she had been dragged through her dreams. Her room, normally a sanctuary, now felt oppressive, the shadows of the night lingering in the corners like unwelcome guests.

She moved through her morning routine, each action tinged with the unease that had become her constant companion. Her hand trembled as she brushed her hair, her eyes flickering toward the small drawer beside her bed. She knew what lay inside, the necklace, with its three gemstones, the very one Lillian had spoken of many times. More than a piece of jewelry, it was a symbol of power, a relic of her family's legacy.

But to Gemma, it was also a source of unbearable guilt. Even hidden away, the necklace cast a long shadow over her every thought and action.

She refused to open the drawer, unable to bear the sight of the evidence of her betrayal. Instead, she dressed, avoiding the mirror, avoiding her own reflection. The day ahead promised the usual routine, working alongside Isobel in the store, arranging shipments, serving customers. But nothing was usual anymore. The secret Gemma carried tainted every moment with Isobel.

By the time she made her way downstairs, the soft light of morning bathed the store. Isobel was there, as always, her presence a beacon of warmth and kindness. She greeted Gemma with a smile, her eyes bright and clear, unaware of the storm brewing beneath Gemma's calm exterior.

"Good morning, Gemma! Ready for another busy day?" Isobel asked as she straightened a display near the front window.

Gemma forced a smile, nodding as she joined Isobel. "Yes, of course," she replied, despite the turmoil inside her.

They worked side by side, their conversation flowing, but Gemma moved as if acting in a play, every line rehearsed, every movement calculated. Isobel's laughter, her serene smile, only deepened the ache in Gemma's chest. How could she have betrayed someone who had shown her nothing but kindness?

As they arranged new shipments and discussed plans for the store, Gemma stole glances at Isobel, watching her with a mixture of admiration and guilt. Isobel moved with a grace and confidence that Gemma envied, her every action infused with sincerity. The store was more than a business to Isobel; it was a place where she poured her heart and soul.

Gemma's hands trembled as she adjusted a stack of books, the guilt gnawing at her with every moment that passed. The necklace was a constant weight on her mind, its presence a reminder of the line she had crossed. She had taken something that wasn't hers, something precious and personal, all in the name of power. And now, she was paying the price.

The day wore on, each hour stretching out like an eternity. Gemma's mind was a battleground, the voices of her ancestors still whispering in her ear, urging her to embrace her destiny, to claim the power that was rightfully hers. But how could she, when the cost was so high?

When the workday ended, and the last customer had left, Isobel turned to Gemma with a warm smile. "Thank you for all your hard work today, Gemma. I couldn't do this without you."

Gemma's heart clenched at the words, the sincerity cutting through her like a knife. She wanted to confess, to tell Isobel everything, but the words wouldn't come. Instead, she nodded, forcing another smile. "I'm glad to help."

As they locked up the store together, Isobel's cheerful "Time for something to eat." felt like both a promise and a penance. Gemma's response, a whispered "Yes," carried the weight of all that remained unsaid between them.

Upstairs, in the solitude of her room, while Isobel prepared their evening meal, Gemma allowed herself to pull the necklace from its hiding place. The metal was cold in her hands; the gemstones gleaming in the dim light. She held it up, staring at it as if it would somehow give her the answers she sought.

"What have I done?" she whispered to the empty room, the words echoing back at her, laden with guilt.

She sat on the edge of her bed; the necklace draped over her fingers. "It'll be easier when she's gone," Gemma told herself, trying to convince herself more than anyone else. If Isobel was miles away at nursing school, perhaps the sting of her betrayal wouldn't feel so acute. She would explore the power of the necklace without the heavy gaze of guilt watching her every move.

But even as she tried to justify her actions, she knew the truth. The necklace wasn't only an object; it was a piece of Isobel's history, a connection to her mother who she lost when she was very young. To take it was to sever that connection, to claim something that wasn't hers to take. How had the necklace end up with Isobel or her mother? It was part of her legacy, her family.

With a heavy sigh, Gemma placed the necklace back into its hiding place, her movements slow and deliberate. She knew she was only delaying the inevitable. One day, she would have to face Isobel and confess what she had done. But for now, she was unable to bear it. She needed more time, more distance. She crossed the room, opened the door to find two places set at the table, and Isobel's big smile as she announced, "Dinner is ready."

Gemma sat, her fingers tracing the grain of the wood as she tried to focus on the meal before her. The savory aroma of stew filled the room, mingling with the warmth of baked bread that Isobel had prepared. The scene should have been comforting, a quiet dinner shared between friends after a long day, but the tension within Gemma's chest made it impossible to enjoy the simple pleasure.

Isobel, sitting across from her, looked up with a warm smile as she ladled a generous portion of stew into Gemma's bowl. "I think I finally perfected the recipe," she said. "I hope you like it."

Gemma managed a tight smile, nodding her thanks as she picked up her spoon. "It smells wonderful, Isobel," she replied in a flat tone. The stew, rich with flavors of tender meat and vegetables, tasted as good as it smelled, but each bite felt heavy on her tongue, weighed by the guilt that gnawed at her insides.

The meal continued in a strained silence, punctuated only by the soft clinks of silverware against ceramic. Gemma kept her eyes on her bowl, avoiding Isobel's gaze as she struggled to keep her thoughts from drifting to the necklace hidden in her room.

Isobel set down her spoon and looked across the table with concern. "Gemma, you've barely said a word all evening. Are you alright?"

Gemma's heart clenched at the gentle question, guilt surging through her like a wave. She forced herself to meet Isobel's gaze, trying to keep her expression neutral. "I'm fine," she lied, betraying a slight tremor. "Just tired, I guess."

Isobel's brow furrowed with worry, but she didn't press further. Instead, she offered a sympathetic smile. "You've been working really hard lately. Maybe you should take it easy tomorrow. I can handle the store."

The kindness in Isobel's voice only deepened the ache in Gemma's chest. Here was Isobel, offering her care and understanding, unaware that Gemma was harboring a secret that might shatter their friendship. The necklace, with its cool metal and glittering stones, burned against her conscience even from its hidden place in the drawer upstairs.

As they ate, Isobel tried to fill the silence with light conversation, mentioning the day's customers and plans for the upcoming season. "I was thinking of ordering more of those embroidered handkerchiefs," she said with a smile, her eyes bright with the joy she found in running the store. "People really seem to love them."

Gemma nodded, her lips forming responses at the right moments, though her thoughts drifted far away. Isobel's words flowed, but each one twisted the knot of guilt tighter in Gemma's chest. The casual warmth of their shared meal, the clink of dishes, the comfort of breaking bread, only made the distance between them more glaring. Gemma's eyes flickered to Isobel's, but quickly darted away, the weight of what she hid pressing heavily on her shoulders, a silent wedge widening the space between them.

As the meal drew to a close, Isobel rose from the table and cleared the dishes. Gemma moved to help, but her hands trembled as she reached for the plates. The day's weight, combined with the burden of her secret, made even the simplest tasks like insurmountable challenges.

Isobel noticed the tremor and took the plate from Gemma's hand. "Why don't you go rest? I can take care of this," she offered, her tone kind but firm. "You've done more than enough today."

The offer, meant to be a kindness, felt like another twist of the knife in Gemma's heart. She nodded, unable to trust her voice not to crack, and murmured a quiet, "Thank you, Isobel."

Once inside her room, Gemma closed the door behind her and leaned against it, her breath coming in shallow gasps. The day's events replayed in her mind, but it was the image of Isobel's trusting smile that haunted her the most. How would she face her friend, knowing what she had done?

She crossed the small room to the drawer where the necklace lay hidden. Her hand hovered over the handle, trembling as she contemplated opening it, but she was unable to bring herself to do it. The weight of the necklace, both physical and symbolic, was too much to bear.

Instead, she turned away and sat on the edge of her bed; her mind was a storm of conflicting emotions. Claire, her grandmother, echoed in her thoughts, urging her to embrace the power the necklace represented, to take her place in the long line of witches that came before her. But the weight of the cost pressed down on Gemma. A sense that the power she sought came at the expense of something far more valuable, her friendship with Isobel.

As she lay back on her bed, staring at the ceiling, Gemma knew sleep would not come easily. The guilt, the stolen necklace, and the unspoken truths between her and Isobel would keep her awake, turning over the events of the day and the choices she had made. The tension between the allure of power and the weight of her conscience pulled at her, each tug threatening to unravel the fragile peace she had built in Tin Creek.

Tomorrow, she would have to face Isobel again, to continue the charade of normalcy while the necklace remained a secret between them. But Gemma knew that the truth would not stay hidden forever. Eventually, the consequences of her actions would come crashing down, and when they did, she feared they would be more than she could handle.

Chapter Thirteen

THE MORNING SUN BATHED Tin Creek in a warm glow, casting golden rays over the brand new train station. The building stood proud and stark against the horizon, its fresh paint still gleaming, a beacon of progress and change. Around it, the towns-folk gathered, excitement buzzed in every hushed conversation and eager glance along the tracks. Children darted between the adults, their laughter ringing out like the chimes of a clock. Older residents leaned against the wooden fences, their expressions a mix of curiosity and nostalgia.

Gemma lingered at the edge of the bustling crowd, the vibrant hum of families sharing stories and dreams for the future, doing little to ease the knot in her chest. The train station, brimming with promises of new beginnings, felt to her like the last note in a bittersweet melody, the end of the living arrangements she shared with Isobel. Soon, Isobel would leave for Chicago, bound for nursing school and the life waiting for her after, coming back to marry John and work alongside Doc. Gemma, meanwhile, would manage the store with the steady presence of Marisol and Jane to guide her. The thought left her feeling untethered, as if a part of her would depart with Isobel on that train. Even John, who had promised to wait, embodied the ache of anticipation, and Gemma couldn't decide if she pitied him or envied his hope.

Gemma's gaze drifted to a young family nearby, their faces alight with anticipation as they pointed toward the tracks where the train would soon appear. The mother held her child close, whispering something that made the little girl giggle, her sticky fingers clutching a half-eaten candy apple. The scene twisted Gemma's heart. This moment, this gathering of the town to welcome the train, should have been about connections. But all Gemma had was the growing distance between herself and the life she had known, especially with Isobel preparing to leave.

The crowd's excitement grew, marking the train's imminent arrival. Conversations lulled, and a collective breath hung in the air, suspended in anticipation. Gemma's eyes locked on the curve in the tracks, her heart pounding with a mixture of dread and longing. This train, this metal beast, was about to take Isobel away from her, pulling her friend into a future where Gemma might not have a place.

Isobel stood on the platform, her silhouette outlined against the soft light of the morning. Her stance was poised, confident, the confidence Gemma admired and envied in equal measure. Isobel adjusted the straps of her old leather suitcase—a suitcase filled with more dreams than belongings, Gemma knew. The sight of her, so full of purpose, made Gemma's throat tighten with unshed tears. This was the girl who had become her closest companion, the one who had made her feel less alone in the vast, untamed world of Tin Creek. And now she was leaving.

The platform buzzed with farewells, but to Gemma, the world had narrowed to only the two of them. She wanted to reach out, to hold on to Isobel and beg her to stay, but the words stuck in her throat, choked by the weight of all that remained unspoken between them.

Isobel turned to face the crowd, her gaze sweeping over the gathered townsfolk before landing on Gemma. For a moment, their eyes met, and in that silent exchange, the full force of what was about to happen hit Gemma. Isobel's face, usually so animated with laughter and mischief, now held a quiet resolve. She was ready for this, for the adventure that lay ahead, and Gemma couldn't find it in herself to hold her back, no matter how much it hurt.

Nearby, Henry stood with John's parents, their small group exuding warmth and support. Henry's large hands rested on Isobel's shoulders, his expression a mix of pride and sorrow. He adjusted Isobel's scarf, his fingers lingering for a moment longer than necessary, as if trying to imprint this memory in his heart. The love between them was a stark contrast to the complicated, fractured relationship Gemma had with her own family. Watching them, she held a pang of longing for the bond that came naturally to others.

As the train whistle pierced the air, Gemma's stomach twisted into knots. The distant rumble grew louder, signaling the train's approach. The crowd's anticipation swelled, excitement mingling with the bittersweet reality of what the train represented. Wisps of smoke curled into the sky, and the train's silhouette emerged from the bend, powerful and unstoppable. Its engine roared as it thundered into the station, sending vibrations through the ground beneath Gemma's feet.

The train came to a halt with a final hiss of steam. A door slid open to reveal the conductor, his uniform crisp against the metal beast behind him. The arrival was a spectacle, the train a symbol of progress and change. But to Gemma, it represented a force pulling everything apart.

Isobel stepped forward, her hand resting on the cool metal of the carriage as she prepared to board. The platform fell into a hush; the crowd holding its breath. Gemma's heart broke with each step Isobel took. She wanted to call out, to say something, anything, to make Isobel stay. But all she could do was watch as her friend ascended the steps, each footfall a drumbeat in Gemma's chest.

Isobel turned one last time, her eyes finding Gemma's in the crowd. She lifted her hand in a last wave, a gesture that carried the weight of every moment they had shared, every secret they had whispered in the dark. Gemma raised her own hand, her movements slow, as if she could somehow freeze time, hold on to these last few seconds before everything changed.

The conductor gave the last call, and the train moved, slowly at first, then picking up speed. Wheels clacked against the tracks; the sound echoing in Gemma's ears like a death knell. Isobel's figure in the window became smaller, fading into the distance until she was a blur, a memory disappearing with the smoke trailing behind the train.

The crowd's cheers of farewell washed over her, distant and hollow. The platform, once bustled with life, now empty, echoed the hollow space in Gemma's heart where Isobel used to be. She stood there, long after the train had vanished, staring at the tracks that stretched out into the horizon. The town moved forward, but Gemma remained behind, anchored to a past that was slipping further and further away.

Gemma's thoughts drifted to the necklace hidden away in her room. It was supposed to be her legacy, but now it was more of a burden, the guilt of her actions weighing on her.

As the last of the townsfolk drifted away, Gemma turned from the tracks, her heart heavy, knowing that this was the beginning of a long, lonely road. The promise she had made to herself, to one day follow her own path, became distant and unreachable.

She walked from the station, the echo of the train's whistle still ringing in her ears, a reminder that the future was coming, whether she was ready for it or not. Shadow trotted beside her, his small paws padding against the dirt. He looked at her with his bright eyes, sensing her sadness, and chittered.

Gemma paused, her eyes stinging with unshed tears. She kneeled, scooping Shadow up into her arms. His fur was soft, and she held him close, burying her face against his striped body. The warmth of his small frame and the gentle rhythm of his breathing grounded her in that moment, providing a comfort that nothing else could. She hugged him, taking in a deep breath, the familiar scent of him bringing a small but vital sense of reassurance.

Shadow nuzzled her cheek, his chittering now soft and soothing, as if he were trying to tell her she wasn't alone, that he would always be by her side. Gemma closed her eyes, allowing herself a moment to hold on to him, to find solace in his unwavering presence.

With Shadow still cradled in her arms, Gemma straightened, her heart feeling a little lighter. She gave the raccoon a grateful smile, whispering, "Thank you, Shadow. I don't know what I'd do without you." He chittered again in response, and Gemma walked once more, the weight of her loneliness easier to bear with her faithful companion held close.

In the quiet stillness, Gemma stood before the small mirror that hung on the wall in her room. The moonlight, soft and ethereal, streamed through the window, casting silver beams across the dark wooden floor. Gemma reached for the silver trinity necklace resting on her dresser. The necklace shimmered, as though it carried secrets too deep for words.

Shadow sat on the edge of the dresser, his dark eyes watching Gemma. His ears twitched at every small sound, sensing the tension in the air. As Gemma's fingers trembled while she reached for the necklace, Shadow let out a soft, almost questioning chitter. Gemma paused for a moment, her gaze meeting his, and she managed a small, strained smile.

"It's okay, Shadow," she whispered, though the words were meant more for herself than for her raccoon familiar. She picked him up, pulling him into a hug, her fingers burying into his soft fur. Shadow nuzzled against her neck, his warmth comforting her in the cold uncertainty of the moment. But the necklace still called to her, its weight more than just physical, it was a pull she couldn't ignore.

With a deliberate motion, Gemma set Shadow back on the dresser, her heart heavy. He chittered, pacing on the wooden surface, his eyes never leaving her. Slowly, Gemma clasped the necklace around her neck. The gemstones caught the moonlight, flaring for a moment and casting strange shadows that danced across the walls, causing the room to close in on her. As the necklace settled against her skin, cold and heavy, the air thickened with an energy that whispered of ancient magick and hidden realms.

Shadow let out a low growl, his tiny paws pressing against the edge of the dresser as he leaned forward, watching the necklace with clear unease. Gemma stared into the mirror, her reflection gazing back at her with eyes that held a mix of determination and fear. The surrounding room shrunk, the walls creeping closer, drawn by the power of the artifact now resting on her chest. The familiar sounds of the town at night, the creak of wood, the distant call of an owl, faded into the background, leaving only the eerie silence of her room.

Shadow's restless movements drew her attention for a moment. He hopped from the dresser to the floor, padding closer to her feet. He tugged at the hem of her dress, his small paws insistent. Gemma looked at him, her heart squeezing in her chest. "Stay close, Shadow," she whispered.

A sharp gust of wind swept through the room, cold and biting, spiraling around her with a force that made her shiver. Shadow squeaked, scampering backward, his fur standing on end as the wind whipped. The candles flickered before being snuffed out one by one. Darkness enveloped the room, thick and suffocating, pressing against her eyes and quickening her pulse.

Gemma stood frozen, her breath coming in short, rapid bursts. Shadow let out a soft, fearful chitter, moving to press against her leg, his small body trembling. She reached down, her hand brushing his fur, grounding herself for just a moment. But the dread only deepened. The shadows in the room grew darker, more pronounced, as if they were alive, pulsing with a sinister intent.

Shadow darted away, his form barely visible in the darkened room as he scurried to the window. He pawed at the glass, his chittering now frantic, as if trying to find a way out of the oppressive darkness that had taken hold.

The room dissolved around her, solid walls and floor giving way to a swirling mist that obscured everything she knew. The vertigo of descent overwhelmed her, as if she were being pulled through a tunnel that defied the laws of physics and reality. Her surroundings blurred and twisted until she was no longer in her room but standing in a vast, moonlit clearing.

The ground beneath her feet sank with each step, damp and cold, the dew-soaked grass glistening under the eerie glow of the moon. Gemma stumbled, her vision warping as the world shifted, her breath catching, strangled by the wrongness that surrounded her.

The forest surrounding the clearing transformed into a realm of darkness and distortion, a waking nightmare that defied conceal-ment. Tree branches clawed at the sky, their jagged outlines stretch-ing in a desperate reach for an unattainable salvation.

The cursed necklace pressed against her throat, humming with a malevolent energy that weighed her down. Gemma's fingers hovered near it, tempted to tear it away, but she froze, her heartbeat pound-ing a warning through her veins.

A faint rustle made her turn, and there, in the thick of the shad-ows, emerged three figures.

Her breath hitched. The eldest stood at the center, her posture regal, her eyes sharp and cruel. The dark robes she wore flowed like shadows, and her silver hair gleamed in the dim light, a stark contrast to the ominous energy surrounding her. Next to her, Margaret, her great-grandmother, and Grace, her grandmother, stood like sentinels, cold and imposing, their faces emotionless masks. Their eyes, however, glowed, filled with an ancient, predatory hunger.

Here they were. The witches from her family's past, her ancestors. Her bloodline.

"Welcome, child," the older woman said, smooth as silk but undercut with a malice that chilled Gemma's bones. "It's time."

Gemma took a step back, her gaze darting from one witch to the next. "Where... where am I?" she managed trembling as her mind struggled to process the surreal nightmare before her.

Hannah's smile was thin and cruel. "You're home. I'm your great-great grandmother, Hannah. I've been waiting for you."

The fog thickened around Gemma's ankles, as though the earth itself wanted to hold her. The weight of the necklace burned against her skin, as if it were alive, a part of this strange, twisted place. She glanced down, watching the faint glow of the gemstones pulse with each beat of her heart.

"I don't belong here," Gemma said. She had to keep control, had to push back the fear overwhelming her.

"Oh, but you do," Hannah purred, taking a step closer. The air warped and twisted, and the trees groaned in response to her presence. "You've always belonged here, Gemma. You've felt it, haven't you? The power inside you, restless, waiting."

Gemma's throat constricted, panic rising like a tide. She wanted to rip the necklace away, fling it far into the shadows, but her body refused to obey. The earth clung to her feet, rooting her to the spot, trapping her in the nightmare. Her trembling hand moved toward the cursed necklace, her fingers brushing the cold metal. A sharp gasp escaped her lips as a jolt of energy surged through her, dark and relentless. For an instant, it consumed her, a torrent of ancestral power that coiled around her heart, choking her with its sinister intent. Fear gripped her, tightening its hold as the darkness spoke promises she didn't dare listen to.

"I don't want this," she whispered, the sound almost lost to the wind.

Hannah chuckled, low and cold. "You have no choice, child. You were born for this. To embrace your true nature. Stop pretending you're something you're not. Accept your destiny."

Gemma's head spun, her pulse quickening. Her hand dropped from the necklace, trembling. "I'm not like you."

A hiss echoed through the clearing as Margaret stepped forward, her eyes narrowing into slits. "You are exactly like us," she said. "Our blood flows through you. You have the power to become something greater than you can even imagine. Stop fighting it."

The shadows slithered toward her, enveloping her in a suffocating shroud. Their icy fingers brushed against her skin, sending chills deep into her bones, as if the forest had come alive with malice, its dark will pressing in on her from all sides. Gemma's breath hitched, her heart pounding in her chest. Panic clawed at her mind, and she stumbled backward, her legs shaky, the weight of the darkness bearing down on her. She had to escape, had to break free from this living nightmare before it swallowed her whole.

But Hannah stopped her. "Look around, Gemma. This is your world. This is where you truly belong."

The trees groaned as if in agreement, and the darkness swirled closer, tighter, wrapping her like a noose.

A flash of light, bright, warm, and defiant, cut through the suffocating darkness.

Lillian.

Gemma's breath caught in her throat as her great-aunt stepped into the clearing, her form shimmering with the glow of light magick. She was not quite solid, as if the very nature of this dark forest resisted her presence, but she stood firm, her gaze locked on Gemma.

Gemma's heart twisted as she took in the sight of Lillian, her great-aunt, her mentor, the woman who had taught her about magick and its consequences. The woman who had saved her from darkness more than once. For so long, Gemma had held onto the hope that she would see Lillian again, alive, in the flesh, that somehow, her great-aunt would return to her. But here she was, caught in that ethereal glow, her face bearing the calm but weary wisdom of someone who had crossed beyond the veil.

The reality struck Gemma, a deep ache settling into her bones, Lillian was gone. Truly gone. She had always known, deep down, that this day would come, that her great-aunt would not be there to guide her forever. But facing it now, seeing her like this, the hollow ache in her chest expanded into something almost unbearable. Lillian had always been a constant in her life, a source of strength, and a reminder that, even in darkness, there was someone fighting for her.

The urge to reach out, to embrace her, washed over Gemma, a futile, desperate desire to feel her great-aunt's arms around her once more, to be a young girl again, safe in Lillian's protection. She blinked, fighting the tears that pricked at her eyes. Lillian had crossed into the afterlife to stand with her once more, to help her fight. Even in death, she hadn't abandoned her. But the finality of it gnawed at Gemma's heart, a wound that couldn't be closed. She wanted to hear Lillian in person, not as an echo across the veil.

"Gemma, you don't have to listen to them," Lillian said strongly, despite the strain in her face. "Take off the necklace. You have a choice."

Gemma's heart pounded in her chest. Could she do it? Could she break free of this nightmare?

Hannah's laughter rang out, cold and sharp. "Lillian. Always late, always useless." Her eyes gleamed with malicious delight. "You couldn't control your own hunger for power, and now look at you. Nothing more than a fading ghost."

Lillian's form flickered, but she stood her ground. "I'm not here for you, Hannah. I'm here for Gemma."

"Pathetic," Hannah sneered, her power rippling through the air like a storm ready to break. "You think you can save her? You couldn't even save yourself."

Gemma's head spun as she looked between the two women, one offering the dark, raw power she had always feared, the other a fragile lifeline, flickering in and out of existence.

"You don't have to do this, Gemma," Lillian said. "You're stronger than I ever was. Walk away. You don't need their power."

But the shadows twisted closer, and Hannah's voice oozed into Gemma's mind like poison. "Walk away? From what you're meant to be? Don't be a fool, Gemma. You have greatness in you, the kind of power that will bend the world to your will. With us, you can finally stop being weak."

Gemma's pulse quickened, the necklace burning against her skin as the weight of her ancestors' expectations crashed down on her. The power was right there, within reach, whispering promises of strength and control. She could take it. She could finally stop being afraid.

But then she saw Lillian's eyes, filled with pain and desperation.

"Please, Gemma," Lillian whispered. "Don't let them do to you what they did to me."

The shadows swirled around Lillian, pressing in, and her form flickered. Gemma's heart lurched as she watched the darkness consume her great-aunt, threatening to snuff out her light.

"Enough!" Hannah boomed through the clearing, her power surging. The shadows lashed out, wrapping around Lillian, choking the life out of her fading form.

"Gemma!" Lillian screamed as she was dragged into the darkness. "Don't let them take you!"

Gemma's heart raced, her hands shaking as she reached for the necklace, torn between the power it offered and the light that flickered in Lillian.

Hannah's voice slithered into her ear, soft and commanding. "There is no escape, Gemma. You are ours. You always have been."

The weight of her words pressed on Gemma, the necklace burning against her skin, searing into her very soul. She could feel the darkness pulling her in, promising her everything she had ever feared, and everything she had ever wanted.

But then she heard Lillian, faint but clear, like a lifeline in the storm.

"You're stronger than this, Gemma. You're stronger than her."

Gemma's breath caught, her hand trembling as it hovered over the necklace. She had to choose. Power or freedom. Darkness or light.

Chapter Fourteen

As Gemma stumbled away from the eerie moonlit clearing, the world around her twisted, distorting like she was looking through warped glass. The familiar streets of Tin Creek blurred, their edges softening until everything lost its solidity. A chill settled in her bones, deeper than any winter cold, a hollow, haunting chill that clawed at her very essence, drawing her life force into the gemstones that now weighed on her chest.

She tried to move, but her legs refused to obey. Panic shot through her, a caged bird flapping its wings, desperate to escape, but her limbs hung limp, unresponsive. The once-familiar sounds of Tin Creek, the distant barking of a dog, children's laughter echoing from some forgotten corner, Jane's cheerful greeting, morphed into muffled echoes, slipping away from her as if she were plunging into deep water.

Gemma opened her mouth to scream, to call for help, but no sound came. Her throat seized, each breath a laborious fight against some unseen force pressing down on her chest. She fought to drag air into her lungs, her vision shrinking, blackness creeping in at the corners until the world narrowed to a pinprick of light. And then that too vanished.

Darkness swallowed her, absolute, inescapable. She hung there in the void, trapped. Her senses told her she was still standing, but there was no floor beneath her feet, no air, no warmth, only nothingness and the icy weight of the necklace against her skin. The gemstones pulsed, growing colder, heavier, like they thrived on her fear.

Shadows shifted in the darkness, moving closer, their forms amorphous and unsettling. Whispers started, a chorus of malevolent voices speaking in a language she didn't understand. The hairs on her neck stood on end. She sensed their ancient power, their hunger. These were not only specters. They were witches, long-dead, old, and relentless. They had waited for her, and now she was here, bound by the cursed necklace. She was the vessel they needed, and she felt their dark intentions seeping into her mind.

Gemma's pulse quickened, each beat a frantic drum in the suffocating silence. She struggled to fight them, but her arms hung like lead, her fingers numb. The shadows crowded her, their whispers rising to an urgent pitch, closing in tighter. She attempted to twist away, but they wrapped around her, their forms pressing in a strangling mass of dark power. She wasn't just surrounded, she was drowning in them.

"Leave me alone," she tried to shout, but the words were swallowed before they even left her lips.

The icy touch of their fingers brushed against her skin, skeletal and invasive. They whispered of unimaginable power, of ruling with them, of a world plunged into darkness, hers for the taking. They promised her the world, but it came laced with a sinister intent. Queen of the Damned, ruler of a wasteland.

Gemma's heart pounded, her mind frantic as she sought to find a way out. Her hands shook, her fingers curling instinctively as she called upon the air. She focused on the feeling of the wind, the energy that had once moved easily through her, the power that had flowed in response to her will. The slightest stirring, a cool breeze brushed against her skin, rustling the leaves. The air shifted, and for a fleeting moment, hope surged within her, maybe, just maybe, she could use her magick to drive the darkness back.

She clenched her fists tighter, her eyes narrowing as she tried to force the air to obey her, to gather, to swirl, to push away the shadows closing in. But the power slipped through her fingers, like trying to hold on to smoke. The breeze faltered, the movement dying before it even began. Panic clawed at her chest, her confidence crumbling as the magick dissipated, leaving nothing but stillness.

The air became heavy, suffocating, as though the forest itself turned against her. She couldn't grasp it, couldn't control it. Her heart sank, the crushing realization washing over her, she wasn't strong enough. The wind was beyond her command, her magick failing her when she needed it most. Her breaths came in ragged gasps, each one more desperate than the last, as if the very air she tried to summon refused to enter her lungs.

She had lost her connection, and now, in this dark place, surrounded by the relentless voices of the witches, she couldn't find it again. Her magick, once a part of her, now felt like a stranger, distant, unreachable. Her own inadequacy pressed down on her, the fear of failing, of not being enough, tightening its grip on her heart.

The necklace anchored her in place, making her too heavy to move. The shadows grew thicker, darker, until all she saw, all she comprehended, was darkness pressing in on her. Each breath came shorter, her body giving way, the fight within her ebbing.

The witches' voices swelled, piercing her thoughts like needles threading through fabric. She fought to block them out, but her strength faltered. Their presence dulled her mind, each word chipping away at her sense of self. Bit by bit, she drifted, her identity dissolving under the crushing weight of the encroaching shadows. The necklace pulsed against her chest, its cold stones digging into her flesh, binding her closer to the witches' will.

The full moon was coming, and with it, the end of everything she had ever known. She would be claimed, body and soul, and become their dark queen, the instrument of their vengeance against the world. The thought filled her with a cold, hollow dread, but there was nothing she could do to stop it.

She was trapped, and no one was coming to save her.

As the night dragged on, the darkness deepened, the shadows closing in around her until they were all she could see, all she could feel. The witches' whispers grew louder, more insistent, filling her mind with visions of the world they would create, a world of maleficence and despair, ruled by their dark magick.

Gemma's last thought before she slipped into unconsciousness was a silent, desperate plea for someone to find her, to stop what was coming. But there was no answer, only the cold, unfeeling evilness, and the knowledge that when she awoke, it would be too late. The witches would have her, and the world would burn.

Early morning sun bathed Tin Creek in a warm, golden glow, painting the town in soft hues of amber. The usual tranquility of the dawn, however, did little to soothe the unease gnawing at Jane's heart as she approached the store. It wasn't like Gemma to be late; she was always the first to open shop, her energy and punctuality as reliable as the sunrise itself.

A movement caught Jane's eye as she neared the entrance, a small, dark shape scratching at the window. Shadow, Gemma's raccoon companion. His tiny paws pressed against the glass, his sharp claws making faint scraping noises. He spun his head towards her, his dark eyes locked on, chittering with an urgency that made her heart skip a beat.

"What is it, Shadow?" Jane murmured, frowning.

Shadow's scratching intensified for a moment, then he darted away from the window, disappearing from sight. Without waiting for her to approach the door, he leaped up the narrow staircase that led to the upper quarters of the store. His chittering echoed, and he paused, turning his head to ensure she was following him.

Jane's sense of concern deepened as she pulled out the key from her pocket, the one Isobel had entrusted to her. She unlocked the door and stepped inside, the click and the dim, silent interior only heightening her apprehension. The usual morning activity was absent; the "Closed" sign still hung in the window, a disconcerting sight at this hour.

Shadow's small, striped tail flicked at the top of the staircase. He waited long enough for Jane to see him before turning and dashing into the living quarters above the store, his insistent chittering continuing.

Something was wrong.

Jane's footsteps echoed in the cool, dim space as she moved to follow Shadow up the stairs. Her fingers tightened around the railing as she climbed, her heart pounding. At the top, she paused, taking a deep breath to steady herself before turning towards Gemma's room, the door ajar.

When she pushed it open, her breath caught in her throat.

Gemma stood motionless in front of her mirror, her eyes wide and vacant. Her lively presence appeared drained, hollowed out. The morning sun filtered through the window, but it clashed with the tension hanging in the air, out of place at this unsettling moment.

Shadow scurried over to Gemma's feet, climbing up onto her legs, his paws gripping the hem of her skirt. He glanced at Jane, his eyes pleading and filled with the same urgency he had shown at the window.

Jane saw his unease in his small, twitching movements, in the desperate way he clung to Gemma. "Gemma?" She took a few hesitant steps into the room. The unnatural stillness in Gemma's expression made her stomach drop.

She reached out, her hand brushing Gemma's shoulder. Her skin was cold to the touch, and Jane's concern turned to panic.

"Gemma, can you hear me?" Jane said louder. But Gemma remained unresponsive, her eyes staring into the mirror with a glassy, empty look.

Shadow chittered, his tiny claws scratching at Gemma's skirt as he tried to pull her attention away from whatever held her in this trance. But it was no use. The young woman's gaze stayed fixed, her mind elsewhere.

The raccoon looked at Jane, then at Gemma, his dark eyes wide with distress, and Jane's own heart twisted in response. She had to do something, anything, to help Gemma.

Panic surged as Jane fumbled to check Gemma's pulse, her fingers trembling against Gemma's cold wrist. The faint thump of a pulse met her touch, but it was weak, slow, almost as if Gemma's life was slipping away. Shadow chirped again, a mournful sound that echoed Jane's own rising fear.

Jane spun around, her heart pounding, her thoughts a chaotic blur. She needed help, and fast. Every second slipping away was a second too many, each heartbeat a reminder of the urgency pressing down on her.

She rushed for the door, sparing one last glance at Gemma and the raccoon, who stayed by her side, his presence a small but fierce symbol of protection. Jane sprinted down the stairs, the wooden steps groaning beneath her hurried movements. The morning sunlight outside blazed with an almost cruel brightness, its rays cutting across the room, a harsh contrast to the dark fear twisting in her chest.

The street was quiet, her footsteps the only sound as she dashed towards Doc's office, the urgency of the situation propelling her forward. Every second counted, Gemma was fading, and Jane wouldn't let her go.

Doc's office came into view. Jane's heart leaped with a mix of relief and dread as she reached the front door, her hand pounding on the wood. The sharp sound cut through the quiet morning, and within moments, the door swung open to reveal Doc, his expression shifting from surprise to concern as he took in Jane's distressed state.

"Jane, what's happened?" Doc was calm, a stark contrast to the panic that had taken hold of her.

"It's Gemma," Jane gasped. "Something's wrong, her breathing's shallow, and she's so cold. I didn't know what to do, so I came to get you. Please, you have to come quickly!"

Doc's expression hardened, his years of experience kicking into gear. Without wasting another moment, he grabbed his medical bag from the nearby table. "Lead the way, Jane," he said as he followed her out the door.

The two of them hurried back through the streets, the urgency of their mission reflected in the quickness of their steps. The serene morning was now charged with a tension that hung heavy in the air, every sound amplified by the silence of the town waking up around them.

Jane's heart raced as they reached the store, and she led Doc up the stairs to where Gemma remained in her unresponsive state. The room turned colder than before, the silence more oppressive as Doc set his medical bag on the floor with a quiet thud. Jane hovered by Gemma's side, her eyes never leaving Doc as he began his examination.

Doc's movements were efficient and precise as he checked Gemma's pulse, listened to her heart, and examined her eyes. But as the minutes ticked by, Jane saw the lines in his face deepen, his calm demeanor beginning to crack under the weight of the situation.

"What's wrong with her, Doc?" Jane trembled as she watched him work, her hands wringing together to keep herself from falling apart.

Doc didn't answer right away. He finished his examination and stepped back, wiping his brow with the back of his hand—a gesture Jane had never seen him make before.

"Jane," Doc began, low and hesitant, "I've done all I can with what I know, but she's not responding to any of the usual methods. Her condition is... unlike anything I've encountered before. It's as if she's here physically, but her mind is somewhere else, somewhere I can't reach."

Jane's heart sank, a wave of despair washed over her. "But there must be something we can do," she pleaded. "Isn't there anything that might help?"

Doc shook his head, his eyes filled with a helplessness that Jane had never seen in him before. "What she needs might be beyond my help, Jane. Perhaps beyond conventional medicine altogether."

The room grew even colder; the reality of the situation settled around them. Jane's chest tightened under a crushing weight as she looked at Gemma, standing still and silent in front of the dresser.

The silence in the room was snapped by the sound of the front door opening and quick footsteps approaching. Jane turned to see Marisol entering the room, her face etched with concern as she assessed the situation.

"What's happened?" Marisol asked, her voice breathless as her eyes landed on Gemma's pale, motionless form.

Doc summarized his findings, steady but tinged with frustration. Jane filled in the details of how she had found Gemma that morning, her narrative punctuated by the worry that had only deepened with time.

Marisol listened. After a moment, her eyes lit up. "We need Isobel," she said, turning to Jane and Doc. "Her knowledge of herbal medicine might have something to help Gemma. This isn't something ordinary, perhaps Isobel's approach is the key."

Marisol's suggestion filled Jane with a surge of hope. It was fragile, but it was something to hold on to. Without hesitation, the three of them drafted a telegram to Isobel, explaining the severity of the situation and their need for her expertise.

Marisol took the slip of paper. "I'll send it as soon as I leave here."

A weight lifted from Jane's shoulders, replaced by the tentative belief that help was on the way. "We can't leave her like this."

Jane, Doc, and Marisol exchanged a glance; silent nods passed between them. With careful movements, they positioned themselves around her.

"On three," Doc said. "One, two, three."

Together, they lifted Gemma, her body limp and cold in their hands. Shadow scampered beside them, chittering as they moved her towards the bed. Jane tried to steady her trembling fingers as she cradled Gemma's head, while Marisol held her feet, their eyes full of shared concern.

They laid her on the bed, arranging the quilt over her to ward off the chill clung to her skin. The room fell into a hushed silence as they stepped back.

Shadow climbed onto the bed, his small, striped body pressing against Gemma's side, as if his presence alone could ward off whatever dark force held her captive. He curled up close to her, his usual playful spirit replaced by a quiet, determined protectiveness. His ears twitched at every sound, and his dark eyes remained half-closed, vigilant despite the tense atmosphere surrounding them.

Jane stood by the headboard, her fingers brushing against Gemma's brow, her worry etched deep in the furrow of her brow. The coldness of Gemma's skin sent a shiver down her spine, her chest tightening. Shadow nestled close beside Gemma, his small body pressed against her, a faint warmth amidst the chill. Jane swallowed hard, her gaze flicking to the raccoon and back to Gemma. The uncertainty of what lay ahead lingered, a weight pressing down on her shoulders, refusing to lift.

Marisol kneeled beside her, her fingers brushing through Gemma's hair in a soothing gesture, though her eyes held a depth of concern that belied the calm exterior. Doc hovered at the foot of the bed, his brow furrowed in thought as he reviewed his limited options.

In the center of it all, Shadow's presence was a silent testimony to the bond he shared with Gemma, his vibrant energy subdued by the heavy, unspoken fear that weighed down the room. Despite the humans gathered around, Shadow remained steadfast, his little body a barrier between Gemma and the unknown forces that had taken hold of her.

CHAPTER FIFTEEN

THE WIND WHIPPED THROUGH the Druid's Altar with a biting chill, carrying whispers that only the dark could understand. Gemma stood alone in the circle of stones, the cold seeping through her thin shoes as she tried to steady her breath. The air pulsed with evil energy, ancient and unnerving, as if the ground itself was alive. Above her, the stars dimmed, their light barely penetrating the oppressive shroud of darkness that wrapped the night like a blanket.

She was not alone.

The witches, her ancestors, surrounded her, their presence more perceived than seen. Cloaked in shadow, their eyes gleamed with a sinister light, pinpoints of malice that cut through the darkness. The wind picked up again, swirling around the stone circle, and the eerie rustle of leaves and branches sounded more like mocking laughter than the sigh of nature.

Hannah stood at the forefront, her silhouette tall and commanding. Her silver hair, shimmering in the dim starlight, made her appear regal. There was no warmth in her gaze, only the cold, calculating hunger of someone who had waited centuries for this moment. The ground bent toward her, as if recognizing its master.

"You belong with us, Gemma," Hannah's voice slithered through the air, smooth as a dagger's edge. "You were born to wield the power within you. Stop fighting it."

Gemma's heart hammered against her ribs. The seductive lure of power that promised control and promised safety pulled at her. Her fingers twitched toward the necklace she wore, its presence a burning reminder of the curse she had unwittingly accepted.

"Look at her," Margaret, her great-grandmother, hissed from the shadows. "She weak, trembling like a leaf. She doesn't deserve the gift we offer."

Margaret stepped forward, her dark eyes flashing with disdain. The wind bowed in her presence, reflecting her dominion over air. She circled Gemma like a predator, her gaze sharp and predatory. "Do you really think you can refuse this? Do you think you can escape what's in your blood?"

Gemma clenched her fists, her knuckles white. "I don't want your power. I'm not like you."

The witches chuckled, a low, mocking sound that rippled through the stone circle like a wave of venom. Grace, her grandmother, stepped forward next, her lips twisting into a cruel smile. "You don't get to choose, child," she purred. "You were born for this. Born to be more than the pathetic creature you are now."

The ground beneath Gemma's feet trembled, and the stones around the altar hummed with energy. A sensation crawled up her legs, cold and invasive, seeking entry into her very bones. The pressure mounted as the wind swirled faster, and the surrounding trees groaned in response to the witches' gathering power.

Hannah raised her hand, and the wind stopped. Complete, oppressive silence settled over the circle.

"You seek to defy us," Hannah said, soft but laced with menace. "But you can't deny what's inside you, Gemma. The darkness is already there, growing, waiting. Why fight it?"

Gemma's chest tightened as the weight of their words pressed down on her, suffocating. The necklace at her throat pulsed with a sickly warmth, a constant reminder of the power she had tried to reject. Her breath came in ragged gasps as her mind raced. She wouldn't let them win. She wouldn't let herself become like them.

But then the air shimmered, and the world shifted.

The cold altar vanished, replaced by a grand hall bathed in golden light. Gemma blinked in confusion as she stood before a throne of black stone, her body draped in a flowing violet gown. She looked down at her hands and saw a crown for her head, her fingers adorned with rings of power.

Around her, people bowed. Not just any people, powerful men and women, their eyes wide with awe and fear. They spoke her name with reverence. They obeyed her every command. And standing beside her, smiling with pride, was Marisol.

"You've done it, Gemma," Marisol said. "Protected us all. You've saved us."

Isobel appeared glowing with admiration. "You've made me proud, Gemma."

The scene overwhelmed her senses. The weight of the crown and the heat of the power coursed through her veins. This was everything she had ever wanted, control, admiration, the ability to protect the people she loved. No one to hurt her, no one to touch her.

But something felt off. As intoxicating as the vision was, a small voice whispered at the back of her mind. This isn't real.

Her heart clenched. She reached out to touch Marisol's hand, but her fingers passed through her like smoke. The warmth drained from the room, and the faces of those bowing before her began to warp and twist, their features contorting into grotesque masks of malice. Marisol and Isobel's smiles turned sharp and cruel, and the golden hall dissolved into shadow.

"No," Gemma whispered, shaking as the vision crumbled. She tried to step back, but the ground shifted again.

She was on a battlefield. Bodies lay broken at her feet, her enemies vanquished. She stood at the head of an army, victorious, untouchable. Power surged through her, dark and terrible. She would stop anyone from ever hurting her or the people she loved again.

The witches' voices swirled around her like a poison cloud. "You can save them all, Gemma. You can stop the pain, stop the suffering. Just give in. Take the power."

The images were so vivid, so real, she tasted the victory. Her knees buckled as she sank to the ground, her hands trembling as they reached out for the power the witches offered. The darkness hummed, eager to consume her, to fill the void that screamed for control.

But then something snapped, a fragile but unyielding tether to the truth.

"No," Gemma said. "This isn't real."

The witches' laughter echoed around her, cruel and mocking. "You can't escape, Gemma," they hissed, their voices like the rustling of dead leaves. "You belong to us."

Gemma gritted her teeth, forcing herself to remember why she had come, why she was fighting. Her mind conjured the faces of Marisol, Isobel, Jane, the people she loved, the people she had sworn to protect. She wouldn't let the darkness win. She had to show herself that they were still out there, still waiting for her, safe and whole. Drawing on the fragile threads of her remaining magick, she tried to weave an illusion, an image of them standing with her, their smiles bright, their love surrounding her.

The illusion shimmered in front of her, the colors soft and hazy, like a half-remembered dream. She could almost see Isobel's eyes, filled with warmth, and Marisol's comforting smile. She tried to focus, to bring the image into sharper relief, to make it real. For a heartbeat, their presence, the warmth of their love cut through the darkness like a lifeline.

But the illusion sputtered. The edges blurred, the colors fading into murky shadows. Marisol's face twisted, becoming indistinct, her smile disappearing into the encroaching darkness. Isobel's eyes dulled, her form flickering like a dying candle. The illusion collapsed, dissolving into nothingness, leaving only the cold, suffocating reality of the witches' whispers.

Desperation clawed at her chest, a raw, aching need that made her heart feel as though it might shatter. She had failed. The people she loved were slipping away from her, beyond her grasp. Her magick, once her shield, her connection to the world, now crumbled to dust in her hands. The shadows closed in, wrapped around her like a vice, their weight pressing down until she believed the earth itself was swallowing her whole.

The visions tightened their grip on her mind, wrapping around her like chains. Her resolve slipped, and her strength ebbed away. The witches were too strong. She was drowning in their promises, their illusions. The line between reality and fantasy blurred, and she clawed at the ground, desperate to hold on to something real.

"You're losing, child," Margaret sneered. "You were never strong enough."

Gemma's body trembled as she fought against the pull of the dark magick, her breaths coming in ragged gasps. She grappled with the necklace around her throat, the cursed object that tethered her to this nightmare. If she could only remove it...

A hand, gentle yet firm, touched her shoulder.

She looked up, her vision blurred, and saw a figure standing above her, Lillian, her great-aunt, her face filled with determination and sadness.

"Gemma," Lillian said, "you don't have to do this. You don't have to be like them."

The witches hissed in unison, their shadows tightening around Lillian, trying to choke her out of existence. But Lillian held firm, her ghostly form shimmering in the darkness.

"You have a choice," Lillian whispered into the howling wind. "You're stronger than them. Stronger than this."

Gemma's hands trembled as she gripped the necklace. The darkness swirled around her, the witches' voices growing louder, more insistent. But she focused on Lillian's face, on the flicker of hope in her eyes.

Gemma's heart pounded as she yanked at the cursed necklace, her fingers scraping against the cold metal. Panic surged in her chest when she realized it wouldn't budge. No matter how hard she pulled, it stayed fused to her skin; the gemstones glowing brighter with each frantic tug. A cold sweat broke out on her forehead, and the eerie chanting of the witches echoed around her, growing louder, more menacing.

"You can't escape us," Hannah purred. She stood outside the circle, watching with her arms crossed, her eyes gleaming like polished stone. "You are bound to us now, Gemma. Forever."

Gemma's breath hitched as the shadows writhed at the edge of the clearing, creeping closer, suffocating her with their weight. The dark energy in the air thickened, like a storm about to break. The twisted branches of the ancient trees stretched toward her, their bark cracking under the force of the malevolent magick filling the space.

"Let it happen, child." Margaret stepped forward from the darkness, her presence commanding, her long, dark robes swirling as if caught in an invisible wind. "You were born for this. Stop fighting. Embrace what you are."

"No..." Gemma whispered, trembling. Her hands dropped to her sides as her strength drained away. The necklace tightened, its cold metal digging into her skin as though it were alive, feeding off her resistance.

A gust of wind whipped through the clearing, smelling of earth and decay. The witches closed in, their forms shifting like shadows in the moonlight. Margaret's eyes gleamed with cruel delight, while Grace remained in the background, silent and watching. The anticipation hung in the air like a knife waiting to drop.

"You're almost there," Hannah whispered, stepping closer, her breath chilling Gemma's skin. "Stop resisting, and you will become more powerful than you've ever imagined. You will be free."

Gemma's pulse roared in her ears as her mind spun, the weight of the witches' words pressing on her like a vise. The ground beneath her feet tilted, as if the very earth was conspiring to push her into the darkness. A flicker of doubt, then more—images of herself wielding untold power, bending the world to her will, unstoppable. It was a tantalizing offer, whispering promises of protection, control, and safety.

But what kind of monster would she become?

"Don't listen to them!" Lillian's voice pierced through the thickening air, desperate but fading. Her spectral form flickered near the edge of the clearing, the shadows pulling at her, trying to drag her back. "You're stronger than this, Gemma! Fight them! Don't let them take you!"

Gemma's gaze locked onto her great-aunt, her chest tightening with fear and anger. She wanted to scream, to run, but the necklace pulsed with each beat of her heart, a sinister rhythm that synced with the witches' chant. Her head spun as the magick from the necklace seeped deeper into her bones, whispering to her, luring her into the darkness.

With each pulse, the world around her dimmed. The moon's light faded, replaced by a suffocating blackness that swallowed everything. The witches' voices grew louder, stronger, their power pressing down on her, binding her to the earth, to them.

Her vision blurred, and for a moment, she saw herself, a twisted reflection in the darkness. Her eyes burned with the same icy fire as Hannah's, her hands crackling with dark energy, her mouth curled into a wicked smile. The power in that vision was intoxicating, irresistible.

"No!" Gemma shouted, forcing herself to look away, to cling to her own fading sense of self. But it was slipping, slipping away like water through her fingers.

"You're already ours, Gemma," Hannah whispered, her icy hand resting on Gemma's shoulder. "There's no going back."

Gemma's breath caught, her body frozen, and for the first time, she sensed it, the darkness inside her, waiting, growing. A part of her wanted to give in, to stop fighting, to have control. The necklace pulsed in time with her thoughts, its power intertwining with hers, drawing her deeper into the void.

She heard Lillian calling her name, distant now, fading as the witches' power overwhelmed her senses. The ground beneath her feet trembled, the symbols carved into the stones around her glowing with ancient magick. A fragile boundary separated the worlds, thin enough to tear open at any moment. Gemma stood on the precipice, teetering on the edge.

The necklace tightened one last time, its cold, metal grip like shackles around her throat. Gemma's chest heaved as her vision darkened, her limbs growing heavy, too heavy to lift. She was being pulled deeper, falling into the abyss that waited beneath the surface.

And then the darkness whispered, What will you choose?

Her heart raced, her mind screaming for a way out. But there was no escape. Not this time.

A crack echoed through the clearing, and Gemma's eyes shot open as the ground beneath her split apart, tendrils of black mist seeping from the earth, wrapping around her ankles. The witches' chanting grew louder, more fevered, and their power pulled her down, pulled her into them.

And as the darkness swallowed her whole, Gemma heard a faint voice, her own voice, distant and unfamiliar, whispering from deep within.

But the words were lost, drowned by the witches' final chant as the world disappeared around her.

The last thing she saw before the shadows consumed her was Hannah's cold, triumphant smile.

And then everything went black.

But deep within the void, something stirred.

And Gemma was not alone.

CHAPTER SIXTEEN

ISOBEL STOOD IN THE kitchen of her aunt's brownstone in Chicago, measuring out herbs for a remedy. The sharp ring of the doorbell jolted her out of her reverie, the sound slicing through the stillness of the morning like a knife.

Her heart skipped a beat. The herbal leaves fell from her fingers, forgotten. Wiping her hands on her apron, she hurried to the door, an inexplicable sense of dread tightening around her chest. The early light streamed through the windows, casting a soft glow on the wooden floorboards, but the warmth it offered did nothing to ease the icy knot forming in the pit of her stomach.

The door creaked as she opened it to reveal the telegram boy, his expression somber as he extended a small, sealed envelope toward her. Isobel's fingers trembled as she reached out, her breath catching in her throat. Telegrams are never good news. She dug out a nickel from her apron and handed it to him. He gave a quick nod, turned on his heel, and hurried down the steps, disappearing into the morning light.

Isobel barely noticed him run off as she stood in the doorway, staring at the envelope in her hands. Her fingers were clumsy, the paper rough against her skin. With a quick, practiced motion, she tore open the seal, her heart pounding in her ears as she unfolded the thin sheet of paper inside as she walked back to the kitchen.

The words leaped off the page at her, each letter stark and cold in the dim light of the hallway. "Gemma... dire circumstances... lifeless..." The room spun for a moment as the telegram swam before her eyes. She blinked, forcing the words into focus, her breath catching as the weight of the message settled into her bones. Gemma was in grave danger. The details were sparse, but the urgency was undeniable. A curse? A hex? Isobel's mind raced, flipping through her knowledge of both medicine and the mystical arts. This wasn't something a country doctor could mend. If it were, Doc would have handled it.

Dropping the telegram onto the kitchen table, Isobel pressed a hand to her forehead, trying to still the rising panic. Her herbal remedy, the morning routine before her nursing classes, everything around her faded into the background. All she saw was Gemma's face. Her hands shook as she reached out to steady herself on the edge of the table. She had left Tin Creek for nursing school and then would return to start a new life with John. But now, she was being called back to face the unknown.

Isobel took a deep breath. She had to act and fast. There was no time to dwell on the what-ifs. She needed to return to Tin Creek.

Aunt Stella's footsteps echoed down the hallway. Isobel's heart clenched as she heard the familiar sound, her resolve hardening. She wanted Aunt Stella's guidance, her wisdom, and her strength. Picking up the telegram, Isobel moved toward the parlor where the morning light streamed through tall windows, casting a warm glow that was out-of-place given the gravity of the news.

"Aunt Stella," Isobel called. Stella appeared in the doorway, her eyes locking onto the paper in Isobel's hand. Without a word, she crossed the room, her presence both comforting and commanding.

"What is it, my dear?" Stella's eyes held a flicker of concern as she took the telegram from Isobel's trembling hand.

As Stella read the words, her expression darkened, her brow furrowing in deep thought. She looked up, meeting Isobel's eyes. "This sounds serious, Isobel. We must go to Tin Creek. Now."

Isobel nodded. "Yes. I fear this is not an ordinary illness. This... this might involve the dark ways."

Stella's eyes sharpened, the implications of Isobel's words sinking in. The dark ways—the family's knowledge of curses and protections—these were things they had not spoken of in some time. But now they were being called back to those very traditions.

"You think it's a curse?" Stella asked as she handed the telegram back.

"I do," Isobel replied, the fear gnawing at her. "Gemma is strong, resilient. If something has laid her so low, it must be something beyond the ordinary. Something dark."

Stella's face hardened with resolve. "Then we must go prepared. I'll gather what I can from my supplies—herbs, tinctures, anything that might be of use. We don't know what we're walking into, but we won't walk in blind."

As Stella moved to prepare, the weight of the situation settled on Isobel's shoulders. She had always admired her aunt's strength, her ability to face any challenge with calm determination. Now, Isobel would need to draw on that asset for herself. At least she would not tackle this journey alone.

The atmosphere in the brownstone shifted as the two women moved with purpose, gathering what they require for their trip. Isobel's hands worked quickly, folding clothes and collecting her nursing and herbal tools, while her mind raced through the scenarios that awaited them.

Isobella helped Stella pack her own bag with the care and precision that had always defined her—a mixture of practical items and the mysterious, all wrapped in cloth and tied with twine.

As they worked, the weight of the task ahead pressed down on them, unspoken but unmistakable. Stella's calm efficiency was a steadying force for Isobel, whose thoughts kept drifting back to Gemma—her friend, caught in the grip of something malevolent.

When the last bag was closed, Isobel returned to look around her bedroom. The morning light had illuminated the space, highlighting the comfort and safety she had found here. But now, it was time to leave that behind. With a last glance at the familiar surroundings, Isobel squared her shoulders and turned to face Stella, who was already waiting by the door.

"Ready?" Stella asked.

Isobel nodded, her resolve firm. "Ready."

Their journey from Chicago to Tin Creek was long, marked by the rhythmic clatter of the train wheels and the ever-changing scenery outside the windows. Each passing mile took them closer to the heart of the mystery of the telegram.

Days later, as the train pulled into the small station at Tin Creek, the cool air smelling of pine and earth filling her lungs as she stepped onto the platform. It was a scent that spoke of home, but now, it carried an edge of danger, of the challenges that lay ahead.

\# \# \#

Isobel's hand trembled as she gripped the brass doorknob, its cold surface biting into her palm. The familiar creak of the door, which had always been a comforting sound in the upstairs living quarters, now echoed through the silent hall. Her heart pounded in her chest as she pushed the door open, the soft morning light filtering in behind her as if hesitant to enter the room.

Gemma lay motionless on the bed, her form still beneath the heavy quilt. The sight stopped Isobel in her tracks, a wave of icy dread crashing over her. The room, usually warm and filled with the quiet sounds of Gemma's daily life, felt silent, as if time itself had paused in this small, dim space. Isobel's breath caught in her throat as she stepped closer, her eyes sweeping over her friend's pale face. Gemma's vibrant spirit, always bright and lively, was gone, leaving behind only an eerie shell of the person she had known.

As Isobel approached the bed, a glint of metal captured her eye. Her heart skipped a beat as her gaze landed on the necklace draped around Gemma's neck—a delicate silver chain with an intricate pendant that gleamed in the low light. The sight of it hit Isobel like a punch to the gut. Her necklace she had thought lost, the one that had vanished when Tom and Paul kidnapped her, was lying against Gemma's chest, innocuous yet sinister.

Isobel's fingers shook as she reached for the pendant, half-expecting it to burn her skin. Instead, the metal was icy cold, as if it had absorbed the life from Gemma herself. Memories flooded back to her—her mother's cryptic warnings, Stella's stories about the necklace's dark history, and her own foolish decision to wear it. Guilt twisted in her chest. Had her actions, her inability to keep the cursed object away, brought this upon Gemma?

A soft rustle by the bed startled her. Isobel saw Shadow, Gemma's raccoon familiar, curled up against her side, his small body pressed against hers as if trying to warm her. The raccoon's usual bright, curious eyes were half-closed, his energy subdued as he rested against his unresponsive mistress. Even in this moment of deep stillness, Shadow refused to leave her side, his loyalty unyielding. His tail twitched, a acknowledgment of Isobel's presence, but he remained snuggled beside Gemma.

The room felt colder, darker, as if the necklace itself was drawing the warmth and light from the space. Isobel's mind raced, searching for answers. This wasn't just an illness. It couldn't be. The necklace, with its cursed history, had somehow found its way to Gemma, and now trapped her in some unnatural state.

"Gemma," Isobel whispered, trembling as she crouched by the bed, reaching out to touch her friend's chilly hand. "I'm so sorry. I promise to fix this."

The door creaked again behind her, and Aunt Stella entered the room, her sharp gaze locking onto the necklace. Her lips pressed into a thin line as she stepped forward, her presence commanding yet calm.

"Isobel," Stella said, filled with a gravity that made Isobel's stomach twist. "That necklace... This is worse than I had imagined."

Stella urged Isobel to sit beside her on the edge of the bed.

Isobel asked, "How did it get to Gemma? This is all my fault."

Stella held up a hand, stopping her. "It's not your fault. Cursed objects have a means of finding their path, especially to those with power or those connected to its past. You didn't lose it, Isobel. It was waiting. Waiting for the right moment, the right person. One thing we know for sure now is that Gemma is related to our line."

Isobel listened, her eyes fixed on Stella, absorbing every word with a growing sense of dread and realization. "She's family?"

Stella took Isobel's hand in hers and nodded, offering a tactile reassurance as she delved deeper into the past. "The story goes that one of our ancestors made the necklace under a blood moon. Full of intentions that weren't even from this world." She paused, eyes narrowing. "And all those stories—people who wore it, losing themselves, pushed right over the edge into darkness. When my mother had it, strange things happened. Her desire and draw to the dark arts was troubling. I suspect it drove your mother to do things…"

The room grew colder with each word, as the weight of Stella's knowledge settled around them like a thick fog. "Your decision to wear it was unwise, and now it seems to have found its way to Gemma," Stella said, a hint of sorrow lacing her tone.

Isobel's heart raced, her mind piecing together the fragmented warnings of the past with the grim reality before her. The connection was clear and chilling: Gemma, vibrant and curious, had likely been drawn to the necklace by its deceptive allure, unaware of its dark core.

"I never intended for this to happen," Isobel said. Her mind went to her deep attachment with Gemma from the first moment they met. She couldn't lose her now.

Stella squeezed her hand, interrupting. "We know not how these things come to pass, my dear. But we do know that we must act, not only to save Gemma, but to perhaps finally break this cycle of a curse that clings to our lineage."

Stella's expression hardened. "We will break the curse."

Isobel nodded, though fear gnawed at the edges of her resolve. Breaking curses was dangerous, and there was no guarantee they would succeed. But what choice did they have? Gemma was slipping away before their eyes, and the necklace was the key.

CHAPTER SEVENTEEN

THE AIR AT DRUID'S Altar crackled with an otherworldly energy, thick with the echoes of centuries-old magick. The gnarled stone pillars stood like sentinels, casting long shadows in the faint light of a crescent moon. Gemma shivered, though the cold that crept over her wasn't from the wind but from the oppressive atmosphere pressing in on her.

At the center of the circle, Gemma's heart pounded as witches circled her, slow and deliberate. Their dark cloaks billowed out behind them, whispering against the ground as they chanted in low, rhythmic tones. The sound sent a chill down her spine, but she held her ground, determined not to show the fear gnawing at the edges of her resolve.

"We have come again, child," one witch hissed, sounding like the rustling of dead leaves. "But this time, we offer you a truth you cannot deny."

Gemma lifted her chin, meeting the gaze of the witch who had spoken. "I'm not here to listen to your lies," she said, her hands trembling at her sides. "I make my own choices and I choose not to embrace your dark magick."

The witches laughed, a cruel, mocking sound that reverberated through the air. Their leader, a tall figure with hollow eyes, stepped forward, her skeletal fingers outstretched. "It is not a choice, foolish girl," she whispered. "It is your birthright."

Without warning, everything around Gemma shifted, rippling like a pond disturbed by a stone. Shadows materialized from the ground, swirling around her in a dark, oppressive fog. Figures formed within the mist, tall, regal shapes with sharp features and eyes that glowed with a cold, ethereal light. Gemma's breath caught in her throat as she realized who they were.

Her ancestors.

The spirits stood before her, their expressions a blend of disdain and expectation. Each one had once walked the path of dark magick, wielded immense power, and fallen prey to the curse that Gemma now fought fiercely to escape.

"Gemma!" Hannah was smooth, but she had an undeniable edge in her tone. Her robes flowed as if they had a consciousness of their own. "You carry our blood, our legacy. The power that courses through your veins is not something you can run from. It is who you are."

"I don't want your legacy," Gemma replied. "I want to live my life free from the darkness you've embraced."

Hannah's eyes flashed with a mix of pity and anger. "You are young, naïve. You think you can escape what is woven into your very essence?" She stepped closer, her presence overwhelming, almost smothering. "You speak of choice, but there is no choice when it comes to blood. You were born for this."

Gemma's heart pounded harder, her thoughts swirling. "I was born to make my own decisions," she said, louder now, trying to muster the courage was slipping away. "I choose my path, not yours."

More spirits emerged from the shadows, their spectral forms flickering like dying embers. Their voices wove together with Hannah's, creating a chilling chorus that surged through the air. The sound coiled around Gemma, a relentless refrain of inevitability, each word a reminder that her path to darkness was inescapable. The harmony pressed against her like a heavy shroud, whispering that resistance was futile, that her bloodline had already sealed her fate.

"Do you think you can run from who you are?" Margaret asked, deep and echoing.

"You cannot deny the power that lies within you," Claire added, her tone both soothing and menacing.

Gemma's head spun as their voices grew louder, surrounding her, closing in. She was being pulled in every direction at once, their words tugging at her, their promises of power and greatness twisting her thoughts.

The temptation was overwhelming. They offered her the ability to protect those she loved, to command the world around her, to never be helpless again. The weight of their promises crushed down on her, making her knees weak.

"You can save them all," Hannah whispered, stepping closer. "With our power, you can ensure that no one you love will ever suffer."

Gemma clenched her fists, her nails digging into her palms. "No," she said. "That's not the way."

Hannah's expression softened, almost motherly. "Oh, but it is. You think you can fight against the inevitable, but all you are doing is delaying your destiny. You will come to us, in time. Better to do it willingly."

Gemma's heart ached with uncertainty. Were they right? Is this to be her only path? The desire to protect those she loved, to prevent any more pain or loss, weighed on her. What if embracing the dark magick was the only way?

The spirits appeared to sense her doubt. They closed in, their forms shifting and blurring as they circled her. Their voices filled her mind, drowning out her own thoughts.

"Why resist?" Margaret murmured.

"Join us," Grace urged, "and you will never be powerless again."

Gemma pressed her hands to her head, trying to block them out, but they were relentless.

"You dishonor us with your defiance," Hannah said, cold and harsh. "You are not only betraying yourself, you are betraying all of us."

The accusation struck Gemma hard, like a physical blow. She had always been proud of her family's history, their strength, their resilience. But now they used that pride against her, twisting it into something dark and repulsive. They made her feel small, weak, unworthy of the legacy they had built.

Tears burned at the corners of her eyes as their words tore at her resolve. They spoke of duty and tradition, of a lineage that wrapped around her like unyielding chains. Their words carried the weight of an immovable force, etched deep into the marrow of her existence. How could she rise against the roots from which her life had sprung?

Gemma's spirit faltered under their accusations. Guilt overwhelmed her, crushing her until it felt like she had already lost. Foolishness clawed at her resolve, thinking she could forge her own path had been naïve. The power they offered loomed as her only option, a dark fate she would embrace, no matter what she wanted.

"No," she whispered, but her conviction was slipping away.

"You cannot escape us," Hannah said, sounding as a final judgment.

Gemma's breath hitched, each inhale sharp and shallow as the oppressive weight of their presence closed in. The shadows of her ancestors loomed as a strangling shroud, pressing against her chest, heavy with the dark magick and power they had wielded. Their legacy coiled around her like an unbreakable chain, tightening with every heartbeat. Escape felt like a distant dream, her defiance swallowed whole by the crushing inevitability of their will.

Gemma's knees buckled, and she fell to the ground, her hands trembling as they pressed against the cold stone beneath her. The persistent voices in her mind crushed her spirit and tore at the fragile threads of her courage.

She had failed. The fight drained from her, leaving her hollow, unable to bear the relentless weight of her own bloodline. Their promises of power loomed too vast, their accusations cut too deep, slicing through her resolve like a blade. Gemma's shoulders sagged, her head bowing under the crushing tide of guilt and exhaustion. Her body quaked, not from fear, but from the despair that seeped into her bones, threatening to extinguish the last flicker of her defiance.

But even as she kneeled there, broken and defeated, a small spark of rebelliousness remained buried deep within her. A voice, faint but steady, whispered from the depths of her soul. *This isn't over.*

Gemma gritted her teeth, her fingers curling into fists. In a desperate attempt, she reached out with her mind, trying to grasp the familiar connection that had always been there with Isobel. She focused on her friend's presence—the warmth of her voice, the strength she could rely on, the love that was like an anchor when everything else crumbled. "Isobel", she called, her thoughts straining against the distance. *I need you. Please... help me.*

But there was nothing. No spark of recognition, no comforting reply. Just silence. The void stretched between them, the reach too vast, her power too weak. Isobel was in Chicago, hundreds of miles away, and Gemma was alone—utterly, frighteningly alone. The realization gnawed at her already fragile resolve, a hollow ache settling in her chest.

She squeezed her eyes shut, fighting back the despair that threatened to consume her. She had no one here to help her fight, no one to lend their strength. But she aspired to be someone that Isobel would be proud of, who could stand against the darkness even when it seemed impossible. The thought of Isobel's unshakeable determination sparked something within her, a fire, however small, refusing to be extinguished.

With a shaky breath, Gemma forced herself to her feet. Her body screamed in protest, her mind shattered, but she stood, though her legs wobbled under her. She stared at the shadows of her ancestors, the oppressive fog of their presence swirling around her.

"I won't give in," she whispered, hoarse but resolute.

The spirits hissed in displeasure, but Gemma refused to back down. Defeating them was beyond her right now, but surrender wasn't an option. She stood her ground, determined to fight, to resist, even if hope carried the air as lost.

Hannah's cold eyes narrowed, her form looming larger as she stepped closer. "You will come to us, Gemma," she said, "whether you want to or not."

Gemma swallowed hard, her heart pounding, but she held her ground. "Maybe," she said, despite the fear clawing at her. "But not today."

And with that, she turned and walked away from the altar, leaving the spirits and their dark promises behind—for now.

Isobel and Aunt Stella passed through the wooden gate of the cemetery. The thick silence that hung in the air swallowed the sound of their footsteps soft against the dirt path. The landscape lay silent under the new moon's darkness, cloaked in shadow, only faint starlight giving an eerie glow. Each tombstone cast long, somber shadows that danced in the breeze, a reminder of the lives once lived and the secrets buried beneath the earth.

The wind whispered through the trees, smelling of damp soil and something else, older, darker. The path stretched ahead, winding through rows of gravestones like a trail leading into the heart of their family's history. Each step they took grew heavier, burdened by the weight of the past they were about to confront. Neither woman spoke, but the tension intensified with every step, as if the cemetery itself held its breath.

Isobel shivered, pulling her coat tighter around her as they neared their destination—a single grave at the far edge of the cemetery. Mary, her mother's grave. Over the years, the stone angel her father,

Henry, had placed endured the weather. Its graceful figure remained untouched, wings outstretched as if guarding the soul below. The moonlight softened the worn edges of the angel's face, casting it in an ethereal glow that made it seem almost alive.

Isobel paused, her heart pounding in her chest as they stood before the grave. The air thickened around them, charged with a sense of anticipation and old, buried secrets. She kneeled beside the headstone, her hand brushing the cool stone as she closed her eyes. The few memories she had of her mother flooded her mind—memories of warmth, laughter, and the comfort only a mother could give. But also memories of whispers, of things left unsaid, of a darkness that had always hovered right out of reach, lingering at the edges of their lives.

Aunt Stella, sensing the turmoil in Isobel, placed a comforting hand on her shoulder. "This place holds more than memories, Isobel," she said, barely louder than the rustling leaves. "It holds answers. But only if we're willing to listen."

Isobel opened her eyes and stood, her gaze fixed on the grave. "What if I don't want to hear them?" she whispered, the fear betraying her calm facade.

Stella's grip tightened, a gesture meant to steady her niece. "We don't always get to choose what we hear. Sometimes the truth finds us, whether we're ready or not."

As they stood in the moonlit graveyard, the surrounding silence deepened, becoming almost oppressive. The air was thick with an energy Isobel couldn't quite explain, a presence, as if the ground beneath their feet was alive, waiting for something. She noticed it, a connection to the earth, to the history buried in this place, and to her mother. As if the cemetery itself urged them forward to un-cover what had been hidden for too long.

The wind shifted, and with it came the faintest sound carried on the breeze. Isobel stiffened, her breath catching in her throat. She glanced at Stella, who nodded, confirming that she had heard it too. The sound started softly, indistinct, but as the wind picked up, it grew louder, more urgent. It was a woman's sorrowful tone, tinged with a darker edge.

"She is Grace's grandchild..." came the whisper, faint but un-mistakable.

Isobel's heart skipped a beat. The sound of her mother, Mary, echoed in her ears. She remembered the name. But she wasn't sure who Grace was.

"Stella, I have seen Mother and Gemma at Druid's Altar along with grandmother Hannah... and Margaret and Claire." The whisper grew stronger, and the chill in the air intensified. Isobel's breath clouded the air as she listened, her mind racing to make sense of what she heard.

"Gemma's destiny is to be the dark witch over all who dwell on the other side," Mary continued, each word heavier than the last. "She was told she had a choice, but Hannah is holding her against her will until the next full moon... when the transition will occur."

Isobel's blood ran cold. Her breath came in short gasps, the re-ality of her mother's words crashing over her like a wave. Gemma wasn't only cursed, she was being held. Bound by something far more dangerous and powerful than they had expected. Hannah, a name spoken in hushed whispers, had somehow claimed Gemma, dragging her into a legacy of darkness that stretched back cen-turies.

Stella inhaled at the mention of her aunt, grandmother and great-grandmother's name. Her face, usually composed and strong, faltered for a moment. She closed her eyes, steadying herself against the flood of emotion. It had been decades since she had spoken to her sister, beyond the occasional letter before Mary's passing.

"Mary..." Stella whispered. "It's been so long since we've spoken." The wind stilled, as if the air was listening, waiting for her to continue. "I never thought I would hear you again like this or have to face Hannah's legacy again. But we're here now, and we're going to do everything in our power to stop this."

"Stella..." Mary sighed, weary and bittersweet. "You never expected this, did you? None of us did. We were children, playing with powers we didn't fully understand. I thought I could outlive the past, escape the shadows of those who came before us. See where I ended up?"

Stella clenched her fists, her knuckles turning white as she fought to keep her composure. Isobel glanced at her aunt, seeing the pain etched into her face, the sorrow of old wounds being torn open. Stella looked so vulnerable.

"Mother..." Isobel said, soft but desperate. "How do we stop this? How do we free Gemma from Hannah's grasp? There must be a way."

When Mary spoke, she sounded sorrowful and resigned. "Hannah's power is strong. Too strong. She holds Gemma's spirit now, keeping her tethered to Druid's Altar until the full moon. On that night, the veil between our world and hers will be thin, and Hannah will try to force the transformation upon Gemma. She will become what Hannah could not, a dark witch with dominion over everything."

Isobel's chest tightened. Gemma, trapped and helpless, enslaved to a fate she had not chosen, overwhelmed her. The Gemma she knew, though anxious and unsure, was brave, spirited, full of life, none of which matched the image of a dark witch ruling over the dead. She refused to accept that this was the end for her friend, her cousin.

"There has to be a way," Isobel said, trembling with both fear and determination. "We won't let that happen. We can fight. Tell us how."

For a long moment, Mary was silent, as though the spirits themselves were considering Isobel's plea. Then, her mother spoke, quieter, but filled with a strange hope.

"Gemma's heart still beats with the strength of her own spirit. That is her salvation. Hannah cannot take what Gemma will not freely give. She cannot complete the transformation without Gemma's willing submission."

Stella straightened, her eyes narrowing with sudden clarity. "Then we must reach her," she said. "We must break through to her spirit, give her the strength to resist Hannah's influence. If she can hold on until the full moon passes, Hannah's power will weaken, and Gemma will remain herself."

But a grim warning tempered Mary's words. "It won't be easy. Hannah will fight, and she has the power of generations of our family at her command. Gemma is strong, but she is alone. You must be there for her, to give her the strength she needs to endure."

A surge of resolve course through Isobel. She would not let Gemma fall victim to the same darkness that had haunted their family for generations. They would fight, no matter the cost. She turned to her aunt, strong and unwavering. "We'll find a way to bring her back," Isobel vowed, "by reaching her and showing her that she's not alone."

Stella nodded, her expression hardening. "We have to hurry. The full moon is coming soon, and we'll need every bit of strength we have to stand against Hannah's power."

As the wind stirred once more, carrying with it the faintest whisper from Mary, Isobel had a strange sense of peace settle over her, despite the peril ahead.

"Be strong, my sister," Mary said. "Be strong, my daughter, and remember that love is the most powerful magick of all. It's how you saved me once, and it's what will save Gemma now."

Isobel closed her eyes, letting her mother's words sink deep into her heart. When she opened them again, the cemetery sounded quieter, more still. The chill in the air remained, but the oppressiveness had vanished. In its place was a challenge—a call to action.

"Let's go," Isobel said, turning to Stella. "We have work to do."

With one last glance at her mother's grave, Isobel and Stella walked back through the cemetery gate.

CHAPTER EIGHTEEN

THE WIND HOWLED AROUND the ancient stones of Druid's Altar, carrying the sinister whispers of the witches who circled Gemma. Their dark cloaks fluttered like raven wings in the night air. A moonless sky above, thick with clouds, cast a heavy shadow over the clearing. The atmosphere was suffocating, making it hard to breathe.

She stood in the center of the stone circle again, her heart pounding, her mind swirling with confusion and fear. Each step toward freedom was like walking against a tide, the pull of dark magick growing stronger with every attempt she made to resist. The witches had tried tricks, illusions, and even the weight of her own family's legacy to bring her to her knees. Each time, Gemma fought back, but her strength waned, her resolve weakened.

"You're fighting a losing battle, child," Margaret hissed, low and venomous. She stepped forward, her face hidden beneath a hood, but her eyes glowed in the darkness, burning with malevolent intent. "Every moment you resist only makes things worse for you. You cannot escape what's inside you."

Gemma swallowed hard, her throat dry, her muscles tense. She knew they were right, she could not focus. She had fought through illusions that preyed on her desires, confronted the spirits of her ancestors who had tried to bind her to the darkness of her lineage. But now, as she stood before them, her energy drained and her mind clouded with doubt, she wasn't sure how much longer she could hold on.

"Why do you continue to resist?" Hannah stepped forward, her tone softer, more coaxing. "We offer you a way out. No more struggle, no more pain. Think of your loved ones, Gemma. Think of Isobel, Marisol, and Jane, and all the people of Tin Creek."

At the mention of Isobel, Marisol, and Jane, Gemma perceived a strong pang in her chest. She had always been protective of them, especially Isobel, who had been more like a sister than a friend. They had shared much together, laughter, secrets, fears. And Marisol, with her wisdom and unyielding support, had become a second mother to her. Anything happening to them sent an icy dread crawling up her spine. Jane was a confidante and Gemma looked forward to Jane's baby being born.

The witches pressed closer, their words turning into a malignant melody of temptation. "You want to protect them, don't you?" Grace asked, dripping with false sweetness. "We can give you that. We can make sure they are safe, untouched by harm. All you have to do is accept what's already within you. Embrace the dark magick. It's the only way."

Gemma's heart thudded in her chest. They showed her a vision, a future where Isobel, Marisol, and Jane lived in peace, the town of Tin Creek thriving, its people happy and safe. She stood at the edge of the town, watching over them like a guardian.

Her breath caught in her throat. The beautiful and perfect image made her want to reach out and touch it. To make it real.

The witches circled her, their voices rising in a harmonious chant. "It's all within your grasp, Gemma. You can have this future. You can ensure that no harm ever comes to the people you love. All you have to do is surrender."

Tears pricked at the corners of Gemma's eyes. The weight of the decision pressed down on her, the temptation nearly unbearable. Could she do it? Could she give in to the darkness if it meant that everyone she cared about would be safe? Losing Isobel or Marisol, or letting them face any danger, was a fear she could not comprehend. And the witches knew that. They were using it against her.

Her fingers curled into fists at her sides, her nails digging into her palms. "If I accept... they'll be safe?" she whispered, biting her cheek.

"They will be safe," Hannah purred, stepping even closer until she was only inches away. "They will live out their days in peace, free from harm or the dangers that lurk in the shadows. And you, Gemma, will be their protector with the power to keep them safe."

Gemma's vision blurred with tears. The idea of being strong enough to protect everyone she loved shimmered like a distant oasis, so tempting and beautiful that it almost shattered her resolve to stay away from the darkness. She teetered on the edge of surrender, the promise of safety and security pulling her closer.

But then, something in the vision shifted.

It was subtle at first, a flicker in the air, a strange distortion around the edges of the idyllic scene the witches had conjured. And then Gemma saw it. She was not a protector; she was a prisoner.

Her movements were rigid, her eyes devoid of light, her expression cold and empty. The power the witches promised wasn't hers to wield, it was theirs. They controlled her every action, every thought.

She was a puppet, bound to their will, enslaved to the dark forces that had consumed her.

"No," she whispered. Then, louder, more forceful, "No!"

The vision crumbled, the perfect future dissolving into ash and shadows. The witches recoiled, hissing with fury.

"What are you doing?" one of them snarled, her face twisted with anger. "You can have everything! Why do you throw it away?"

Gemma's chest heaved with the force of her breaths as she took a step back, shaking her head. "Because it's a lie," she said, trembling. "You don't want to help me protect them. You want to control me!"

The witches' eyes narrowed, their expressions darkening. "You think you can protect them without us?" Margaret hissed, dripping with malice. "Huh, you're weak, Gemma. You will fail, and they will suffer because of you."

Their words cut deep, making Gemma flinch. Fear gnawed at her, whispering doubts she that wouldn't silence. Maybe they were right. What if she wasn't strong enough? Her refusal to embrace dark magick might lead to the very thing she was trying to prevent. And what if Isobel and Marisol ended up paying the price for her defiance? The notion twisted inside her, a heavy burden she struggled to shake.

The image of herself as a slave to the dark magick that consumed her soul was a twisted mockery of safety and peace. And she knew, deep down, that she wouldn't trade her freedom, her soul, for a lie.

"I won't do it," Gemma said, firm despite the tears that slipped down her cheeks. "I won't become your puppet."

The witches were furious, their forms shifting and darkening as they surrounded her. "Foolish girl," Margaret snarled. "You will lose everything."

Gemma stood her ground, though her body trembled with exhaustion and fear. "I'd rather lose everything than lose myself."

For a moment, the witches were silent, their eyes gleaming with anger and something darker, more insidious. They retreated, their forms fading into the shadows as their voices echoed around her.

"You already lost, Gemma. You just don't know it yet."

The words chilled her to the bone, but she stood tall, refusing to let them see the fear that still gnawed at her insides. She had come close to giving in, too close. The emotional manipulation had been a bit more than she could bear. They had preyed on her deepest fears, her love for her friends, and used it against her. And for a moment, she had almost believed them.

But she had pulled back. She had seen the truth hidden behind their lies. And though she was battered and weary, she was still standing and fighting.

As the last of the witches disappeared into the night, the oppressive weight of their presence lifted, but the damage was done. Gemma looked at her empty hands, shaking all over, her spirit crushed beneath the choices she had almost made. She had resisted, but the emotional toll was heavy, leaving her feeling powerless and alone.

She sank to her knees, her body trembling with silent sobs as the enormity of the battle ahead settled over her. The witches were relentless, their power immense, and she wasn't sure how much longer she would hold out. Each failure chipped away at her strength, her resolve, and the self-doubt gnawed at her like a raging tide.

Wiping the tears from her face, Gemma took a deep, steadying breath. She would keep fighting. For Isobel, Marisol, Jane, and herself.

No matter how many times she failed, she would not surrender to the darkness.

But as the night closed in, swallowing her in its shadows, the fear gnawed at her, whispering that the witches were right, that all her defiance had been for nothing.

Isobel and Stella moved with a hushed urgency through the cemetery, the air thick with tension. Between them, Gemma lay limp, her body a stark reminder of the life she had lost hold of. Moonlight, faint and flickering through the clouds, barely lit their path. Branches of nearby trees cast eerie, elongated shadows that danced around them.

The ground beneath their feet was soft and dewy, each step sinking slightly, making their progress slow. The air smelled of damp earth and decaying leaves, a fitting scent for the place of the dead. As they neared Mary's grave, an angel statue stood like a sentinel in the darkness, watching over them, reminding them of the depth of their task.

Shadow, Gemma's raccoon familiar, trailed behind, his little paws silent on the wet ground. He stayed close, his sharp eyes darting around the cemetery, alert for any danger. As they reached Mary's grave, Shadow scampered ahead, circling the spot where they would lay Gemma down. He chittered, looking between Isobel and Stella, urging them to move faster.

Isobel shivered, and it wasn't the night chill. The heaviness of what they were about to attempt weighed on her like a stone. The weak moonlight barely illuminated the grave, but it was enough for Isobel to see her hawk familiar perched on the headstone, a silent guardian watching over them. Despite the tranquil setting, dread gnawed at her, whispering that they were about to cross a line that couldn't be uncrossed.

Stella, her face set with a forced calm, laid Gemma down beside the grave. The rustle of clothes and Gemma's soft breathing echoed in the otherwise silent cemetery. Both women stood still for a heartbeat, their breaths coming in visible puffs, as if gathering strength for what came next.

Shadow climbed onto Gemma's chest, curling up against her. His dark eyes stayed fixed on her face, and he nudged her chin with his nose, trying to coax a response. He chittered, his small body trembling as if he too understood the gravity of what was happening. Gemma's fingers twitched, and Shadow pressed closer, his warmth a stark contrast to the cold, unfeeling night.

The cemetery, meant to be a place of rest, now became the setting for a desperate bid for life, a clash between the living and whatever lay beyond the veil. Isobel shared a look with Stella, a silent acknowledgment of their fears and the risks they were about to take.

Stella set a bowl of embers between them, the gentle glow pushing back the night's darkness. The fire, though small, burned steadily, a reminder of life's fragility and resilience. The flickering flames illuminated their lips, pulled in a straight line, and their darting glances at every little sound.

They arranged the ritual components around the grave, stones for the earth, feathers for the air, and water collected under the moon. Each item held a significance that connected them to the natural world. The jar of moon water, placed next to the bowl of embers, shimmered, a reflection of hope. Its soft glow bound them to the night sky, reminding them of the greater forces at play.

Stella's brows drew together as she whispered, "We're using blood magick tonight." There was no need to say more; they both understood the risks. Blood magick was powerful, dangerous, every spell carried a price.

Isobel took the small silver knife Stella offered, her heart pounding. She pricked her finger, and Stella did the same. Each allowed a drop of blood to fall into the bowl of moon water, watching as it mixed with the shimmering liquid. It glowed with an energy that pulsed with their heartbeats.

Shadow's eyes stayed on Gemma, his small paws holding onto her sleeve as if anchoring her to life. He produced a low, mournful chitter, his gaze never leaving her face. Stella chanted, growing stronger with each word, calling upon the ancient energies bound by blood, water, earth, air, and fire. Isobel joined in, their voices intertwining, their intent focused on the ritual at hand.

But then, something shifted. The darkness of the new moon became an obstacle they hadn't fully expected. The moonlight, which they had counted on to aid their spell, was nonexistent, hidden behind thick clouds. Without its light, Mary's spirit, whom they had hoped would lend her strength, remained beyond reach.

Isobel's heart clenched as she glanced at Stella. The embers flickered, casting long shadows, the dim light doing little to dispel the creeping dread. Stella's brow furrowed, her steady demeanor faltering. "The moon isn't strong enough," she whispered, her eyes searching the sky for a break in the clouds that didn't come.

Panic swelled in Isobel's chest. She scanned their surroundings, looking for something that could help. "What if we amplify the light we have?" she asked, looking at the jar of moon water. Stella hesitated, then nodded.

Stella fed the embers, coaxing the flames to grow, while Isobel placed the jar close, letting the firelight reflect off the water. The shimmering grew stronger, casting a faint glow that wrapped around them like a protective shield. Isobel took a deep breath, feeling a glimmer of hope as they resumed the chant, their voices rising into the still night.

The air thrummed with power as they pushed forward, the amplified light flickering in time with their incantations. Isobel clung to the belief that they could bring Gemma back, that their love and determination might be enough to overcome the darkness.

The spell built to its peak; the symbols drawn in the earth glowing. Shadow curled tighter against Gemma, his watchful eyes wide. His ears twitched at the silence that settled over the cemetery as the last words of the incantation fell from their lips.

They stood frozen, hands still raised, staring down at the glowing symbols. The stillness pressed in on them as though the earth itself waited to see what would come of their efforts.

"Did it work?" Isobel whispered, not wanting to shatter the fragile silence.

Stella lowered her hands. "I don't know," she replied. "Sometimes, these things take time."

They turned to look at Gemma, her body still and pale alongside Mary's grave. The glow from the symbols faded, leaving behind only darkness and uncertainty.

Isobel kneeled beside Gemma, taking her chilly hand in her own. The air grew colder, the quiet more profound. Stella stood next to her, eyes locked on Gemma, the worry clear in the lines of her face.

And then, as the first hint of dawn touched the horizon, Isobel felt it, a subtle warmth in Gemma's hand. Her breath caught as she watched Shadow shift, his little head lifting as Gemma's chest rose with a deeper breath. Gemma's face twitched, her lips parting, as if answering some distant call.

Stella leaned closer, her experienced hands moving to check for more signs of life, while Shadow nudged Gemma's face. The long, dark night gave way to the first light of dawn, and with it came the hope that they had succeeded—that Gemma was still with them.

CHAPTER NINETEEN

GEMMA STOOD IN THE center of the Druid's Altar. Her body trembled, her spirit crushed beneath the weight of countless failed attempts to break free. The once-clear sky had darkened, clouds swirling above in a chaotic storm, blocking any light that might have offered her comfort.

The wind howled through the desolate stones of the altar, carrying the eerie chants of the witches who encircled Gemma. Their voices wove together, forming a dark melody that thrummed with sinister power, reverberating through the earth beneath her feet.

The witches, their cloaked forms shifting like shadows around her, chanted louder. Their eyes gleamed with malevolent delight, sensing her weakening resolve.

"You can't fight it forever, Gemma," Margaret hissed, the sound cutting through the chanting like a sharp blade. "This is who you are."

Gemma's knees buckled, and she dropped to the ground, her hands sinking into the cold, damp earth. Her body shook with fatigue, her breaths coming in shallow, desperate gasps. The ground pulsed beneath her, as if the stones of the altar were alive, feeding on her despair.

"I... I can't..." she whispered, drowned by the witches' rhythmic chanting. The words slipped from her lips, heavy with defeat, and the darkness tightened its grip, pressing in closer, suffocating her resolve. Gemma had fought for so long, resisted their lies, their illusions, their manipulations. But now, the end was here. She had nothing left to give.

The witches closed in, their figures looming over her like specters of doom. Their voices rose in a triumphant crescendo, the air crackling with the dark magick they had wielded for centuries. "It's time, Gemma," they whispered in unison. "It's time to accept your destiny."

Gemma's heart sank. She had been sure that she could find a way out, sure that she could fight this and come out on the other side. But now, her body refused to move, her mind clouded with fear and doubt. She was on the verge of giving in, of letting go and surrendering to the darkness that had pursued her relentlessly.

Something pierced through the chanting. A faint voice, soft but steady, calling her name.

"Gemma..."

Her head jerked up, eyes wide with disbelief. It couldn't be. Gemma strained to hear through the oppressive noise of the witches' spell, and there it was again—stronger this time.

"Gemma, hold on. We're coming."

Isobel.

A fragile spark of hope ignited in her chest, but the oppressive force of the witches' magick smothered it. The air grew heavy, pressing against her lungs like a vice, while unseen chains wrapped around her limbs, locking her in place. Their chanting swelled, a relentless tide of sound that drowned out all other noise, its rhythm hammering through her skull. The witches drew closer, their movements slow and deliberate, their dark hoods casting deep shadows over faces she couldn't see, yet she could feel their intent, cold, unyielding, and terrifyingly close.

Gemma's vision blurred as the darkness crept into the edges of her mind. But before it could consume her entirely, a familiar presence, a warmth, a force of love that cut through the cold broke through.

The ground beneath her shook. A blinding flash of light illuminated the altar, and the witches' chanting faltered, their rhythm breaking. Gemma gasped, her head snapping up to find Isobel and an older woman break through the swirling storm of magick. They stood at the edge of the stone circle, their faces resolute, their hands clasped together in a powerful bond.

"Gemma!" Isobel called. "You have to fight! You have to choose!"

Isobel's companion raised her arms as she chanted ancient words, first low and steady, her eyes glowing with the power of a protective spell. The air shimmered with magick, not the dark, twisted kind that the witches wielded, but something pure, something pulsed with love and life. Protective magick weaved through the space, creating a barrier between Gemma and the witches.

The witches screamed in fury, their hold on Gemma slipping as the woman's magick pressed against them. But they fought back, their voices rising again, scratching her arms, determined to pull Gemma into the abyss.

"Gemma, listen to me!" Isobel shouted, stepping forward. Her eyes locked onto Gemma's, and in that moment, the world around them quieted. "You don't have to do this. Don't give in. You are stronger than this magick, stronger than them."

Gemma's heart pounded in her chest. "How do I fight them," she cried. "I've tried so many times."

Isobel's face softened. "You know how, Gemma. You have the power inside you, not the power they're trying to force on you, but your own strength. Use your own light. It's what makes you who you are."

The witches hissed in anger, their magick crackling around them as they tried to regain control. But the mystery woman's protective barrier held strong, and for the first time, the weight of the witches' influence lifted.

Isobel said, "You are not defined by your family's choices. Not this darkness. You get to choose your own path, Gemma."

Tears filled Gemma's eyes as she looked at Isobel, at the unwavering love and belief shining in her best friend's eyes. It was the lifeline she had been searching for, the reminder she needed. She wasn't alone. She had people who loved her, people who believed in her. And that was where her strength came from, not from dark magick, but from the love and light within her heart.

"I believe in you, Gemma," Isobel whispered. "We all do."

The gray-haired woman's chanting grew louder, the protective spell surging with energy. The witches shrieked in frustration, their hold on Gemma slipping further.

Gemma closed her eyes, taking a deep, steadying breath. She opened her heart to the warmth around her. Isobel's friendship, steadfast, wrapped her in comfort. Even the chanting woman's guidance, fierce and protective, stood like a shield at her side. And the quiet nods and hushed words of her neighbors carried a strength she hadn't allowed herself to lean on before. This was her strength. This was her power.

"I choose my own path," Gemma whispered, stronger with each word. She opened her eyes, her gaze locking onto the witches. "And I choose not to follow you."

A powerful surge of light erupted from within her, bursting forth like a tidal wave and pushing the witches back. Their screams filled the night, their dark forms writhing and twisting as they tried to resist the onslaught of light and love that emanated from Gemma's heart.

"No!" Hannah shrieked. "You cannot escape us!"

But Gemma stood tall now, her body glowing with an inner light that eclipsed the darkness surrounding her. The weight of the witches' magick fell away, like chains breaking, and she was free.

"I am not yours to control," she said. "I am my own."

With a final, deafening scream, the light consumed the witches. Their forms disintegrated into shadows, swept away by the powerful energy that radiated from Gemma's soul. Except Hannah.

The storm above them cleared, the clouds dissipating to reveal a clear, star-filled sky. The stones of Druid's Altar fell silent, the darkness that had once clung to the place now banished by the light of Gemma's choice. Isobel and Stella were gone, but their effect hung on her shoulders like a warm blanket.

Gemma, her body still trembling with the aftermath of the battle, smiled through her tears. She had done it. She had fought the darkness and won, not with magick, but with love, with light, and with the strength of her own heart.

As she left the altar behind, walking away from the shadows and into the warmth of a new beginning, Hannah said, "I will have you by the full moon. Don't fool yourself that it ends here."

Gemma shrugged.

As the cool night air settled around them, a soft rustling in the distance caught Gemma's attention. She turned her head, her eyes finding a small shape skittering over the ground toward her.

Shadow appeared, his dark eyes gleaming with focus as his small paws moved soundlessly over the soft earth. He darted through the underbrush in quick, fluid motions, weaving between branches and leaves until he was by her side.

"Shadow," Gemma whispered as she reached out with trembling hands. She gathered the raccoon up, hugging him close to her chest. The warmth of his furry body seeped into her, grounding her in the moment. Shadow chittered, a gentle sound of reassurance as he nestled into her arms, his bushy tail wrapping around her protectively.

"Thank you," Gemma whispered. Her hands stroked Shadow's fur as he leaned into her touch. "For being here. For... for finding me."

As Gemma's eyes fluttered open, the moon's soft, ethereal glow filtered through the branches above, casting a gentle light that seemed to welcome her back to consciousness. Everything sharpened in delicate fragments—the dim light, the silhouettes of trees, and the faint voices nearby.

Her gaze shifted upward to two faces hovering above her. One was familiar: Isobel with worry etched into her features. The other, however, was a stranger, an older woman with a guarded but concerned expression. The one who chanted the protective spell at Druid's Altar.

"Gemma!" Isobel gasped as she kneeled closer. Her eyes shimmered with unshed tears, and her hand reached for Gemma's, squeezing it. "I'm happy you're awake. Where did you get these scratches on your arm?"

The warmth of Isobel's touch and the concern in her voice tethered Gemma to the present, pulling her further from the dark abyss she had just escaped. She blinked, her mind piecing together what had happened.

"Isobel..." Gemma croaked, her throat dry. "Ancestors? I don't know. What... what happened?"

Before Isobel could respond, the older woman leaned forward. Her presence was steady and strong, yet her eyes held a mixture of curiosity and shock. Gemma noticed how this stranger kept looking at her, as if searching for answers in her face.

"You're safe now," the woman whispered. "The spell broke the necklace's hold on you. We pulled you back."

Gemma's eyes flickered between Isobel and the woman, confusion swirling in her chest. "Who... who are you?"

The woman's expression softened, but a guarded tension remained in her posture. "I'm Stella, Isobel's aunt," she introduced herself. "Your... aunt, I suppose. We share blood, though we've never met." Stella's gaze swept over Gemma. "I didn't know you existed until now."

Gemma's heart skipped a beat. Aunt? The words echoed in her mind, and a thousand questions surged to the surface. Isobel had mentioned Stella many times before, but never in a way that prepared her for this moment. She had never known about this side of her family. It had only been her and Lillian until she came to America.

As Gemma struggled to sit up, her body still weak from the weight of the curse that had nearly consumed her, she had an overwhelming need for answers. Every breath she took was a reminder that she was alive, but the questions pressing against her chest were too many, too urgent to ignore. She looked between the two women, Isobel, who she had grown to trust, and the other, familiar, connected.

Stella place a hand behind Gemma's back, helping her sit. "Well, we share more than blood, we share magick, passed down through generations of our family."

Magick. Gemma had always known she was different, that the power within her was something unique, but this revelation wasn't enough. She needed more. She stroked Shadow, comforting them both.

Stella inhaled deeply, her gaze steady on Gemma. "My mother, Lillian, was a powerful witch, like her mother, Margaret, and Margaret's mother, Hannah. Our lineage runs deep, through blood and the magick that's been passed down since before even Hannah and her daughters."

Gemma's thoughts tangled around the names, Margaret, Hannah, women she met at Druid's Altar and whose power had shaped her without her even knowing. But nothing Stella said explained why she knew Gemma, or how this all connected to her life back in Ireland.

"I know who Lillian and Margaret are," Gemma said. Her eyes locked on Stella, seeking answers. "Who are you?"

Stella's jaw tensed, a shadow of emotion crossing her face before she spoke again. "I left Ireland many years ago to come to America with my sister, Mary." She paused, her eyes softening as she continued. "Leaving behind our family, our home... everything. For a long time, I believed I'd lost that connection forever." Stella leaned closer, her eyes searching Gemma's. "But tonight, something shifted. I felt it, a pull, a magick so familiar. You carry the same power."

Gemma's breath caught, the weight of Stella's words sinking in. America. The name "Mary" hung between them, unanswered questions rippling through her mind. How did this stranger, who had left her homeland long before, find her now? And why did Stella's explanation feel like a revelation wrapped in riddles?

"I..." Gemma hesitated, her fingers fidgeting with the edge of her sleeve. "My grandmother was Grace." She saw Stella's eyes widen with recognition. "She had a daughter, my mother, Claire. But Claire..." Gemma swallowed hard, her throat tightening. "She left me when I was still a child." She trembled as she spoke the name, the memories raw beneath the surface. "It was Lillian who raised me until... until she sent me here, to America."

Stella's face paled. Her mouth opened, but no words came out at first, as though she could no longer speak. "Lillian?" she whispered, disbelief lacing her tone. "My mother?"

Gemma nodded, the confusion growing. "Yes... Lillian was your mother?" The realization hit her even as the words left her mouth. Lillian was a stern but loving guardian, someone who had taught her about herbal medicine but never spoke about her life. She had never told Gemma she had children.

Stella's hands trembled as she pressed them to her lips, her eyes distant as if trying to reach back in time. "I thought she died decades ago." Her voice cracked, the pain of old wounds surfacing. "I left Ireland with Mary, my sister, because there was nothing there for us. I had no idea my mother survived."

The revelation hung between them, heavy and unsettling. Gemma watched as Stella grappled with the truth, her face a mixture of shock and sorrow. Isobel remained quiet, her hand squeezing Gemma's and Stella's for reassurance, but her own expression reflected the weight of the discovery.

"Lillian never told me much about her past," Gemma said. "She was always secretive about her life before she found me. Never said she had children..."

Stella's eyes filled with tears. "Didn't think I'd hear her name again," she whispered. "I didn't know she had lived... Gemma..." She paused. "I had no idea." Her eyes softened, her hand reaching out to cover Gemma's. "Lillian was always determined, always thinking ahead. She wanted you safe. She sent you here because she knew, somehow, that we would find each other."

For a long moment, silence stretched between them, broken only by the soft rustling of the wind through the cemetery. The revelations hit Gemma like waves crashing against a fragile shoreline, each one more forceful than the last, pulling at her, leaving her breathless and disoriented. As the truths about Lillian and their tangled family ties unraveled, Gemma's emotions swelled.

Stella stood rigid, her shoulders tense, her eyes darting between Gemma and Isobel as if searching for solid ground in the middle of a storm.

Gemma didn't need her powers to sense the turmoil radiating from her aunt, an undercurrent of shock, confusion, and something darker, something rawer. Betrayal? Fear? Whatever it was, it reverberated throughout the cemetery, making the space smaller, suffocating. Stella's guarded expression couldn't mask the way her hands trembled at her sides, her control slipping at the edges.

"I thought I was alone," Gemma said. "After Lillian sent me away."

Stella reached out, taking Gemma's hand in her own. Her grip was firm, yet tender, the touch of someone trying to hold on to a fragile connection. "You're not alone," Stella said. "We're family, Gemma. You, me, Isobel, we're bound together by more than blood."

The words were a balm to Gemma's weary soul. Family. It was a word that had always seemed distant, elusive. But now, sitting in the cold, quiet cemetery, surrounded by the weight of history and the magick of their lineage, that connection coursed through her bones, grounding her.

"I never met Grace," Stella said. Her expression darkened with regret. "So much of our family was lost, scattered."

Gemma nodded, her heart heavy, understanding that they had both been living in the shadows of secrets and silence. "Lillian tried to protect me," she said. "But there were things she wouldn't talk about. I never understood why."

Stella sighed, her shoulders slumping under the weight of everything unsaid. "Our family has always carried... burdens," she said. "Darkness, secrets, curses. Lillian believed she was protecting you by keeping you in the dark. She didn't want you to be pulled into the same struggles she had faced."

"But now..." Isobel said. "Now we're here. Together. We'll figure it out. No more secrets."

Gemma looked between Stella and Isobel, her heart swelling with gratitude and a strange, newfound hope. She wandered through her own life like a stranger, never sure where she fit in. But now, with these women beside her, a spark of belonging ignited within her, a sense of connection she had never known before.

The moon cast a soft glow over the cemetery, illuminating the path ahead. As they sat together, surrounded by the weight of their shared history, the chains of isolation loosen. Gemma wasn't alone anymore. They would face the past, uncovering the truth of their family and forging a new future from the ashes of secrets long kept hidden.

"Thank you," Gemma whispered. "For being here. For... for finding me."

Stella smiled, tipping her head. "We're family," she said. "That's what we do."

Gemma's mind spun. Family. A foreign word to her, almost unattainable. She had believed she was alone, abandoned first by her mother and then by fate. But now, these two women, Isobel and Stella, beside her, bound to her by blood and magick, promising a connection she had longed for but never expected to find.

As the cool night air settled around them, something shifted deep within her. The darkness that had once consumed her was no longer suffocating. The weight of the cursed necklace on her neck had been lifted, and with it, the sense of isolation that had clung to her.

"I always felt... like I didn't belong anywhere," Gemma said. "But now, with you both here, I feel..." she trailed off, struggling to find the words.

"Like you've found your place," Stella finished.

Gemma nodded, tears slipping down her cheeks. "Yes."

Stella and Isobel moved closer, surrounding her with the warmth of their presence. The moonlight bathed them in its soft glow, casting long shadows across the cemetery, but the darkness no longer threatened her. In this moment, surrounded by family, Gemma had a sense of belonging.

"We have so much to uncover," Stella said. "Our family's history, the magick that binds us, it's all connected. We'll face it together, Gemma. You don't have to carry this burden alone. Now we must break the curse of the necklace. Together."

Chapter Twenty

Wrapped in a quilt infused with faint but soothing scents of lavender and sage, Gemma lay motionless, her body nestled in the comfort of her bed. Beside her, Shadow curled up, his rhythmic breathing offering a quiet sense of stability. But the peace of her room did nothing to calm the storm raging in her mind. Despite the cozy surroundings, darkness clung to her thoughts, the weight of the visions she had endured lingering like a heavy cloud.

The flickering candlelight bathed her room in soft, dancing shadows, casting ominous shapes on the walls that only deepened the tension Gemma wrestled with. She clutched the quilt tighter, as if it somehow protected her from the horrors that had haunted her unconscious state. Stella and Isobel sat on the bed, their expressions a blend of concern and anticipation. Their presence, though comforting, only reminded Gemma of the gravity of her situation.

Gemma broke the stillness, low and steady but tinged with fear. "The visions... they wouldn't stop." Her hands gripped the edges of the quilt tighter. "I saw ancestors I didn't recognize, shadowy figures, speaking of things I never wanted to know." Her throat tightened as the words spilled out, and she forced herself to continue. "They whispered of a destiny. They want me to become... the most powerful dark witch, to control spirits and shadows."

The candle's soft crackle was the only sound in the room as her words hung in the air. Gemma's gaze drifted toward the window, where thick curtains hid the night sky and the looming full moon. She didn't have to see it to feel its pull, an invisible force tugging her to the fate she feared.

"The full moon," she whispered, strained. "It's close... so close. October first. It feels like it's waiting for me to... change."

Isobel's hand found Gemma's. The warmth of her touch offered a flicker of reassurance, though it did little to quell the cold dread that had settled deep in Gemma's bones. "We won't let that happen," Isobel said. She squeezed Gemma's hand, her eyes filled with a fierce determination. "You won't face this alone."

Gemma's eyes flickered toward Isobel, but the solacing couldn't shake the grip of fear constricting her chest. "It all felt so real," she whispered. "Even now, it's like the shadows are still clutching at me, refusing to let go. I can't breathe sometimes... like I'm being suffocated by something I can't see."

Stella's expression hardened with concentration, her gaze fixed on Gemma. "These aren't dreams," Stella said, taking on a grave tone as she stared into the flickering candlelight. "They're warnings... or worse, commands. From the past. The bloodline that ties us together isn't only a gift, Gemma—it's also a curse, one that shapes our futures if we are not careful."

Gemma's heart pounded harder against her chest. She had always sensed something different about her tied to her lineage. But now, knowing that her ancestors wanted her to follow the dark path, to wield a power that would consume her, was almost too much to bear.

"I don't want this," Gemma said, her hands clutching the quilt so hard her knuckles turned white. "I don't want any of it if it means losing myself to the darkness." Her eyes darted back to the window. "But I'm scared that I won't be able to escape it."

A heavy tension settled over the room after Gemma's confession, the silence pressing in from all sides. The flickering candlelight dimmed, casting deeper shadows that made the space tighter, the air thick with unspoken dread. Gemma's fear hung thick, an almost suffocating presence that swallowed any words, leaving everyone frozen under the weight of what had been revealed.

Stella leaned forward, her face lit by the flickering light. "You won't lose yourself, Gemma," she said with conviction. "We'll figure this out together. The necklace, the full moon... there's a way to fight this. We have to find it."

Isobel's hand tightened around Gemma's. "You're not alone in this," she whispered. "Whatever it takes, we'll do it. You don't have to face this destiny. We'll make sure of it."

The weight of their words and the fear gnawed at her, clawing at her resolve. "The moon is calling me," she said. "Like it's pulling me toward something... dark. And every minute that passes brings me closer to it."

The room grew still again, the only sound the rustling of Shadow as he shifted beside her, his presence a slight comfort. The impending full moon loomed, an invisible force driving the urgency. Stella's expression became more resolute as she stood, the resolve in her stance unmistakable.

"We can't wait any longer," Stella said, cutting through the heavy silence. "That necklace... it's the key to all of this. It has to be destroyed."

Gemma looked up at Stella, her heart racing as she realized the enormity of what needed to be done. Destroying the necklace felt like severing a piece of herself—a dark, malignant piece. The thought of it both relieved and terrified her.

"We'll need to hurry," Stella said, pacing the room. "The full moon is only two weeks away, and with it comes the culmination of the curse that's tied to our bloodline."

Isobel stood, joining her aunt in the planning. "There's a binding spell we could use, one that might neutralize the necklace before the full moon rises."

"And if we combine it with a purification ritual, we might strip the necklace of its power," Stella added, her eyes scanning the grimoires that lay scattered on the nearby table. "But it won't be easy. The power tied to it is ancient and strong."

Gemma sat up a little straighter, her resolve hardening as she listened to their plan. The fear was still there, gnawing at the edges of her mind, but for the first time in days, there was a glimmer of hope. "Whatever we need to do," she said, "I'll do it."

Urgency charged the room as Stella and Isobel exchanged ideas, their words overlapping in their haste to cover all options. But the clock in the corner continued its relentless ticking, a reminder of how little time they had.

The oppressive weight of the full moon pressing down on Gemma, the knowledge that her time was running out filling her with a renewed sense of dread. Every tick of the clock echoed in her ears, a countdown to when she would have to confront her fate head-on.

"We'll find a way," Isobel said again with determination as she glanced at Gemma. "We have to."

Gemma nodded. The fear burrowed in her chest eased at the sight of Isobel and Stella standing strong beside her. She wasn't alone. No matter what the full moon brought, they would face it together.

Isobel stepped through the doorway of the dining room of the Bitterroot Hotel, her breath catching as the atmosphere enveloped her. The room hummed with life, a celebration in full swing. The soft glow of candlelight flickered against the polished surfaces, casting warm, dancing shadows across the elegantly set tables. Laughter rippled through the room, punctuated by the clinking of glasses and the murmur of friendly conversation. The smell of fresh flowers mingled with the aroma of the evening feast, creating a heady mixture of warmth, love, and community.

Isobel stood still, letting the scene wash over her. She scanned the room, her eyes flitting over the smiling faces of friends and neighbors, each one a reminder of how far she had come since her arrival in Tin Creek. These people had woven themselves into her life, and now they gathered to celebrate her engagement to John, a moment she hadn't expected, but now embraced with her whole heart.

As Isobel took a step forward, something brushed against her ankle. Startled, she glanced down in time to see Shadow darting through the crowd. His small, striped body moved with surprising agility between the legs of unsuspecting partygoers. Shadow paused long enough to snatch a piece of bread that had fallen from a nearby plate, his paws working quickly as he stuffed it into his mouth.

"Shadow," Isobel muttered under her breath, shaking her head with an amused smile. The raccoon looked up at her with a gleam of mischief in his eyes, almost as if to say, "What? It's a party, isn't it?" Then, with a quick chitter, he scurried off, weaving between the guests once more.

Isobel spotted Gemma across the room, her cousin laughing at something Marisol said, her eyes bright and animated. And there, at Gemma's feet, was Shadow, now perched on his hind legs, eyeing the dessert table with a look of intent focus. Gemma seemed oblivious, lost in conversation, but Isobel knew that the little rascal would soon make his move.

A soft but firm hand touched Isobel's shoulder. She turned to see Stella, her aunt, with a gentle smile lighting up her face. "Are you just going to stand there, or are you finally going to go and enjoy yourself?" Stella asked, her eyes warm but searching as they met Isobel's.

Isobel laughed, shaking her head. "I was taking it all in. It's a bit overwhelming, isn't it?"

Stella gave her a knowing look, squeezing her shoulder. "You deserve this moment, darling. Don't let it pass you by."

Isobel's heart softened, and she leaned in to hug Stella. "Thank you, Aunt Stella. For everything."

Stella returned the hug with a tenderness that spoke of all the support she had given over the years. "Now go on," she said. "Have fun."

Isobel smiled, her heart full. "I'm going. But you'd better not stay in the corner, you're part of this family too, you know."

Stella chuckled. "I'll leave the dancing to the younger ones, but I'll be here, watching over you all."

With that reassurance, Isobel moved forward, sensing the warmth of her aunt's presence behind her. As she stepped closer to John, she caught sight of Jane speaking with a small group of townsfolk, her laughter as bright as the flickering candlelight. Isobel's heart swelled further, surrounded by all these people who had woven themselves into her life in ways she hadn't expected.

John appeared at her side, his warm, steady smile meeting hers. His hand found the small of her back, grounding her amid the swirl of the evening. "Everything looks perfect, doesn't it?" John said, low and filled with pride, his eyes crinkling at the edges as he glanced around the room.

Isobel nodded, her eyes glistening as she looked up at him. "It's more than perfect," she whispered, her fingers tracing the back of his hand. "It's more than I ever imagined." She gave a quick nod toward Gemma and Shadow. "Although it looks like Shadow's got his own ideas about how to celebrate."

John followed her gaze in time to see Shadow climbing up a chair to get closer to a slice of cake. Gemma, catching the movement, looked down and scooped him up into her arms. "Not today, Shadow," she said, laughing as she held him, giving his nose a gentle bop. Shadow chittered in protest but settled into her arms, his paws crossed over his chest as though annoyed that his plans had been foiled.

John chuckled, shaking his head. "That raccoon is trouble."

Isobel leaned into John's side. "He's loyal trouble. Gemma wouldn't have it any other way."

The room continued to buzz with excitement, laughter echoing off the walls. Shadow's antics had added an extra layer of light-heartedness to the evening, reminding everyone that even in times of celebration, a little chaos could make the moments even sweeter.

Isobel's heart twisted. She wanted to believe everything was fine, but the nagging fear that had settled deep in her bones wouldn't let go. The full moon was two weeks away, and Gemma's ordeal wasn't over yet.

"You're still worried about her," John said, pulling her from her thoughts. He could always read her so well.

Isobel offered a small, tired smile. "I can't help it. Something still feels wrong."

"She looks back to her old self," John said her, his hand squeezing her waist. "But whatever's going on, you'll find a way to help her."

Isobel nodded, her heart grateful for his unwavering belief in her. Still, the shadow of doubt clung to the edges of her mind. She couldn't let herself dwell on it tonight, not when they had come this far and had much to celebrate.

A sharp chime rang through the room, cutting through the hum of conversation. All eyes turned towards Anna, John's mother, stood with a glass raised high. Her eyes sparkled with delight as she prepared to make a toast.

"Ladies and gentlemen," Anna said, "tonight, we're here to celebrate something truly special, Isobel and John's engagement." Her smile widened as she looked at them. "We all know these two were meant for each other, and it brings me more joy than I can put into words to toast to their future together."

Cheers erupted across the room, glasses clinking as the guests joined in the toast. Anna wasn't finished, though. "And let me tell you," she said with a mischievous grin, "I've already got some ideas for the wedding. Grand ideas. You'll just have to trust me."

Laughter rippled through the crowd, and Isobel laughed along with them. Anna's enthusiasm was infectious, and Isobel knew she was in for quite the journey with the wedding planning.

As the room settled once more, Anna raised her glass higher. "To Isobel and John, may your love be as strong as the bonds we've built here in Tin Creek. We wish you all the happiness, laughter, and joy the world has to offer."

The room filled with cheers and more clinking glasses. Isobel's heart swelled with gratitude as she looked around, taking in the faces of those who had become her family. She glanced at John as he gave her hand a gentle squeeze, and for a moment, the rest of the world fell away.

As the evening wore on, Isobel moved through the room, greeting friends and family, who came to offer their congratulations. She laughed, shared stories, and soaked in the joy that surrounded her. As the hours passed, she noticed her father, Henry, standing near the edge of the room. His gaze rested on her, a mix of pride and something more, something deeper that tugged at her heart.

Excusing herself from talking with Jane and Marisol, Isobel made her way to him. Henry had always been her rock, but tonight, she sensed a shift. An unspoken truth lingered between them, waiting for the right moment to emerge.

"Father," Isobel greeted him as she reached his side. Calling him that after years of uncle was natural.

Henry turned toward her, his face softening as he took her in. "You look radiant tonight, Isobel," he said, carrying a depth of emotion that startled her.

"Thank you," she replied, her eyes searching his. "I... I wanted to thank you. For everything."

Henry shook his head, a small smile tugging at his lips. "You don't need to thank me, Isobel. I've only ever done what any father would do."

Isobel paused, glancing down briefly before meeting his gaze again. "I wouldn't be here without you. You insisted I come to take care of George." The memory of George still stung, but it had led her here, to this life, to John.

Henry's expression softened even more, and for a moment, they stood in silence, the weight of the past settling between them. Then, after what felt like a lifetime, he spoke again, lower, more serious. "I never thought I'd see this day. Watching you grow, watching you find love, it's more than I could've ever hoped for."

Isobel's heart tightened, her emotions swelling. "Father..."

Henry placed a gentle hand on her arm, his grip firm but tender. "I worried for so long," he said. "Worried that you'd never let anyone in, that you closed yourself off. But John... John's different, isn't he?"

A smile ghosted across Isobel's lips. "He is. He's everything I never thought I'd find."

Henry's eyes glistened, unshed tears pooling at their edges. "Then that's all I could ever ask for."

They stood there for a moment longer, the weight of unspoken fears and hopes easing between them. Henry pulled her into a tight hug, his arms wrapping around her as if to protect her from everything the world might throw her way.

"I love you, Isobel," he whispered, thick with emotion.

"I love you too, Father," she replied against his shoulder.

When they pulled apart, Isobel couldn't resist a teasing smile. "What about you and Marisol?" she asked, her eyes twinkling. "What's going on there?"

Henry's face flushed a deep crimson. "I don't know what you're talking about," he mumbled, touching her elbow before making a hasty retreat toward a group of new friends.

Isobel laughed as she watched him go, her heart light and full. The rest of the evening passed in a blur of happiness, surrounded by the people she loved most. She had John by her side, her father's blessing, and the warmth of a community that had become her family.

CHAPTER TWENTY-ONE

ISOBEL'S HEART FLUTTERED AS she followed John down the familiar, winding path that led to his favorite fishing spot by the Bitterroot River. Here, amidst the rustling leaves and the gentle flow of the river, they had shared their first picnic.

As they emerged into the clearing, the sight of the river, with its calm waters reflecting the clear blue sky, soothed her. John spread the picnic blanket with a practiced ease, his movements familiar and comforting. The river's tranquil murmur, a constant backdrop to their reunion, washed away the noise of the chaotic world beyond this secluded haven.

"Feels like coming home, doesn't it?" John said with a gentle smile as he handed her a sandwich, his eyes crinkling at the edges with genuine warmth. Isobel nodded, her response caught in a laugh that bubbled up, lightening her heart. The ease of their interaction, the way their conversation flowed as naturally as the river beside them, reminded her how deeply entwined her soul had become with his.

They sat close together on the blanket, shoulder to shoulder, sharing food and stories with a laughter that echoed off the water, blending with the sounds of nature. Every joke he made, every shared memory they revisited, reignited the deep connection that had first drawn them to each other. In these moments, with the soft rustle of the riverbank foliage and John's comforting presence, a profound peace enveloped Isobel. The weight of her worries dissolved, carried away by the river's current.

This reunion by the Bitterroot River, in their special spot, rekindled the joy and simplicity of their early days together. It was a poignant reminder of the pure happiness they found in each other's company, acting as a healing salve to the weariness that had crept into Isobel's life. Here, with John, surrounded by the beauty of nature and the ease of their love, she anchored herself, whole and grateful, savoring the serenity this moment offered.

As the afternoon sun dipped lower in the sky, casting a golden sheen across the flowing Bitterroot River, Isobel and John settled closer to each other on the soft blanket. The sunlight danced on the water's surface, creating a mesmerizing pattern of light that wrapped the couple in a secluded world of their own. The serene beauty of their surroundings, coupled with the hidden nature of the spot, lent an intimate air to their reunion.

John reached over, taking Isobel's hand in his, his touch gentle but filled with unspoken emotions. The physical connection reignited their bond, a tangible current of affection flowing between them, warming them more deeply than the afternoon sun. Isobel turned to John, their eyes locking in a silent exchange that conveyed everything words could not. Their love, tempered by time and distance, now resurfaced with a tenderness and passion that was deeper than before.

They leaned into each other, savoring the warmth of being close again. No words were needed; they spoke through gentle touches and knowing glances, each gesture drawing them nearer. The laughter from earlier softened into something deeper, an exchange of looks and smiles that uttered volumes, expressing what words never could.

As they watched the sunlight playing on the water, the beauty of the moment amplified their feelings, making the heart swell with emotion. John brushed a strand of hair from Isobel's face, his fingers lingering on her cheek, a gesture filled with affection and a hint of protectiveness. Isobel closed her eyes, savoring the warmth of his touch, allowing herself to be present, immersed in the love that surged through her.

In this secluded spot by the river, where they had found joy in each other's company many times before, emotions overflowed. The peaceful setting, away from the world's demands, became a sanctuary where their love was renewed and celebrated. The gentle sounds of the river, the rustling leaves, and the soft warmth of the sun enveloped them, creating a perfect backdrop for their moment of reconnection.

This was more than a physical reunion; it was a spiritual homecoming, a return to the deep, abiding love they shared. Here, by the Bitterroot River, Isobel and John allowed themselves to be swept away by the intensity of their feelings, lost in a world of their own, bound by love and the timeless rhythm of the flowing water. No one witnessed their transgression.

As the golden hue of the afternoon gave way to the softer light of early evening, Isobel's heart, full of joy and affection, clouded with an unease. The laughter and warmth shared with John now became tinged with a shadow of guilt that crept in unbidden, marring the perfection of the moment.

Sitting beside the river, Isobel's thoughts drifted to her mother's past, a history fraught with choices that had borne societal repercussions. The parallels between their lives, once a mere whisper in her mind, now roared like the rapids. Mary's journey, marked by love but scarred by judgment, mirrored Isobel's own fears, each step a reminder of the path she dreaded following.

A heavy burden settled upon her shoulders, a mix of shame and fear that tightened her chest and dimmed the light in her eyes. The fear of judgment, of repeating her mother's history, of not living up to the expectations she had set for herself, all these thoughts swirled in her mind, casting long shadows over her happiness.

John, ever attuned to her shifts in mood, noticed the change. He reached out, his touch gentle on her arm, a wordless question hanging between them. Isobel forced a smile, but it did not reach her eyes, which remained distant and clouded.

"The fear of others' judgments haunts me," Isobel said, barely above a whisper against the gentle sounds of the river. "I love you, and I cherish what we have, but I can't escape the fear that I might somehow be repeating my mother's mistakes."

The air between them thickened with the weight of her admission, the idyllic surroundings a stark contrast to the turmoil brewing within her. Her gaze drifted to the flowing water, its surface shimmering with the last rays of the setting sun, a metaphor for the flow of life, ever moving, ever changing, but shaped by the rocks and eddies that lay beneath.

John's eyes, full of concern and empathy, met hers. "Isobel," he said, soft but firm presence in the cooling air, "whatever happened in the past, we are not bound to repeat it. You are not your mother, and our story is ours to write."

His words, meant to console and fortify, were like a beacon in the stormy sea of her doubts. He squeezed her hand, reinforcing his words with the warmth of his touch. "I'm here, with you, every step," he said, "but I know this is a journey you must figure out for yourself. Just remember, you're not alone."

Isobel listened, the sincerity and resolve in John's voice acting as a counterweight to the swirling fears that threatened to overwhelm her. His support was a lifeline, yet she knew the true battle lay within her own heart and mind. She looked out over the river, its waters flowing beside them, a perfect metaphor for her thoughts.

The river, she realized, was never the same from one moment to the next, its waters forever changing, moving, shaped by the landscape but always carving its own path forward. Like the river, her life too was a flow of experiences, of joy and sorrow, of choices and their inevitable consequences. This realization brought a sense of clarity and a measure of peace.

Isobel turned back to John, a soft smile beginning to break through the clouds of her uncertainty. "Thank you," she said, steadied now. "Seeing life as this river, ever flowing, ever changing, it helps. I know my fears, my choices. They're part of this flow. And like the river, I will find my way through them."

John nodded. They sat together in silence for a moment longer, watching as the last light of day danced upon the water, turning it to molten gold.

Isobel paced the narrow length of her modest apartment, the floor-boards creaking beneath her boots as she stepped. Above the dry goods store she now owned, the small space was both comforting and claustrophobic. The soft, fading hues of dusk, purple and or-ange, painted the sky, a serene contrast to the turmoil twisting inside her chest.

She paused, eyes drawn to the window. The beauty outside should have calmed her, but it only magnified the conflict within. The peaceful evening scene was at odds with the storm of indeci-sion brewing in her heart. Every step she took, every glance out the window, reminded her of the chasm between her old life and the one she was building here.

In her hands, she gripped a telegram from the nursing school in Chicago. It dragged her back to a world she had temporarily left behind. The words, clear and urgent, laid out a choice: return to school soon, or forfeit her place. It was an ultimatum she hadn't expected to face so soon, and it was one that demanded an answer she wasn't sure she had.

Her feet carried her back and forth across the room as her thoughts tangled. The path she had planned for herself, nursing school, a career, had been so certain once. Now, that life was distant, abstract to her, and the world of Tin Creek, with its raw, untamed edges, had drawn her in, deepening its hold with each passing day.

She turned the paper over in her hands, tracing the creased lines with her thumb. Her school in Chicago was calling her back, but her heart was anchored here, in Montana. There was Gemma, still fighting the dark curse that threatened to consume her, and the town itself, which depended on her budding medical skills. Her connection to these people, their struggles, their stories, was more tangible than anything in the sterile, academic halls of her nursing school.

A soft knock at the door jolted her from her thoughts. Isobel turned and found John standing there, his broad shoulders filling the frame. His presence grounded her, as it always did, offering her a tether to the present when her mind threatened to spiral into uncertainty.

"Everything okay?" John asked, stepping into the room. His gaze was steady, reassuring, as he took in the sight of her pacing, the paper still clenched in her hands.

Isobel nodded, but didn't speak right away. She was grateful for John's unspoken understanding, the way he read her turmoil without her needing to explain it. He moved closer, his hand finding the small of her back in that familiar, comforting way.

"Still thinking about Chicago?" he asked, though it wasn't really a question.

Isobel sighed, her eyes drifting back to the window, where the last light of the day was fading into night. "It feels far away now," she whispered. "But this... it's a reminder. I can't ignore it."

John's fingers traced gentle circles on her back. "You don't have to decide tonight," he said. "But I know whatever choice you make, it'll be the right one."

His confidence in her was unwavering, and it was both comforting and daunting. Isobel leaned into him, grateful for the moment of respite he provided from the chaos in her mind. But even as she took comfort in his presence, the reality of her situation loomed large. She couldn't keep putting off the decision.

"I thought I had everything planned," she said after a long pause. "Chicago was supposed to be my future. I was going to finish my studies, become a nurse, and then return... But now?" Her voice wavered, betraying the depth of her uncertainty. "Everything here, the people, Gemma... It's like they need me."

John listened, his hand never leaving her back. "It's not just them that need you, Isobel. You've built something here, too. You've become a part of this place."

Isobel swallowed hard, her thoughts flickering to Gemma, to the fragile smile she'd seen on her cousin's face earlier that day. Gemma was still fighting—fighting the darkness that threatened to pull her under, the curse that clung to her like a shadow. How could she leave now, when Gemma needed her more than ever?

As if sensing her thoughts, John said, "Gemma's stronger than you think. She's got you and Stella looking out for her. Whatever happens, she's not alone."

Isobel nodded, but the weight of the decision pressed heavier with each passing moment. She pulled away from John, moving to the window and resting her hand against the cool glass. The town below was quiet now, the streets empty.

"Every time I look out there," Isobel murmured, "It's like I'm being pulled in two directions. Chicago is the nursing school I always wanted, but here... Here, I'm needed."

The air thickened with her words, the gravity of the situation settling between them. John approached her from behind, resting his chin on her shoulder as they both stared out into the night.

"Maybe it's not about choosing one or the other," he said. "Maybe it's about figuring out where your heart is."

Isobel closed her eyes, letting his words sink in. Henry's way of life had shifted in Tin Creek, finding a new purpose, a new love, even with Marisol. Seeing him happy was unexpected, but it made her realize that sometimes the life you plan isn't the one you end up needing.

"Henry's happy here," Isobel said, more to herself than to John. "I didn't think he would be, but he's found something here. Something worth staying for. He's selling his business and house in Chicago."

John's arms wrapped around her, pulling her closer. "And what about you? Have you found something worth staying for?"

The question lingered in the air, its weight undeniable. There were the people in the town, the friendships she forged, the small victories she shared with the community. And John, solid, dependable John, had become her anchor.

"I have," she whispered, the answer rising within her like a quiet truth she wouldn't ignore anymore.

The decision wasn't about abandoning her dreams; it was about recognizing that her dreams changed. The life she planned in Chicago no longer fit the person she had become in Tin Creek. Here, in this small town, she found purpose beyond the sterile world of textbooks and hospital wards. She found a community, a family, a place where she would make a real difference. And she found love that had deepened with every shared moment, every challenge faced together.

Isobel turned in John's arms, looking up into his eyes. "I'm staying," she said with conviction. "I can't leave this place, not now. Not with everything that's happening."

John smiled, the relief clear in his eyes. "I'm glad," he murmured, pressing a gentle kiss to her forehead. "Because I don't think I could imagine this place without you."

The tension that had coiled inside her for days unwound. The letter from Chicago still sat on the table, but it no longer held the power it once did. Her future was here, in Tin Creek, with the people she loved and the life she was building. The dreams of the past were no longer as bright as the reality of her present.

Together, she and John stood by the window, watching as the last of the day's light faded into night. In the stillness, a deep sense of peace settled over her. The decision had been made, and for the first time in weeks, she was certain. She wasn't turning her back on her dreams, she was choosing a fresh path. One that led not to the bustling streets of Chicago, but to the quiet, steady rhythms of life in Tin Creek.

CHAPTER TWENTY-TWO

GEMMA PERCHED ON A stool by an old wooden table in the general store, her fingers digging deep into Shadow's fur. Shadow curled on her lap, his warm body a steady presence as he gazed at the cursed necklace resting in front of them. The dark chilling energy radiating from the necklace pulsed with every beat of her heart. Anxiety wrapped itself around her like a second skin, tightening with each breath she took.

The scent of burning sage filled the room, its smoke curling through the air, mingling with the dim glow of candlelight. Candles sat on all available surfaces, their flames flickering and casting flighty shadows along the walls, as though they were alive, whispering secrets only they understood. A heavy, unspoken tension swirled around, covering everything.

Stella and Isobel moved back and forth across the creaking floorboards, their pacing a restless rhythm that filled the space between the counter and the table. Their eyes flicked toward the necklace, their expressions hardening each time, as if expecting it to strike. Every few steps, one of them would exchange a glance, their whispered conversation crackling with urgency.

Isobel halted mid-step, her brow furrowed in deep concentration. "We're running out of time," she said. "The full moon is less than two weeks away, and we still haven't figured out how to stop this curse."

She stopped, the weight of the consequences hanging between them like a storm cloud ready to burst. Silence filled the room, heavy and cold.

Stella paused beside her, her eyes locked on the necklace. "I know," she replied. "But we can't afford to rush this. If we make the wrong move, we could make everything worse." She clenched her jaw, betraying a hint of the worry she kept hidden.

Gemma's heart pounded. Each word they spoke suffocated her with the fear of what lay ahead. The cursed necklace, the source of all her nightmares, pulsed on the table like a heartbeat, and the sight of it stirred something dark and terrible in her. She shifted in her seat, her grip tightening on the edges of the quilt draped over her shoulders.

"What if... what if there's no way to stop it?" she whispered, trembling.

Stella and Isobel both turned, staring at Gemma, their expressions softening. For a moment, neither spoke.

Stella strode across the room with purpose, stopping in front of Gemma. She bent at the waist, her hands braced on her knees, bringing herself to Gemma's level. Her gaze pierced through the space between them, unwavering and fierce as it locked onto Gemma's. "We will find a way," Stella said, steady and resolute. "I won't let them take you. I promise."

Isobel nodded, her arms crossed over her chest. "Stella's right," she added. "We're not giving up. There has to be something we haven't tried."

Gemma swallowed, her throat dry as she nodded. But deep down, doubt gnawed at her. They had tried everything they could think of—every spell, every charm, every counter-curse—but none of it had worked. The options were dwindling, and time was slipping away like sand through her fingers.

"We need something more," Isobel muttered, her eyes scanning the shelves that lined the walls. "Something stronger than what we've already done. We can't just keep throwing protection spells at it and hope it sticks."

Stella straightened, resumed pacing again, her eyes distant. "We could invoke Morgana," she suggested. "Ask her for guidance."

Isobel stiffened, shaking her head. "No. Morgana's power is too unpredictable. If we call on her, we risk losing control. She might see Gemma as an opportunity, a way to expand her own influence. That's too dangerous."

Gemma shivered. The idea of becoming a pawn in some ancient power game terrified her as much as the curse itself. She had no intention of trading one prison for another.

"Then who?" Stella asked, palms up. "We've exhausted almost every option."

Isobel's gaze lingered on the necklace, her eyes narrowing. "Brigid," she said. "She's a goddess of fire and healing, of protection and purification. If anyone can help us, it's her."

Stella stopped pacing, her eyes widening as she considered the suggestion. "Brigid," she repeated, nodding. "Yes, that could work.

Her fire cleanses without destroying. She's known for her compassion and her strength."

A flicker of hope lit up inside Gemma at the mention of Brigid's name. She knew little about the goddess, but the way Isobel spoke of her, with such confidence, made her want to believe.

"Then we'll call upon her," Stella said. "But we must do this properly. We'll need offerings—something to show our sincerity. Brigid doesn't intervene lightly."

"We'll make it right." Isobel nodded, already moving toward the shelves. "Let's get everything ready."

The room shifted as urgency replaced uncertainty. Isobel pulled out their grimoires, flipping through pages with careful precision, her fingers tracing the lines of text as she found what they needed. Stella prepared the altar, moving with practiced ease, her hands steady as she gathered the items they would need.

Gemma stood, her hands still trembling. She crossed the room to where they were working, her eyes on the items they laid out on the altar—a small hammer to represent the forge, herbs for healing, a bowl of burning embers for purification.

"What do I do?" Gemma asked. She didn't like being helpless and wanted direction.

Isobel looked up at her, a gentle smile curving her lips. "You're going to help us call Brigid," she said. "We need your voice, your strength. This is your fight, too."

Gemma nodded, her resolve hardening. She wasn't powerless. Not yet.

As the altar took shape, the energy in the room shifted. The candles burned brighter, their flames steady and unwavering. The heat of the embers mingled with the sage, creating a cozy warmth that pushed back the fear that had taken hold of her.

Stella stood at the head of the altar, her eyes closed as she took a deep breath. Isobel stood beside her, and Gemma took her place on the other side, her heart pounding as she looked at the altar before them.

"Brigid, goddess of the forge, of healing and protection, hear our call," Stella said. "We come to you with reverence, seeking your aid."

Isobel continued, her tone steady but urgent. "A darkness threatens one of our own. We ask for your fire to cleanse, your strength to protect, and your guidance to light our way."

Gemma swallowed hard, her throat tight. When she spoke, she was soft but unwavering. "I ask for your protection, Brigid. Shield me from the darkness. Help me stay true to the light."

Their voices rose together, the energy in the room thickening, the candles flaring as if in response. As they called on the goddess, the air hummed, vibrating with power. The necklace on the table lay still, its dark energy receded, as though listening.

The flames of the candles grew taller, the light flickering in rhythm with their words. A soft, warm glow from the embers cast over the altar, the heat radiating outward, wrapping around them like a protective embrace.

Gemma's heart raced, her pulse pounding in her ears. Was it working? She closed her eyes, focusing all her energy on their plea, willing Brigid to hear them and to answer.

The embers flared, a burst of light, and heat filled the room. The candles flickered, their flames dancing, and for a moment, it felt as though the room itself held its breath.

Gemma's heart raced. Was it working?

But as quickly as it had flared, the light dimmed again; the candles returning to their gentle flicker. The room was still once more.

Stella exhaled, her shoulders sagging. "It's not enough," she whispered, filled with frustration. "We need more time. More power."

Isobel turned to Gemma, her gaze softening, a promise clear in her eyes. "We're not giving up. We'll keep trying and find a way."

Gemma nodded, swallowing the lump of fear that had lodged in her throat. The brief spark of hope slipped away, replaced once again by the weight of uncertainty. She knew time was running out, and the full moon loomed ever closer.

Stella straightened, her jaw set, determination hardening her features. "We need another element," she growled. "A catalyst, something to ignite Brigid's attention."

Isobel tilted her head, considering. "A personal sacrifice," she whispered to herself. "Something precious." She looked at Gemma, her eyes flickering with realization. "The necklace. Brigid must understand its significance."

Gemma's breath caught. "The necklace? You want to offer it?"

Stella shook her head, stepping closer to the altar. "Not as an offering—at least not in the traditional sense. We need to present it, show Brigid that this is what binds you, what threatens you. We need her to see the true darkness we're facing."

Isobel nodded. "The connection between you and the necklace is strong. If Brigid sees that, she may be more inclined to intervene."

Gemma stared at the cursed object, the silver chain glinting under the flickering candlelight. Her heart pounded in her chest, a war of fear and hope battling within her. She took a deep breath, the taste of sage heavy on her tongue, and stepped closer to the altar.

"What do I do?" she asked, trembling.

Stella met her gaze, her expression softening. "You need to touch it. Hold the necklace while we invoke Brigid again. We need to show her the bond between you and the curse."

Gemma swallowed, her eyes locked on the dark stones embedded in the pendant. The idea of touching it again filled her with dread. But this was the only way. She reached out, her hand trembling as her fingers brushed the cold metal.

The moment her skin made contact, a shiver ran through her, the dark energy of the necklace seeping into her bones. She clenched her jaw, her resolve hardening, as she closed her hand around the pendant.

"Brigid, goddess of fire, of healing and light, see what binds me," Gemma said, her jaw set, chin held high. "See the darkness that holds me and help me break free of it."

Stella and Isobel joined her, their voices rising in unison, their words a plea, a command, an invocation.

Flaring once more, the candle flames reached toward the ceiling. The embers glowed brighter; warmth intensified as the room filled with a powerful, tangible energy. The air hummed, vibrating with their words, their plea echoing through the small space.

Gemma closed her eyes, her fingers gripping the necklace. She focused all her energy, all her hope, on Brigid, with her fire, protection, and strength. She imagined the flames burning away the darkness, purifying her, freeing her from the curse that had held her for so long.

The heat in the room intensified, the air thickening with the power they had summoned. A brilliant light that filled the room as the embers blazed, blinding in its intensity. The warmth wrapped around Gemma, enveloping her, seeping into her very soul.

For a heartbeat, everything was still. The power, the light, the heat—it all paused, as if waiting.

Then, a rush of energy surged through Gemma, her eyes snapping open as the power of the goddess filled her. The necklace burned in her hand, the dark energy writhing against the light, fighting, resisting.

"Brigid, help me!" Gemma cried, her voice breaking with the force of her desperation.

The flames roared, the embers blazing brighter than the sun. As if in pain, the darkness within the necklace writhed, twisting and curling. The light pushed against it, relentless.

And then, with a last burst of brilliance, the light shattered the darkness.

The room fell silent, the candles flickering, their flames shrinking back to their gentle glow. The embers dimmed, the warmth receding, leaving only the faint scent of smoke and sage.

Gemma sank to her knees, her hand still clenched around the necklace. Tears welled, her heart pounding as she looked up at Stella and Isobel.

"Did it work?" she whispered.

Stella kneeled beside her, her eyes filled with hope and fear. She reached out, her fingers brushing Gemma's cheek. "We'll see, Gemma," she breathed. "We'll see."

Isobel stepped closer, her hand resting on Gemma's shoulder. "Whatever happens next, you're not alone," she said. "We'll face it together."

Gemma nodded, her tears spilling over as she clutched the necklace to her chest. For the first time in what felt like an eternity, a glimmer of hope sparked within her. They had faced the darkness, and though they didn't yet know if they had won, they had fought together. And that, for now, was enough.

Isobel's footsteps echoed along the wooden boardwalk, each step carrying her closer to Doc's office and the decision that had consumed her thoughts. When she reached the door, she hesitated, her hand hovering over the handle. She closed her eyes for a moment, steadier her breath and gathered her resolve. This moment, this decision, would shape her future, and the weight of it pressed on her like a physical force. She pushed the door open, the creak of the hinges louder than usual, like the room itself welcomed her into this pivotal moment.

Inside, the office glowed from the late afternoon light filtering through dusty windows, casting long, uneven patterns across the wooden floor. The air smelled of herbs and old paper, familiar scents that usually comforted her, but today struck her different—heavier. Doc sat behind his cluttered desk, flipping through a medical journal, his brow furrowed in concentration. When he looked up and saw her, his expression softened with mild surprise, though his eyes narrowed with curiosity.

"Isobel," he greeted her, setting the journal aside. "Didn't expect you back so soon."

She closed the door behind her, the soft click cutting through the silence. Her heart beat fast, and her palms were damp with nerves. She crossed the room, each step measured, and sat down in the worn chair opposite Doc, feeling the weight of her decision settle on her shoulders. The room, a sanctuary of learning and healing, now appeared like a stage for something far more significant.

"Doc, I need to talk to you," Isobel began, steady, though the tremor of nerves beneath it betrayed her inner turmoil. She met his eyes, finding the courage she needed in his familiar, gruff kindness. "It's important."

Doc leaned back in his chair, watching her, his silence an invitation to continue.

Isobel took a breath, feeling the words form in her mind before they left her lips. "I've decided my future—about nursing school in Chicago."

She saw the slight flicker in his eyes, the way his expression shifted, but he said nothing, allowing her to speak.

"I've decided not to go back," she said, the words heavy but also freeing as they hung in the air between them.

For a moment, silence filled the room, broken only by the soft ticking of the clock on the wall. Isobel braced herself, waiting for the weight of her decision to sink in.

"I've been thinking a lot about this, about what I want," she continued, gaining strength. "These last few months in Tin Creek have changed me. I've realized how much this community depends on us. My work here—it's more than treating illnesses. It's about being a part of people's lives, understanding them in ways that go beyond medicine."

She glanced down at her hands, her fingers tracing the edge of the desk. "The relationships I've built here, the trust people have in me... I never expected to find that so fast, and I don't believe I can walk away from it."

Doc's eyes never left her as she spoke, his expression thoughtful, unreadable.

"Working with you, Doc," she added, "has shown me a different side of medicine. It's not only the science. It's about the connection—the immediate, real impact we have on people's lives. I never anticipated how fulfilling it would be."

When she fell silent, the room hummed with the significance of her words. Doc leaned forward, his hands clasped together on the desk, his face thoughtful but calm.

"Isobel," he said, gruff but carrying a warmth that reached her, "I respect your decision, and to be honest, I'm relieved to hear it."

Isobel blinked, surprised by his response. Relief was not what she had expected.

"I've been watching you these past months," Doc continued, his gaze steady and direct. "You've got a gift. Not only the medical part of things, but for the human part. The way you connect with people, the way they trust you—that's something you can't learn in a classroom."

He paused, letting his words sink in before continuing. "I've been thinking about something, and now seems like the right time to bring it up." He leaned back, folding his arms. "What if, instead of going back to school, you stay here and train under me? Full time."

Isobel's heart skipped a beat. Her breath caught in her throat as she processed what he was offering.

"I'm serious," Doc said, seeing the surprise in her eyes. "You've already proven you've got what it takes. I can teach you everything you'd learn in Chicago, and more. Practical, hands-on experience. You've already seen what it's like here—every day is different, and the people depend on us in ways they never would in a city hospital."

The proposal settled between them like a tangible thing, heavy with opportunity.

"You could make a real difference here, Isobel," Doc said. "And I'm not just talking about treating patients. I'm talking about being a pillar in this community, someone people look to, someone they trust. You've already started building that foundation."

Isobel stared at him, her mind racing. This wasn't what she had expected, but now that the offer was in front of her, it had all the signs of being.. right. More than right. It came across like it was everything she'd been searching for, even without realizing it.

Doc watched her, waiting for her response, his expression calm but intent.

"I don't know what to say," she whispered.

Doc smiled, a small, knowing tilt of his lips. "You don't have to say anything right now. Just consider it."

Isobel took a deep breath, the weight of the decision still pressed on her, but now, for the first time, it was a decision she could make with certainty. The thought of staying in Tin Creek, of training under Doc, of being part of something bigger than herself—it filled her with a sense of purpose.

She met Doc's eyes, steady as she said, "I don't need to. I want to stay. I want to do this."

The warmth of his smile deepened, and he nodded, a look of pride in his eyes. "Then welcome to Tin Creek's medical team, Isobel. This is the start of something good."

Isobel exhaled, a slow, relieved breath that carried away the last of her doubts. For the first time in months, she belonged and was part of a bigger thing. As she stood and shook Doc's hand, she knew that this decision, this path, was her own, and it was the right one.

Chapter Twenty-Three

GEMMA THRASHED BENEATH THE tangled sheets, her body twisting as if fighting an unseen force. The fabric wound around her limbs, constricting her like vines, trying to drag her deeper into the darkness. Her skin prickled, every inch of her hypersensitive, as though the sheets themselves were alive, determined to hold her down. The room felt oppressive, thick with an unnatural stillness, except for the thin sliver of moonlight creeping through the window, casting faint silver stripes across the floor.

With a gasping breath, Gemma's eyes fluttered open, but the line between wakefulness and dream blurred. The room dissolved like the fog under the rising sun, and she was pulled into the eerie, seductive grip of the dream.

Now she stood in a vast forest, cloaked in mist. The air was damp and clung to her skin with a bone-chilling cold, while towering, ancient trees loomed all around, their branches stretching high above her, shrouded in fog. The smell of wet earth and decay filled her lungs, sharp and almost overpowering. She hesitated with each step she took, the undergrowth soft beneath her bare feet as the mist swirled, parting just enough to reveal the clearing ahead.

There, standing in the center, was Lillian.

Gemma's heart stuttered in her chest at the sight of her great-aunt. Lillian looked as she remembered, tall, regal, with that same piercing, ghostly beauty. Her once-dark hair had turned luminous white many years ago. It cascaded over her shoulders in shimmering waves, and her sharp green eyes glowed in the pale mist. But something about her appeared different. She was distant and cold in her stance like she was less human, more... something else.

"You cannot escape your destiny, child," Lillian said, soft but ominous. The sound reverberated through the trees, as if the forest itself were speaking with her.

Gemma's breath hitched. She took a step forward, drawn to her great-aunt, the one person she had always trusted. But dread coiled in her stomach. This Lillian was not her Lillian; she was too distant. Her presence, once warm, was now a chilling reminder of the darkness that had invaded Gemma's life. And the way she stood there, like a statue carved from ice, made Gemma hesitate.

"You can't keep running from what's in your blood," Lillian continued, threaded with something darker. "The power inside you is not a curse. It's your strength. You must embrace it."

Gemma's throat tightened. "I don't want it," she whispered. "Not if it means losing myself."

A bitter smile curled across Lillian's lips, but it never reached her eyes. "Naïve girl. You think you have a choice? The path is already written. Power demands sacrifice. You've seen what it's doing."

Gemma flinched, memories of the dark magick clawing at her mind, of how close she had come to being consumed by the witches on the other side. "I'll find another way," she said. "This power won't consume me. I'll use it for good."

Lillian laughed, a sharp, cold sound that sliced through the mist. "Good? There is no good or evil in power, Gemma. There is only control. You can resist, but the price will be paid. Just as it was for me."

A shiver ran down Gemma's spine, not from the cold, but from the truth woven into Lillian's words. The forest closed in, the towering trees no longer sheltering her, but trapping her, boxing her in. The mist surrounded her like a cage, and every word Lillian spoke was a link in the chain tightening around her heart.

"I will find a way," Gemma insisted, leaning forward, stomping a foot.

Lillian's form flickered, her edges blurring in the mist. The icy authority in her gaze wavered for a moment, and the once-familiar figure became a ghostly blur, like ink spreading through water. Gemma's heart skipped a beat as she blinked, trying to clear her vision.

The outline of Lillian distorted, her sharp green eyes dulling, her hair no longer white but a darker, more sinister shade. The mist twisted, wrapping around her, and for a brief, horrifying second, Gemma saw the truth.

This wasn't Lillian.

The shape solidified again. Standing in her place, wearing Lillian's face like a mask, was Hannah.

Gemma's breath caught in her throat as the realization hit her. She stumbled backward, eyes wide with shock and betrayal. The comforting figure of Lillian, the woman who had raised her, guided her, was nothing but a disguise. A cruel trick.

Hannah's lips curled into a dark, twisted smile as she watched Gemma's dawning horror. "You really thought Lillian had come to save you?" she purred, dripping with venom. "Pathetic. She was never strong enough to resist me. And neither are you."

Gemma's heart pounded in her chest, her pulse roaring in her ears. The realization crushed her. She'd been played, deceived into thinking Lillian was on their side. But it had been Hannah all along, manipulating her, pulling her deeper into the trap.

"No," Gemma whispered. "You're a liar."

Hannah took a step closer, her smile widening, her eyes gleaming with malice. "Oh, you were so eager to believe in Lillian, to trust in the family that failed you. But I've always been here, waiting. Guiding you. You can't escape your blood. You can't escape me."

Gemma's hands clenched into fists at her sides, her breath coming in shallow gasps. Fear and anger churned inside her, mixing into a volatile storm. But she couldn't break free.

"Don't fight it, Gemma," Hannah whispered, low and seductive. "This is what you were meant for. This power, this control—it's yours. All you have to do is let go."

Gemma's legs buckled, her knees struck a stone with a sickening thud, her breath punched from her lungs. Grit scraped against her skin as she braced herself, dirt grinding into the torn fabric of her dress. When she rose, her palms were bloodied, her legs stinging with raw scrapes, but she barely noticed over the weight of her ancestors' voices pressing down on her.

"I won't become like you," she spat, though she wavered with the effort. "I won't."

Hannah's smile never faltered. "You already are."

The darkness around Gemma thickened, swallowing the trees, the mist, and Hannah's twisted form. The power of the witches, Hannah, Margaret, Grace, all pulled her into their grasp, their voices whispering promises of control, of destiny, of a power there was no escaping.

And as much as Gemma wanted to scream, to fight, she couldn't move. It was as if her body, her very soul, was being dragged into the abyss they had created for her.

Hannah's voice was the last thing she heard before the dream dissolved into shadows. "You belong to us now."

Gemma jolted awake, the morning light streaming through the thin curtains of her room. Her heart pounded in her chest as fragments of the night before flickered through her mind like a fever dream. She pushed back the covers and froze. Her knees throbbed with pain, raw and streaked with dried blood and grit, the stinging scrapes visible against her pale skin. The hem of her nightgown was torn, the once-soft fabric now stiff with dirt and grass stains. She ran her fingers over the jagged tears, her hands trembling as she realized the grime and soil weren't just imagined remnants of a nightmare. The soreness in her body anchored her in the reality of it all, a vivid reminder of the Druid's Altar and the fight that had left its mark on her, not just in her memories, but on her very skin.

She wasn't sure she could fight much longer.

Gemma leaned closer, breath held tight, eyes locked on Stella's hands as they turned the brittle pages of Lillian's ancient grimoire. The book exuded an aura of raw power, its cracked leather binding containing the secrets etched across its yellowed parchment. Candlelight danced against the worn cover, shadows flickering along the walls as if the room itself held its breath, eager for revelation.

The air thickened with each turn of the page, tension building until even the floorboards groaned beneath it. Every flicker of a flame, every crackle of wax, added weight to the growing suspense. Gemma's nails dug into her palms, her body rigid with anticipation, a tight coil wound by the unknown. The pages whispered their secrets, their rustle like an old incantation promising truths that could change everything.

Stella's brow knit together, her gaze tracing the looping Gaelic script. "Here," she said, her finger stilling on a particular passage. Her eyes lifted to meet Gemma's. "This could be it."

Gemma's heart pounded against her ribs, adrenaline rushing through her veins. "What does it say?"

Stella studied the faded lines, remaining calm, grounded. "It's a spell of elemental destruction." She paused, measuring each word. "If performed correctly, it will destroy the necklace."

Gemma glanced at the cursed object lying on the table, its presence heavy, charged. The silver chain glimmered innocently, but she knew better; it held darkness, twisted and cruel, that had bound her life in a nightmare. Hope flared, a spark amidst the dread. Yet beneath it, fear whispered. What if they failed? Or this only made it worse?

"What do we need to do?" Gemma said.

Stella exhaled, eyes clouded with the gravity of their next steps. "This spell demands balance. Air, earth, fire, and water—harmony between all four. Each element must reinforce the others. Without balance, the power backfires." She looked at Gemma, her gaze deep and unyielding. "We need perfection."

Gemma's pulse thrummed in her ears. Balance. A word that promised safety but hung precariously beyond their reach. Air and earth were elements at their command. Mary's spirit would bring fire. But water? Water eluded them. Her eyes drifted to the grimoire, its pages taunting her, offering freedom that was hopeless.

"We're missing water," she whispered, the realization settling into her bones like a cold stone. "Without it, we're incomplete."

Stella snapped the book shut, her hand resting atop the ancient tome as if pleading for wisdom hidden between the lines. "We can summon fire. Mary draws strength from the moon, but without water..." she trailed off, the unspoken truth twisting in the silence.

The necklace pulsed on the table, a malevolent heartbeat. Gemma leaned back, her body sagging with the weight of despair. So close to freedom, and yet so far.

Isobel, standing by the window, spoke, her eyes holding an idea. "Maybe there's another way. Lillian's texts might hold answers. Could we amplify the other elements? Substitute for what we're missing?"

Hope sparked in Stella's eyes. She flipped open the grimoire once more, determination tightening her grip. "Amplify... If we could amplify our existing elements, make them stronger. Yes. It's a risk, but it's possible." Her fingers traced the words, searching for guidance, candlelight reflecting in her eyes as resolve burned within.

Time stretched thin, each second carrying the weight of their struggle. Shadow chittered from the corner, his small paws planted on a frayed cushion. His dark eyes followed Stella's movements, as if understanding the tension that held the room hostage. Gemma reached down, running her fingers through his fur, seeking solace in the raccoon's warmth. He leaned into her hand, his presence grounding her.

Stella's eyes brightened. "We amplify what we have, strengthen air, earth, and fire. We push our limits, forge ahead even with one element missing. It will demand everything, but it can work."

Gemma swallowed the lump of fear lodged in her throat. This plan promised freedom, though danger lingered at every step. She straightened, resolve setting her features. "I'm ready. We need to do this."

Isobel stepped forward, her body tense but resolute. "If there's any chance we can make this happen, we have to take it."

Shadow scampered across the room, his tiny paws thudding against the wood. He pawed at the grimoire, glancing between them, ready to help in whatever way he could. Stella managed a quick smile, giving him a light pat. "Brave little one," she said, softening for just an instant before focus returned.

Urgency propelled them into motion. Shadow scampered, gathering items, candles, bundles of herbs, smooth stones that Gemma prompted him for. Stella moved quick, her hands steady as she assembled the components of their makeshift ritual. Isobel and Gemma shared a look—unspoken understanding passing between them. They needed every ounce of strength.

Gemma stared at the darkened window. The moon rode high above, bathing the night in its cold silver glow. The cemetery awaited, its sacred grounds, the thinnest part of the veil, a place where Mary's spirit would flourish. Each gravestone bore witness, a stone guardian of forgotten names. Each step toward the ritual brought them closer to the unknown, and Gemma forced herself not to flinch.

The town of Tin Creek lay silent as they moved through it, the shadows stretching across narrow streets. Shadow darted ahead, his nose twitching at every sound, every movement. Gemma kept her eyes fixed on the path before her, her heart pounding in rhythm with the wind rustling the bare branches overhead. His carefree movements reassured her—a reminder that even here, at the edge of their courage, they still fought for more than just themselves.

They reached the cemetery, moonlight transforming tombstones into pale sentinels. Stella led the way, her feet steady, her eyes never wavering. The clearing near Mary's grave offered itself as their stage. They set to work, positioning the symbols, feathers for air, stones for earth, glowing embers for fire.

Mary's spirit materialized, her form shimmering beneath the moon's gaze. She moved without hesitation, guiding them, arranging candles, adding her energy to the ritual. Her flames flickered brighter, an ethereal warmth enveloping the clearing.

"Take your places," Stella said, edged with urgency.

Gemma inhaled, centering herself. Shadow pressed against her leg, his fur soft beneath her fingers, his presence giving her the courage she needed. She whispered "thank you" to him, then stepped forward.

Stella lifted her arms, chanting into the night, powerful and demanding. "We call upon the sacred forces, those who protect and heal, to hear our plea!" Each word carried weight, commanding attention. The fire roared around them, responding to her invocation.

Isobel kneeled, her palms pressed to the earth as her voice rose, joining the ritual. "We call upon the earth, the foundation of all, to lend us your power. We ask for your strength to balance, to protect."

Gemma drew a breath, her chest tight. She raised her face to the sky, eyes meeting the moon's light. "I call upon the air, the breath of life, the force of freedom. Answer me now, lift this darkness!" Her plea rang out, melding with Stella's and Isobel's. Together, they wove a spell of power and desperation, each word pushing the elements to reply.

The wind gathered around her, tugging at her clothes, her hair swirling with building intensity. Isobel's connection to the earth grounded the storm, and Mary's flames flared, bright and hot, licking at the edge of the ritual circle. The energy within grew with each heartbeat, their collective strength wrapping itself around them.

Gemma stared at the cursed necklace lying in the center of the circle. The silver chain shimmered, taunting her. The wind howled, and the ground beneath them shivered as Isobel channeled her strength. Fire surged, feeding on their words.

Stella stepped closer, her gaze locked on the necklace, her words cut through the chaos. "Elemental forces, lend us your power! Destroy this darkness! Burn its corruption!"

The wind roared, the flames leaped, the earth trembled. Gemma clenched her jaw, the strain of holding the air pushing her limits. The power they called upon converged on the necklace, a twisting vortex of fire and wind and earth.

A flash of light burst from the circle, blinding in its intensity. Gemma turned her head, eyes shut tight against the searing brightness. Heat enveloped her. The ground shuddered beneath their feet, a violent surge of energy unleashed.

When the light faded, silence descended. The candles flickered, their flames weak, trembling in the aftermath. Gemma opened her eyes, blinking against the darkness. She lowered her gaze, her heart dropping like a stone.

The necklace remained. Its silver glimmered beneath the moonlight, untouched. The malevolent aura still clung, its dark energy as potent as ever.

Stella stared at the cursed object, disbelief shadowing her features. Her lips parted, a choked sound escaping. "It... it didn't work."

Isobel stood, her hands brushing dirt from her knees, her eyes filled with regret as she approached Gemma. She touched her shoulder, her expression softened with empathy. "We tried and we'll keep trying."

Shadow nudged Gemma's ankle, his whiskers tickling her skin. She reached down, lifting him into her arms. His small warmth was her only anchor. Tears threatened, but she swallowed them back, refusing to break now. Not here. Not yet.

Gemma looked at Stella, her words tight, but her resolve unbroken. "This isn't over. We'll find another way. We have to."

Stella nodded, her hand resting over Gemma's for a moment. "We will," she promised. "No matter how long it takes."

They stood together, the cemetery dark around them, the moon a distant witness to their silent vow. The chill settled back into Gemma's bones, but she held onto the fire within, a determination that refused to be extinguished.

Chapter Twenty-Four

The blacksmith's forge loomed at the edge of town, its sturdy timber walls scarred by soot and time, a silent witness to countless tools shaped in fire. Orange flames flickered within the wide doorway, their glow spilling out into the night like molten veins, casting the trio in sharp relief. Gemma stood with Isobel and Stella, the heat rolling over them in waves, licking at their faces, and carrying the acrid tang of iron and smoke. The rhythmic clang of hammer on metal rang out, a harsh, relentless melody that set Gemma's nerves on edge. At her feet, Shadow crouched, his keen eyes glinting with the light of the forge, watching the shadows twist and writhe like living things.

"This has to work," Gemma muttered under her breath, glancing at the forge's glowing maw. The cursed necklace gleamed in her palm, the dark energy inside it seeming to pulse in the firelight. The plan was simple: melt the cursed silver and break its hold forever. But nothing about their lives had been simple as late.

Isobel stepped forward, her brow furrowed in thought. "We can't walk in and start using the forge," she said. "The blacksmith will be furious. He's not a pleasant man."

Stella nodded, glancing up the road. "We'll have to ask. There's no other option."

Before doubts could creep further into their resolve, the blacksmith stepped into view. The forge's firelight framed his broad shoulders, casting a flickering aura around him. His soot-streaked face carried the weight of a perpetual scowl, and his hands moved to wipe away the grime with a rag.

Shadow's fur stood on end, a ridge of tension running along his back as a low growl rumbled from his throat. He planted himself in front of Gemma, his sharp eyes locked on the blacksmith. Every muscle in his small body coiled tight, poised to defend her at the slightest provocation.

"What do you want?" The metalworker spoke as rough as the hammer he held, eyes narrowing as they fell on the three women standing outside his shop.

Gemma swallowed hard and stepped forward, the cursed necklace clutched in her palm. "We need your help," she said, faking confidence. "We... need to melt something. It's very important."

The blacksmith's eyes flicked to the necklace in her hand. His frown deepened. "This ain't a place for melting jewelry," he said. "Take that to the assayer."

Stella stepped in, calm and measured. "This isn't ordinary jewelry," she said. "It needs to be destroyed in a fire as hot as your forge."

The blacksmith's scowl didn't waver. "It's a necklace, that's all." His eyes narrowed. "You'll have to do better than that."

"We'll pay you for your trouble," Isobel offered, pulling out a small pouch. "It won't take long. Only enough time for the fire to melt the metal."

He crossed his arms over his chest, glaring down at them. "I don't care how long it takes. This forge is for work, not for your personal needs. Get out. I have work to do."

Gemma's heart sank, but she wasn't ready to give up. "Please," she said, desperation creeping in. "It's cursed. We have to destroy it before the full moon."

The blacksmith's gaze hardened. "Cursed, huh? That sounds like trouble, and I don't invite trouble into my forge." He stepped closer, looming over Gemma. "Get. Out."

Shadow hissed, baring his teeth, and took a step forward, positioning himself between Gemma and the forger. He stood on his hind legs, trying to appear as intimidating as possible. The blacksmith paused, looking down at the raccoon with a mix of annoyance and amusement.

The panic rose in her chest. Gemma sensed the necklace's dark energy swirling beneath its surface, like a snake coiled to strike. She glanced at Stella and Isobel, who were both watching the exchange with mounting tension.

Stella said, "Look, we only need to melt it and pray. That's all. We won't be in your way, and you won't even notice us."

The blacksmith's brow furrowed deeper. "Praying over it, huh? What kind of praying?"

"Simple prayers," Stella spit out. "Nothing more."

The metalworker's grip tightened on the hammer at his side. "You're up to something. I don't want any trouble around here. Get out before I lose my patience."

Gemma's stomach dropped. They couldn't afford to leave. Not now. Not with the curse so close to being destroyed. She stepped closer to the forge, the heat washed over her skin, and pleaded,

"Please. Let us melt it. You don't have to do anything—just let us use the forge."

The blacksmith's eyes narrowed. "No."

He turned his back on them, his dismissal clear as he headed back inside. Gemma's heart raced. This was their only chance.

"Wait!" she called out in desperation.

The blacksmith stopped, turning to glare at her. "You're still here? I said no."

Gemma's hands shook as she held out the necklace. "If we don't destroy this... people will get hurt. We'll leave right after. Please."

The blacksmith stepped closer, his gaze fixed on the necklace. He didn't know the power that radiated from it, but something made him pause. His grip on the hammer tightened, and for a moment, it looked like he might reconsider.

Then he shook his head. "No prayers. I'm not helping you. Now leave before I make you."

Shadow let out another hiss, his fur standing on end, as if daring the forger to take another step. The blacksmith glared down at the small creature, his lips curling into a sneer. "You keep that varmint under control, or I'll make sure he's out of my way, too."

The finality of his words hit Gemma like a blow. The necklace pressed into her palm with an unnatural weight, its cursed energy pulsing against her skin like a heartbeat gone awry. She exchanged a desperate look with Isobel and Stella, who both stood tense and silent.

But before they said anything more, the blacksmith stepped forward, his face dark with anger. "You heard me. Get out of here."

Gemma's pulse quickened as the metalworker advanced, his towering frame casting long shadows across the ground. The hammer in his hand blazed in the firelight.

Isobel stepped in front of Gemma. "We don't want trouble. We're leaving."

But the blacksmith didn't stop, his steps heavy and threatening as he loomed closer. "I don't care what you want. You're not welcome here."

Shadow, undeterred, stood his ground, bristling with defiance. He let out a series of sharp chittering noises, as if scolding the forger for his stubbornness. The sight of the raccoon standing up to the burly man brought a flicker of humor to Gemma's fear, but it faded as the blacksmith's scowl deepened.

Gemma took a shaky step back, her heart pounding in her chest. The curse in the necklace pulsed harder, its malevolent energy feeding on the rising tension in the air.

Stella reached out, her hand gripping Gemma's arm as they backed away. "Let's go," she whispered, tight with fear.

But before they finished retreating, the blacksmith raised his hammer, his eyes locked on them with a dangerous intensity. "Don't come back," he growled, low and threatening. "Next time, you won't be walking away."

The threat hung in the air as the three women hurried away from the forge, Shadow scurrying at their heels, his head held high as if proud of his attempt to protect them. The cursed necklace still clutched in Gemma's trembling hand. Their plan had failed. The forge, their only hope of destroying the necklace, was now closed to them, and the weight of the curse was heavier than ever.

As they made their way through the darkened streets of Tin Creek, the gravity of their failure sank in. The full moon was approaching, and with it, the growing power of the curse that bound the necklace to Gemma's fate. They had no way to destroy it, no way to stop what was coming.

Shadow climbed up onto Gemma's shoulder, nuzzling her neck as if to comfort her. She reached up, scratching behind his ears, grateful for his loyalty. Gemma's heart pounded in her chest, the failure gnawing at her. The curse from the trinity pendant coiled around her neck like a noose tightening with every step, its dark magick pulsing in the night air.

"We need another plan," Isobel muttered, strained with frustration.

Stella nodded, her face pale with worry. "But what? We're running out of time."

Gemma swallowed hard. The full moon was only a week away, and with it, the curse would reach its peak. She had little time left.

"We'll think of something," she whispered, more to herself than to the others. "We have to."

Isobel stood behind the counter, eyes fixed on Gemma. The young woman hunched on a stool, her shoulders tense, hands clasped so tight her knuckles turned white. Afternoon sunlight filtered through the windows, warming the store, but the atmosphere buzzed with unspoken tension. Shadows flickered across the walls, echoing the turmoil brewing on Gemma's face.

Shadow perched beside her, his small paws resting on Gemma's arm. He nudged her elbow, his curious eyes locked on her face, chittering. He radiated comfort, as if trying to tell her, "I'm here." A small smile touched Isobel's lips, but Gemma remained distant, her gaze unfocused.

"Are you all right?" Isobel broke the silence, gentle, hoping to pierce through the thick fog of anxiety that surrounded her cousin.

Gemma's eyes darted from the counter to the ceiling, then toward the window, as if searching for something hidden in the corners. She avoided Isobel's gaze, retreating further each time Isobel tried to engage her. Even Shadow's antics earned only an absent stroke across his back.

Shadow crawled onto Gemma's lap, nudging her clasped hands. He let out a series of soft chirps, eyes fixed on her, insistent. Gemma stroked his fur, her mind elsewhere.

Isobel sighed, picking up a stack of dried herbs, placing them beside Gemma. "It's beautiful outside, isn't it?" she said, moving closer. The store remained empty, but unease hung in the air, as though something dark lingered beyond their walls.

Gemma's eyes flickered to the window before dropping back to her trembling hands. "Yes, it's nice," she replied, distant. She fumbled with the herbs, her shaking fingers betraying her attempts at focus.

Isobel watched her, worry gnawing at her. This wasn't the Gemma she knew—the fearless girl who faced down the shadows of her past. This Gemma shrunk away, her spirit dulled by whatever darkness haunted her. Isobel stepped closer, resting a gentle hand on Gemma's shoulder. "If you need to talk, I'm here," she said. "You know that, right?"

Gemma's head dipped in a faint nod, but her lips remained sealed.

Silence stretched between them, interrupted only by the creaks of the old building and the soft shuffling of Gemma's movements. Shadow settled on Gemma's lap, his head resting on her knee. Isobel kept watch, studying her friend, searching for signs of how deep the curse had twisted its claws. Gemma's hollow eyes, trembling hands, the way she flinched at the smallest sound—all of it spoke of the strain clawing at her.

The store's bell jingled as the door swung open, and Gemma startled, her elbow clipping a jar of dried lavender. The glass teetered on the edge of the counter, and her trembling hands shot out to stop it. Instead, her frantic motion sent it spinning, throwing lavender all across the counter.

Shadow darted, his tiny paws skittering across the surface as he nosed at the mess, his chittering adding to the commotion. Isobel strode over, her steady hands intercepting the jar just before it spun off the edge. "Easy," she said, placing it securely upright on the counter. Her calm voice cut through the tension as she turned to Gemma. "Go upstairs," she urged, her tone firm but gentle. "You need a break. I'll take care of this."

Gemma hesitated, exhaustion etched on her face. She nodded, her reluctance clear. "Maybe just for a while," she said, rising.

Shadow scurried up her arm, settling on her shoulder, chittering as if promising to stand guard. Isobel watched them retreat to the stairs, unease gnawing at her insides. Gemma had been slipping further into herself, muttering to unseen forces, her eyes filled with shadows no one else could see. Isobel heard her restless nights through the thin walls of their rooms upstairs—Gemma tossing, turning, mumbling half-formed, desperate words.

As Gemma disappeared, Isobel sighed, the weight of help-lessness heavy on her chest. Whatever darkness haunted Gemma grew stronger, creeping deeper into her mind, and the full moon loomed near. The cursed necklace wasn't some any old object anymore; it had become a living nightmare, twisting Gemma's thoughts, feeding on her fears.

Later that evening, as the store quieted, Isobel sat behind the counter, her heart heavy with worry. The sun had dipped below the horizon, leaving the room wrapped in the dim glow of a single lamp, its light flickering against the walls like a heartbeat.

Upstairs, muffled sounds filtered through the ceiling—Gemma shifting in her sleep, her soft cries breaking the silence. She called out, her words garbled and frantic, as if trapped in a nightmare she couldn't escape. Each strangled plea twisted Isobel's heart, the sense of looming danger pressing in on her.

Enough. Isobel climbed the stairs, her footsteps light, her pulse pounding. Reaching the top, she paused at the doorway to Gemma's room.

Gemma lay tangled in her blankets, her face pale, drawn. Her chest heaved, hands clenching the sheets, her lips moving in a frantic whisper. Shadow perched beside her, eyes wide, his fur on edge, watching Gemma as if sensing her inner struggle.

Isobel swallowed hard and stepped into the room. She kneeled at the side of the bed, her hand hovering for a moment before resting on Gemma's shoulder. "Gemma," she whispered, filled with concern.

Gemma jolted awake, her eyes wide and wild. She gasped, her gaze darting around, disoriented. Isobel kept her hand on her shoulder, grounding her. "It's all right," she said, her words slow, steady. "You were dreaming. You're safe now."

Gemma blinked, her frantic survey finding Isobel. She swallowed, her eyes wet, haunted. "It's not over," she breathed. "They're coming for me, Isobel. I know it."

The fear in her eyes tore at Isobel's heart. She reached for Gemma's hand, squeezing. "We're not going to let them," she said. "You're not alone. We'll fight this together."

Gemma shut her eyes, her body sagged with exhaustion, and her trembling eased. Shadow nudged closer, resting his head on her arm, his warmth a small comfort. "I don't know how much longer I can fight it," Gemma whispered, barely audible. "Every night, it gets worse. The whispers... I can't tell if they're my own thoughts or if it's the curse."

Isobel leaned in, her forehead almost touching Gemma's. "You're stronger than this," she said. "And I'm with you. We all are. We're not giving up, not now, not ever."

For a long moment, the only sound was their breathing—Gemma's ragged evening out as she held onto Isobel. She looked at her cousin; the worry etched on her face softening, her lips parting in a silent thanks.

Shadow stirred as footsteps approached. Stella entered, her expression grave as she took in the scene. She moved closer, her eyes meeting Isobel's with a shared determination.

"We have to act now," Stella said, hushed but urgent. "The longer this curse binds to her, the stronger its hold becomes."

Isobel nodded, her gaze drifting back to Gemma. "We've tried breaking the necklace's power before. We need something stronger."

Stella's brow furrowed in thought, her scrutiny distant. "We'll have to sever its connection to her, not destroy it. The curse is feeding off her fears—if we cut that bond, we weaken it."

Gemma looked up, her eyes weary, yet hopeful. Shadow let out a soft chirp, his dark eyes fixed on Stella. "We need to do it soon," Gemma said. "I can't keep holding on."

Stella kneeled beside her, brushing a strand of hair from Gemma's face, her eyes gentle. "You won't have to do it alone," she said. "We'll all fight this, together."

Gemma nodded, her lips trembling.

Chapter Twenty-Five

THE GENERAL STORE PULSED with an eerie energy. The warm glow of lanterns danced over the shelves, illuminating an alchemical workshop cobbled together from everyday items and old artifacts. On the counter, a copper cauldron perched atop a charcoal brazier, its surface already gleaming with the heat of preparation. Open grimoires spilled their secrets across the workspace, their faded pages inked with intricate symbols and ancient spells. Jars of dried herbs kept rank like soldiers, their faint aromas mingling into a heady, almost otherworldly perfume.

Gemma stood between Stella and Isobel. The cursed necklace lay before them, its silver trinity setting flared under the lantern light. Each of its stones—ruby, emerald, and sapphire—seemed to hum with dark potential, as if daring them to unravel its mysteries. She clenched her hands at her sides, caught between fear and resolve.

Isobel flipped through the worn pages of an old grimoire, her finger tracing the text with precision. "This should do it," she said, her brow creased in concentration. "We need the strength of the elements to neutralize the curse. It won't be easy, but it's our best chance."

Gemma swallowed hard, watching as Stella mixed the ingredients for the potion that would serve as the catalyst. The scent of sage, juniper, and sulfur filled the room, their pungency sharp enough to tighten her throat.

Shadow scurried across the counter, sniffed at the jars of herbs, and turned his nose up with a gag reflex. He paused beside the copper cauldron, peering over the edge as if trying to assess the bubbling concoction for himself. His presence brought a moment of levity to the otherwise tense atmosphere.

"What are you adding now?" Gemma asked as she watched Stella tip a small vial of silver powder into the vessel. The fine dust caught the light, shimmering before it dissolved into the mix.

"Silver dust," Stella said without looking up. Her tone was calm but focused, her movements deliberate. "It's for purification, to cleanse the necklace of its dark energies."

Gemma nodded, her gaze darting from the cauldron to the cursed necklace, unease gnawing at the edges of her mind. She trusted Stella and Isobel, but the gravity of what they were attempting weighed on her.

As Stella reached for the next vial, she hesitated, her hand hovering over the thick, dark liquid inside. "Pine tar," she said. "It'll act as a binding agent, holding the curse in place while we dismantle it."

Gemma's throat tightened as she watched the viscous liquid ooze into the vessel. The crackling fire beneath the cauldron hissed, and the mixture bubbled. She could feel the dark magick radiating from the necklace—it pulsed in the air like a malevolent heartbeat.

Shadow, picking up on Gemma's unease, climbed onto her shoulder and nuzzled her neck with his small nose. His gentle chittering reassured her, "I'm here. You're not alone." Gemma reached up and stroked his fur, drawing comfort from his presence.

"Isobel," Stella said, stepping back from the cauldron. "Start the incantation."

Isobel nodded. As the potion bubbled, steam rose into thin tendrils. Isobel's voice rang out, steady and clear, weaving through the flickering candlelight. She stood tall, her hands raised over the mixture, fingers whisking the air as if guiding unseen forces.

By earth, by fire, by water, by air,
We summon forth the powers rare.
Bound by blood, by root, by tree,
We call upon our ancestry.
Let sinister ties now break and sever,
Curse be gone, and haunt no longer.
In this cauldron, pure and bright,
We cast away the chains of night.

The room darkened as the incantation flowed. The magick built, swirling through like an invisible current tugging at the edges of her consciousness.

Silver cleanses, flame devours,
Purify this object of its evil powers.
With these words, our will be true,
Cleansing all as light renews.

Stella added another herb to the cauldron, wild rose petals collected earlier that morning. The mixture hissed and spat, the smell of burned pine filling the room. Gemma tensed, her heart racing as the energy in the air became electric, the tension thickening with each passing moment.

As winds of change begin to blow,

Let this cursed necklace lose its hold.

Just as Gemma believed the spell was working, the liquid in the cauldron bubbled more violently. Steam rose from the surface, thick and acrid. Isobel's voice faltered as the temperature in the room spiked.

Without warning, the potion erupted. A column of flame shot out from the vessel, licking the ceiling with violent intensity. Stella jumped back with a sharp cry, clutching her arm where the fire had seared her skin.

"Stella!" Gemma gasped, rushing forward. Her heart lurched as she reached out. The cursed necklace caught her attention as it emanated in the dim light, the malevolence still clinging to it like a living thing.

Shadow leaped from Gemma's shoulder, landing on the counter near the necklace. He hissed at it, his fur bristling as if trying to ward off the lingering dark magick. For a moment, he was defiant against the malevolent artifact.

Isobel abandoned her incantation and hurried to Stella's side. Her hands glowed as she kneeled beside her aunt, the warm light of her healing magick spilling over Stella's arm. "Hold still," Isobel said. The burn on her skin was already red and raw, and Isobel worked to soothe it.

Gemma stood rooted in place, staring down at the necklace that lay on the worn wooden counter. Its dark gemstones pulsed, brimming with sinister energy.

The flames that had shot out moments before died down, leaving the cauldron bubbling. The potion had failed. Whatever magick they'd woven wasn't enough. The room was heavy with the scent of burned herbs, and the remnants of their spell still hung in the air like an unfinished melody.

"We failed," Gemma whispered, the words barely forming through her dry throat. Her body trembled from the surge of emotions flooding through her—fear, confusion, frustration. She had hoped the spell would break the curse, but the necklace remained intact, as dangerous as ever. Dread pooled in her stomach, cold and unyielding.

Stella winced as she pulled her arm away from Isobel's healing touch. Despite her pain, she kept her eyes on the pendant. "Not yet," she said, hoarse but resolute. "This isn't over." She shook her head as if to clear the fog of pain, determination hardening her expression.

"Stella, you're hurt. You need to rest," Isobel said, her face tight with concern.

But Stella refused to back down, clenching her jaw as she pushed herself to her feet. "We don't have time to rest. Not when that thing is still here." She gestured with her good hand toward the necklace, lying on the counter like a coiled serpent. Its malevolent presence appeared larger than ever, as though it still clung to Gemma's spirit.

Gemma watched them, her heart hammering in her chest. "What do we do now?" she asked, shaking as she fought the rising panic. The freedom she wanted slipped away again. The weight of their failure crashed down on her, suffocating her joy before it bloomed.

Isobel turned to her, her expression grim but steady. "We regroup. Something went wrong, but we'll figure it out." She tried to sound confident, but Gemma could hear the edge of uncertainty.

The fear Gemma had kept at bay for so long now swelled, threatening to consume her. She could sense the pull of the dark magick, the whispers that had haunted her dreams for weeks. She glanced at the necklace, glowing, and a cold shudder ran through her. "What if... what if we can't stop it?" she whispered, voicing the terror that had lodged itself deep in her heart.

Stella's expression softened, despite the pain etched across her face. "We will," she said. "This isn't the end. We've come too far to give up now. There's always a way."

Gemma wanted to believe her, but the doubt gnawed at her insides. The curse had already come so close to swallowing her whole.

As they cleaned up the remnants of the spell, the acrid smell of burned herbs stayed—a bitter reminder of their setback.

Isobel insisted Stella visit Doc to have her burn examined. Stella hesitated, preferring to tend to her own wounds, but the searing pain from the now-infected burn demanded attention.

Sitting in the small office, Stella kept her gaze focused on Doc's hands as they worked on her arm. His sharp eyes narrowed as he inspected the burn, a mixture of suspicion and concern crossing his face.

"This isn't an ordinary burn," Doc said, his tone probing. He glanced up at Stella, then shifted his gaze to Isobel and Gemma, who stood nearby, both of them tense and silent.

Stella clenched her jaw, offering a measured response. "We were experimenting with old remedies," she said, shrugging. "It went wrong."

Doc's brow furrowed, his mouth twisted. "What kind of remedies?"

Isobel stepped forward before Stella replied, calm but firm. "We didn't handle the ingredients correctly," she said, trying to divert his curiosity. "It was a mistake, and it won't happen again."

Doc continued to frown, dabbing a pungent salve onto Stella's wound. She winced, the sting biting into her skin, but she kept her expression composed. Doc shook his head, his tone softening, but still cautionary. "You're lucky this didn't spread further. These kinds of experiments can be dangerous if you don't know what you're doing."

The weight of his words pressed on Stella, though she tried not to let it show. She nodded, watching as Doc wrapped her arm with gauze. The secret of their dark magick—the curse they were trying to break—was too dangerous to share. The strain of that burden grew heavier on Stella with each passing day.

When they left the office, the fall air outside was sharp, carrying a biting chill that mirrored the tension lingering between them. Stella pulled her coat around herself, glancing at Isobel and Gemma. They were all tired, worn thin by the constant failures and the looming threat of the full moon.

Stella's mind churned with the recent memories—the makeshift lab engulfed in chaos, flames searing her skin, the potion erupting with explosive force. Every misstep gnawed at her, the weight of each failure pressing down, reminding her of the dangers they faced by daring to toy with these volatile forces.

Inside the store, the once-warm and comforting space had taken on a new tone. The scent of herbs and candlelight, once soothing, now mingled with an air of desperation. Stella sensed it in every corner, the looming deadline of the full moon casting a shadow over everything they did.

She watched as Gemma moved through her tasks in a haze, her face drawn and pale, her hands trembling with anxiety. Gemma was fraying under the weight of the curse. She'd often catch her whispering to herself, her eyes darting around the room as if expecting something to emerge from the shadows. It worried Stella, but she didn't know how to fix it—not yet.

Isobel, too, had grown more withdrawn, her attention focused on poring over ancient texts in search of an elusive answer. She sat now at the counter, her fingers flipping through a grimoire, her expression set in grim determination. Stella admired her niece's tenacity, but the constant setbacks were taking a toll on her as well.

"This isn't working," Gemma muttered one evening, frustration thick as she stared at another failed mixture. "We're running out of time."

Stella wiped her brow, her injured arm aching under the bandages. She met Gemma's gaze, her own expression hardened. "We'll figure it out," she said. "We have to." But even as she spoke, the weight of doubt pressed on her. She wouldn't let it show—not to Gemma, not to Isobel. They were all relying on her strength.

As the moon loomed large on the horizon, Stella approached Gemma where she sat by the window, staring out at the night sky. Her eyes were hollow, her face gaunt. Stella took a deep breath, her heart heavy. "We'll try again tomorrow," she said. "I found something—a spell we haven't tried yet. It's risky, but it might work."

Gemma gave a small nod, but her eyes betrayed her, shadowed with uncertainty that clung like a storm cloud waiting to break. Stella saw the exhaustion etched into her face, the way hope slipped through her fingers like sand. But she wouldn't let Gemma give up.

Not now. The full moon was almost upon them, and the urgency was a tightening noose.

After Gemma retired, Stella had tea with Isobel, but she heard Gemma's restless movements through the thin walls—the murmured words, the sharp gasps as nightmares claimed her. The curse was wrapping itself tighter around Gemma, feeding on her fears. And each day they failed was another step closer to losing her.

Stella made a silent promise to herself. They would break this curse. No matter what it took, no matter how dangerous the magick was—they would find a way. They had to.

Chapter Twenty-Six

THE GHOSTLY MOONLIGHT BATHED the cemetery in silver as Gemma stood, rigid and solemn, beside Mary's headstone. Stella on one side, Isobel on the other. The eerie glow gave the tombstone an unnatural gleam, heightening the tension already knotted tight within her. They needed every advantage of Mary's energy. Every whisper of her power.

The ancient tome lay open on a makeshift altar—a flat piece of gravestone long since shattered—its pages fluttering in the crisp night breeze. Small lanterns lined the perimeter of their circle, their flames flickering and casting haunting shadows that swayed across moss-covered stones. The stillness only amplified the pounding of her heart, the silent plea for this to work.

Shadow darted around, his nose twitching, sniffing at the candles and eyeing the setup with a mix of curiosity and anxiety. He paused at Mary's headstone, his sharp eyes flickering between the preparations and Gemma, as though sensing her fear. His presence anchored her—small, steadfast, determined. He had always been there, always stayed close. If only this ritual could be as dependable.

Mary's spirit materialized beside Stella, barely more than a shimmer in the moonlight—a delicate haze. The sight of her, frail and translucent, stirred a pain Gemma kept buried deep. Mary, who had her own struggle with darkness, whose ghost now stood ready to give for a family left fractured by dark magick. Mary's hand rested on Stella's shoulder, a silent gesture of strength.

Stella spoke, her tone steady, but Gemma could hear the thread of doubt woven through her words. "We believe Hannah might have been the one to curse the necklace." She paused, her eyes catching Gemma's, offering a flicker of hope that Gemma struggled to grasp. "If we can unravel it, break the tie to her…"

Mary's form wavered, a wistful sadness in her hollow eyes. "I know of no one before Hannah," she whispered, her words as fragile as mist. "But whatever darkness that necklace carries, it may be older than her. Far older."

Silence fell heavier than before. The realization sank deep, chilling them more than the night air. Gemma swallowed, her throat dry. Older than Hannah. Something deeper, more twisted than the stories whispered among their family. She glanced at Isobel, catching the furrow of her brow, the fear etched in her gaze.

Isobel shook her head, her thoughts mirroring Gemma's own. "What if it wasn't Hannah? What if it came from her mother, or even further back?" She looked at Stella. "If the curse is that old, we could be chasing shadows—it might never end."

Gemma's chest tightened, panic seeping into her bones. Chasing shadows. The curse felt endless, like a labyrinth with no exit, its walls closing in with each failed attempt to break free. They had to try, though. There was no other choice.

They formed a circle around the grave—Stella, Isobel, Mary's ghostly form, and herself. Their hands linked, the warmth of Stella's grip grounding her, Isobel's hand trembling against hers. They

chanted, each word drawn from the ancient tome before them. The
incantation rolled off their tongues, laden with desperation.

By moon's pale light and night's dark shroud,
We call upon the spirits loud.
Reverse the time, untangle fate,
Lift the curse before it's too late.
Through bloodlines deep and shadows cast,
Reveal the truth from ages past.
With elements of earth and sky,
We seek the truth, we dare to pry.
By fire's burn and water's flow,
By air's whisper and earth's glow,
Unwind the dark, release the hold,
Transform the cursed into pure gold.
Ancestors, hear our earnest plea,
Guide us through this mystery.
From veil to realm, across the night,
Help us set this wrong to right.
From Hannah's hand to times before,
Unravel secrets, unlock the door.
Protect our hearts, guide our sight,
Bring forth the dawn from endless night.

The words flowed, a cadence that echoed through the empty
cemetery, a plea to forces beyond. The tension grew, thickened, until
the air buzzed with the energy they summoned. Gemma's entire
body thrummed, each word vibrating in her bones, her heartbeats
syncing with the incantation. The flames of the lanterns flickered
violently, the wind whipping around them as if alive, carrying the
weight of their hope into the dark.

The energy built, twisting and pulling, straining against the boundary between what was and what could be. Gemma poured every ounce of herself into it, her intent, her fear, her hope—all of it channeled through the words, through the ritual. The fabric of time shuddered, wavered beneath their will.

And then, with a deafening silence, it broke. The energy dissipated, slipping away like water through her fingers. The power they had gathered collapsed, leaving nothing but the cold night air in its place. At the center of their circle lay the necklace still, its malevolent power unchanged, mocking them.

A flash of darkness seared through Gemma's mind. Hannah's face appeared, twisted in a sneer, her eyes dark as night. You think you can break what I've wrought? Her voice hissed inside Gemma's skull, each word dripping with malice. You are nothing, girl. You belong to me now. This ends when I say it ends.

Gemma gasped, her grip on Isobel's hand slipping as she staggered back, her knees giving way. She hit the ground, her palms scraping against the dirt and stone. The image of Hannah lingered, her laughter echoing, an icy, triumphant sound that chilled Gemma to her core.

Isobel dropped to her side, her hands pulling her upright. "Gemma! What happened? Are you all right?"

Gemma blinked, her vision swimming. The mocking laughter faded, replaced by the concerned faces of her family. She swallowed hard, her throat burning. "She was there," she said. "Hannah. She's still... she's still inside it. Watching. She knows everything we're trying to do."

Stella's face hardened, her jaw clenched. She kneeled beside them, her eyes narrowing at the cursed necklace, still lying inert, dark and twisted. "Damn her," she muttered, her fingers brushing Gemma's shoulder. "We'll find another way, Gemma. We're not done yet."

Shadow reacted, unlike any time before. He lunged at the necklace, his body arched, fur bristling, a guttural growl erupting from his throat. He bared his teeth, his small form trembling with rage as he snapped at the cursed object. It was as if he'd sensed Hannah's presence, as if he knew she was taunting them, and he'd had enough. He clawed at the dirt around the necklace, his growls growing louder, more feral, his small body a blur of fury.

"Shadow!" Gemma shouted as she reached for him. She wrapped her arms around him, pulling him back. He writhed for a moment before settling, his chest heaving, his eyes still fixed on the necklace with a hatred she'd never seen in him before.

She held him close, her heart pounding, the adrenaline coursing through her veins leaving her shaky and weak. He settled in her arms, but his eyes never left the necklace. His small body trembled against her, his fury replaced by a low, soft whimper—an expression of his own helplessness against the darkness they faced.

Stella rose, her eyes narrowing as she looked at the necklace. "We need to get out of here. The cemetery—it's too exposed. We'll regroup at the store." Her voice, though controlled, held a steel edge. She moved with purpose, gathering the tome and extinguishing the candles.

Isobel helped Gemma to her feet, her grip firm, her expression etched with determination. "We're not giving up. We'll find another way, I promise you that."

Gemma nodded, her gaze fixed on the cursed object lying at the center of their failed ritual. The laughter echoed in her ears still, but beneath the fear and the despair, anger simmered. She would not let Hannah win. Not now, not ever.

The walk back to the store was slow, the silence between them heavy. Shadow remained in her arms, his eyes alert, his body tense. Gemma's thoughts raced, replaying Hannah's mocking words, the sneer on her face. She'd seen the malice there, the delight in their suffering. It fueled her anger, her resolve.

As they approached the store, Stella turned to them, her expression softening for a moment. "We'll rest tonight. Tomorrow, we start again and look through every spell in every grimoire. There has to be something we're missing."

Gemma met her aunt's gaze, the exhaustion weighing on her, but the fire inside her still burning. She nodded. "We'll find it. We have to."

Stella gave a small, encouraging smile. "We will."

Inside the store, the familiar scent of dried herbs and old wood welcomed them. The warmth of the space wrapped around Gemma, a stark contrast to the cold cemetery. She set Shadow down, watching as he padded over to the corner, curling up but keeping his eyes on the room, ever watchful.

Gemma sank into a chair, her body heavy with fatigue. Isobel sat across from her, their eyes meeting in a silent exchange. They were tired, worn down, but not broken. Not yet.

Stella moved around the store, lighting a few more lamps, their glow pushing back the shadows. She looked at them, her jaw set. "Tonight, we rest. Tomorrow, we fight again."

Gemma nodded, her eyes drifting to Shadow, already asleep but still twitching, his dreams no doubt filled with the same darkness they fought against. She clenched her jaw, her resolve hardening.

Hannah might have the upper hand now, but they weren't finished. They had each other, and they had the will to fight, no matter what lay ahead. They were going to break the curse, to take back their future. And this time, they wouldn't stop until Hannah was nothing but a bitter memory.

The remnants of their failures cluttered the worktable in the back room of the store—burned herbs, a tarnished copper crucible, and crumpled notes from grimoires they had poured over for hours. The shelves, once orderly, now resembled the aftermath of a battle. Everything lay strewn about in disarray, echoing the turmoil churning inside each of them. Surrounded by the faded hope of failed spells, they gathered once more for what they hoped would be their last attempt. This ritual had to work. It had to be their salvation.

The center of the room held a drawn circle. Chalk marks lay smudged and uneven, the sigils for fire, earth, water, and air etched at the cardinal points. Candlelight flickered, illuminating the dim space, casting jagged shadows that leaped and twisted along the floor and walls. At the heart of it all lay the cursed necklace—its ruby, emerald, and sapphire gleamed with an unnatural, malevolent glow, the silver trinity setting reflecting an icy glint. The necklace mocked them, daring them to try again, daring them to hope for something different this time.

Shadow scurried around the perimeter of the circle, his nose twitching as he sniffed at the symbols. He paused by the water sigil, dipping a curious paw into the small bowl representing the element, then pulled back, chittering as if the water's presence was wrong. He moved on, nose twitching, finding a bundle of herbs and attempting to paw at the dried sage, crumbling the leaves between his dexterous fingers. His antics, usually amusing, appeared misplaced amid the tension that thickened the air.

Gemma kneeled beside Isobel and Stella, the three of them forming a triangle around the necklace. Her heart raced as she closed her hand around the sapphire. The cool stone pressed against her skin, heavy with expectation. She swallowed hard, closing her eyes, trying to find a connection to the power she knew should reside within her. But doubt snaked through her thoughts, slipping into every corner of her mind, blurring the edges of her determination.

"Are you ready?" Stella broke through the silence, her fingers wrapped around the ruby. Her jaw clenched, eyes focused on the cursed object, as though sheer willpower alone could shatter it. Exhaustion lined her features—each sleepless night etched in the shadows beneath her eyes—but her determination held fast, a spark of hope still visible.

Gemma nodded, her throat too tight to speak. She held the sapphire with trembling fingers. The tension within her refused to settle. Every breath felt shallow, as though her lungs refused to expand.

Shadow noticed her unease, waddling over to nuzzle against her leg, his tiny claws tapping against her boot. He chittered, his curious eyes staring up at her as though he wanted her to understand he was there for her. Gemma blinked, her vision blurring, her heart aching at the loyalty radiating from her small companion.

Isobel's hands, clasping the emerald, shook as she nodded to Stella's question. She forced a deep breath; the sound escaping her lips louder than intended. "Let's do this," she said, uneven but determined.

They positioned themselves within the chalk-drawn circle, each holding their piece of the necklace—ruby, emerald, and sapphire. The ancient invocation spilled from their lips, the words practiced but heavy with emotion. The chant flowed like a dark melody, resonating through the room, weaving together their voices into something that carried the weight of their combined power. It was hope, desperation, and fury all mixed into one.

Shadow climbed onto the worktable, knocking over a small vial of powdered herbs in his haste. He froze, his ears flicking back, then refocused on the ritual, his paws on the edge as he peered down at the glowing necklace, his eyes reflecting the flickering light.

Isobel pressed her free hand to the floor, the wood rough under her skin, grounding herself as she called out to the element of the earth. "Earth, I call upon you," she said, her words blending with Stella's stronger invocation of fire and Gemma's softer plea to water. Each syllable took more effort, each word harder than the last.

The candles flickered, flames bending and swaying as the energy in the room shifted. Power stirred—Gemma sensed it, a shiver that ran down her spine, a tug beyond reach. The air grew charged, and for a heartbeat, she believed. Maybe this time...

But the energy twisted, buckling in on itself. The air thickened, suffocating. An unsettling stillness fell over the circle, heavy and oppressive, pushing down on them like an unseen hand. The chanting faltered, their voices losing strength as the power dissipated. The candles' flames shrank, flickering as though a gust of wind had swept through the room, their once bright glow reduced to fragile pinpricks of light.

Shadow hissed, fur bristling, darting away. He scrambled up to the shelves, knocking over bottles in his panic, glass shattering on the floor, releasing the pungent scent of herbs and potions that stung Gemma's nostrils. He watched the necklace, ears pinned back, his gaze wary and frightened, washing his paws as if trying to rid himself of the wrongness he sensed.

Isobel pressed her hand harder into the wood. She clutched the emerald until her knuckles turned white, her brow furrowed in concentration, but nothing came. She looked at Stella, desperation etched in her eyes.

"It's not working," Stella said. She held onto the ruby, her eyes wide, pleading, as though willing the stone to ignite. The gem remained cold, lifeless in her hand. "Why isn't it working?"

Gemma shook uncontrollably now, the sapphire slipping from her grasp. "I don't understand." Tears brimmed in her eyes. "Why won't it break?" The necklace lay between them, its gems glinting maliciously. No cracks, no change. The silver trinity frame mocked their every effort.

A chill ran through Gemma, the kind that settled deep into her bones. They had failed. The elements that had once been her allies felt distant, their power unreachable. She exchanged a look with Stella—confusion, fear, and exhaustion reflected at her. Their magick, their greatest strength, came off like a distant dream.

Stella's face paled, her lips trembling. "Did we lose our connection?" The uncertainty in her tone broke something in Gemma. Without their magick, what were they? How could they fight against a force that thrived on their failures?

Gemma stared at the necklace on the floor, her eyes dull, tears streaming down her cheeks. She turned her gaze to Shadow, who had inched from the shelves to the worktable, his small paws trembling. He looked at her, his dark eyes filled with concern, letting out a soft, almost pleading chirp.

Shadow's reaction was sudden and visceral. He leaped from the table, his body arched as he lunged at the necklace. A growl, deep and guttural, erupted from him—a sound Gemma had never heard before. He clawed at the cursed object, vibrating with a rage that startled them all. His teeth bared, he bit down on the chain, yanking as if he could tear the darkness away through sheer will. His fury, his defiance, reflected their own desperation, a primal need to destroy what had caused so much pain.

"Shadow, stop!" Gemma shouted, panic thick in her throat. She lunged forward, grabbing him and pulling him away, his body writhing in her grasp, his claws still outstretched towards the necklace. He let out a long, pitiful whimper, finally going limp in her arms. She held him close, her own body shaking, her heart pounding against her ribs. He trembled, his head buried against her chest, his breaths coming in short, ragged bursts.

Stella rose, her eyes dark with frustration as she stared down at the necklace. "We need to regroup, figure out what we're doing wrong."

Isobel nodded, her hands still trembling as she reached for Gemma, helping her to her feet. She kept her arm around her cousin as they moved away from the circle. The necklace lay untouched on the floor, its dark energy pulsating, an ever-present reminder of their failure. They couldn't afford to give up—not now, not with the full moon in two days—but the endless string of failures was crushing their spirits, making each step away from the ritual space heavier than the last.

Shadow remained in Gemma's arms, his eyes darting, his small body tense, still shaken by the events that had just unfolded. The silence between them was thick, filled with unspoken fears, the weight of their impending deadline pressing down on them.

Stella turned to them, her gaze softening, though her exhaustion showed in the lines of her face. "Tonight, we rest," she breathed. "Tomorrow, we go through everything again. There has to be something we missed—something we overlooked."

Gemma nodded, her eyes hollow, but the fire of determination still flickered within. "We'll find it," she whispered, more to herself than anyone else. "We have to."

Upstairs, the warmth of the space was a stark contrast to the cold dread that had settled in their bones. Gemma set Shadow down, watching as he padded to a corner and curled up, his eyes still watching them, his body curling tight, small whimpers escaping him as he drifted into an uneasy sleep.

Isobel collapsed into a chair, her body aching with fatigue. Across from her, Gemma slumped into another chair, her eyes meeting Isobel's. The despair, the exhaustion—it was all there, mirrored between them, but so was the determination. A stubborn refusal to let this curse win, to let the darkness consume them.

Stella folded a dish towel and placed it beside the woodstove. "I didn't expect this," she said, barely above a whisper, as if trying to convince herself as much as the others. "We'll find a way. We always do."

Gemma sighed, leaning her head back against the chair. The full moon loomed in her mind, a relentless reminder of how little time they had left. But as she looked at Isobel, then at Stella, a flicker of hope sparked deep inside her chest. They weren't alone. They had each other. And that might be enough.

Chapter Twenty-Seven

Isobel settled into her chair in the Bitterroot Hotel's dining room, her eyes tracing the flickering glow of candlelight as it danced along her and John's usual table. She tried to steady her breath, allowing herself to savor the moment, one rare slice of calm amid everything else in her life. John sat across from her, his gaze soft and warm, and the familiar sight made her heart swell. His eyes held a depth she wanted to lose herself in, the love there so obvious that it ached. This dinner had been a time of solace, one that had allowed her to pretend, for a while, that her life was normal.

But even with the warmth of his presence, there laid an undercurrent she couldn't shake, a sense of waiting. She watched John across the table, noticing the way he fiddled with the edge of the napkin, his eyes shifting as though gathering courage. Isobel knew him too well not to recognize the signs, he had something on his mind, and it wasn't only dinner.

She inhaled, her gaze drifting to the menu, but she found it hard to focus on the words. The dining room hummed around them, filled with indistinct murmurs, clinking glasses, and the occasional burst of laughter, but it all seemed distant. John had looked forward to this dinner all week, and Isobel tried to be present for him, but her thoughts kept returning to Gemma, to the curse they still hadn't broken, to the looming full moon and the consequences they all dreaded.

Isobel turned her attention back to John as he cleared his throat, drawing her eyes to him. His brow furrowed, a crease forming between his eyebrows as he leaned forward.

"Isobel," he said, breaking through the comfortable silence that had settled between them. She looked up, meeting his gaze, and saw the determination there mingled with something tender. "I've been thinking." He paused, a small smile tugging at his lips, but his eyes searched hers, as if gauging her reaction before continuing. "About us. About our future."

Isobel blinked, setting her fork down. The sudden shift in tone sent her heart skipping a beat. Her pulse quickened as her curiosity piqued. She noted the gravity of his words, a weight she couldn't ignore.

"Go on." Her chest tightened. She braced herself, sensing that whatever he was about to say would be serious.

John reached across the table, taking her hand in his. His thumb brushed over her knuckles, and the warmth of his touch seeped into her skin, making her throat constrict. "We've talked about waiting," he said, his eyes never leaving hers, "about getting married after you finish nursing school and after things settle down a bit." He hesitated, the corners of his lips softening as he gave her hand a light squeeze. "But things haven't exactly been calm, have they? Not with everything going on here... with Gemma and now you deciding not to go back to Chicago."

Isobel's stomach clenched at the mention of Gemma. She tried to smile, but it came out brittle, and she dropped her gaze to their joined hands. Gemma's condition weighed on her constantly, like an ever-present shadow that threatened to swallow them all. She preferred to tell John, tell him everything about the curse, about the rituals, about why she lay awake at night staring at the ceiling, heart racing with fear for her cousin. But that world wasn't his, and she wouldn't drag him into it. Not now. Maybe never.

She looked back up in time to see the vulnerability in John's eyes as he leaned closer, his expression earnest. "I love you, Isobel," he said. "Why should we wait any longer to get married? I want to face everything together as husband and wife."

The warmth of his hand in hers was grounding, but Isobel's heart twisted. The words hung between them, filled with love but also an innocence that made her chest ache. John had no clue what they were facing, what darkness lurked out of sight, threatening to tear them apart. She wanted to tell him yes, wanted to dive headfirst into the certainty he offered her, to let herself be swept away by his love and the future he imagined. But the timing was wrong.

"John..." Isobel's eyes met his with a tenderness she hoped masked the turmoil roiling beneath her skin. She withdrew her hand, folding it in her lap, her gaze dropping to the flickering candle between them. "I love you too. You know I do." She paused, swallowing against the tightness in her throat. "But there's so much happening right now. Gemma... she's not well. And my work with Doc is just getting started. I don't want us to rush into anything when things feel so... unsettled."

John frowned, his brows knitting together in concern. His hand remained on the table, as if waiting for hers to return. "Isobel, I understand that," he said, his tone gentle. "But having something certain, something we can hold on to, might help get through all of it." His voice carried an insistence, a plea for her to see things from his perspective. The vulnerability in his eyes pierced her, and she hated she was hurting him.

Isobel's heart pounded, torn between her love for him and the weight of everything left unsaid. She wanted to give him the certainty he craved, to promise him a future without hesitation, but the truth was so much more complicated. Her lips parted, but no words came. Instead, she shook her head. Her gaze drifted to the window, where the night pressed against the glass, dark and unknowable.

"John, it's not about my feelings for you." She looked back at him, her eyes searching his face, hoping he understood. "I want to be with you more than anything. But right now... I don't know if it's the right time to add more to everything else we're dealing with. Gemma's health. It's getting worse. And Doc is counting on me. I don't want us to make a decision we might regret because we were rushing."

John's jaw tightened, his eyes narrowing, though not in anger. He looked at her, as if trying to read between the lines of what she was saying. He exhaled, his expression softening. "But life's always going to be complicated, Isobel. There's always going to be something happening." He leaned back, his eyes never leaving hers. "If we keep waiting for the perfect time, we might never get there."

His words struck a chord deep within her, and for a moment, her resolve wavered. He was right. Life in Tin Creek had never been quiet, never been simple for her. There had always been challenges, always something threatening to upend their plans. But what he didn't know was that this wasn't only a matter of day-to-day struggles. The darkness surrounding Gemma wasn't a thing that could be weathered or waited out. It was a storm that threatened to consume everything.

She reached for his hand again, her fingers wrapping around his, squeezing. "Maybe you're right," she said, trembling. "But right now, I need to be there for Gemma. I need to train with Doc." Her eyes met his, her gaze filled with both love and regret. "And I need to know that when we do get married, I can give you everything. You deserve that, John. We both do."

John looked down at their hands, his thumb brushing over her knuckles, his brow furrowing as he processed her words. The silence between them felt heavy, filled with all the things they weren't saying. He nodded, a small, resigned smile tugging at his lips. "I don't want to push you into anything, Isobel. Just want to be there for you, no matter what happens. I don't want to lose you to all that's going on around us."

The sincerity in his words made her heart ache, and she leaned forward, her other hand resting atop his, her eyes locking onto his with an intensity that surprised even her. "You're not going to lose me. You're everything to me, John. But for now, we need to take it one step at a time. Gemma's health is fragile, and I'm still learning so much from Doc. Once life settles down, once we find a way through this, I promise we'll think about our future."

John searched her eyes, and she saw the struggle there, the desire to fight for what he wanted warring with his need to respect her wishes. He nodded, his shoulders relaxing, the tension in his face easing. "Okay." A small, genuine smile curved his lips. "I can wait a little longer. I'm ready whenever you are."

Relief washed over Isobel, and she returned his smile, her heart swelling with love and gratitude for the man sitting across from her. "I know you are," she said. "And I love you for that."

John chuckled, the tension between them dissipating, replaced by a warmth that made Isobel's chest feel lighter. "I guess I'll just have to be patient," he teased, though his eyes kept a seriousness that told her he meant every word. "But don't make me wait too long, alright?"

Isobel laughed, the sound soft, almost fragile, but it held hope. "I won't."

The rest of their dinner passed in a comfortable silence, the weight of their conversation lingering between them but no longer pressing on them. Isobel acquired a renewed sense of determination to would break the curse, to protect Gemma, and keep John safe from the darkness he knew nothing about. And once that was done, she would be ready to start the life they both dreamed of.

As they stepped out of the Bitterroot Hotel and into the cool night air, Isobel leaned into John, her body fitting against his side. His arm wrapped around her shoulders, pulling her close, and his heart beat steady and strong beneath her cheek. The future loomed uncertain, filled with shadows she couldn't understand, but with John beside her, she found a glimmer of light in the darkness.

He glanced down at her, his eyes soft as he took in her expression, and a surge of warmth enveloped her, of love so deep it almost hurt. Whatever happened next, whatever battles they had yet to face, she wouldn't be facing them alone.

Gemma perched at the counter of Isobel's store, her eyes drifting over the mundane, rows of dry goods, bolts of cloth, and household necessities—but her thoughts remained on the back room transformed into a makeshift magickal lab. Tension thrummed beneath her skin, her nerves coiled tight as she watched the preparations unfold through the half-open door. The usual scent of herbs, sage, rosemary, frankincense, drifted, thick and heady, layering with the unease that clung to all surfaces.

The door separated two worlds: the normal life of Tin Creek and the dark, ritualistic world that had occupied their existence. Beyond it, Isobel and Stella worked with a quiet intensity. Every movement carried a weight of experience and precision, each item laid out with a purpose, each motion deliberate. The air itself hummed with energy, and it felt as though each object had taken on its own urgency. This ritual was no ordinary working, it had to be their salvation.

The necklace lay at the heart of their preparations, dark and pulsing with a malevolent glow. An icy shiver traced down Gemma's spine every time she looked at it. On a small table in the center of the room, the necklace, defiant and unyielding, mocked their attempts to break it. The energy emanated from it like a challenge, a silent dare. *Try to break me, if you can.*

Isobel bent over a large circle she had drawn on the floor with salt, an unbroken line to contain whatever the curse fought to unleash. Inside, a pentagram etched in chalk anchored the spell, each point holding a specific purpose, a different facet of protection and cleansing. Stella moved around the pentagram, her hands filled with crystals. "Amethyst for protection," she whispered, placing the deep purple crystal at the lower left. "Tourmaline for absorption of negativity." The black stone took its place at the lower right. "Quartz for amplification." The clear crystal gleamed at the top. "Selenite for purification." The white, translucent shard rested at the upper left. "Hematite for grounding." The metallic stone settled at the upper right.

The air grew denser, the energy collecting, swirling throughout them, each crystal anchoring their intent. Gemma felt it pressing down on her shoulders, a weight that was both reassuring and terrifying.

Shadow skittered around the edges of the room, curiosity leading him to each item. He sniffed at the wreath of herbs, sage to cleanse, rosemary to protect, lavender to soothe, mugwort to enhance the psychic. He pawed at the bundle of sage, knocking it askew. When Stella shooed him away with a gentle "Not now, Shadow," he retreated under the worktable, his bright eyes watching. Somehow, even in his innocence, his presence reassured Gemma, proof that hope still existed amid the dark magick threatening them.

The candles around the room flickered, their small flames dancing with a life of their own, casting long shadows that reached across the walls like dark hands. Gemma pushed away from the counter, her footsteps hesitant as she moved to join them. She took her place between Isobel and Stella, completing the triangle needed to contain the ritual's power.

"This has to work," Gemma whispered, her breath shaky, her eyes locked on the necklace that emanated darkness.

Stella looked at her, her expression fierce despite the exhaustion etched across her features. She reached for Gemma's hand. "This time it *will* work. We've done all we can to prepare."

Isobel nodded, taking Gemma's other hand. "Stay focused. The magick shall guide us."

Their hands formed a link, creating an unbreakable circuit. The energy hummed, a vibration moving through their bodies, joining them together. Anticipation wove through the room. The flames of the candles flared, casting wild shadows that swayed as if they danced to a primal rhythm. They began the chant, each word falling from their lips in unison, ancestral and powerful.

By the light of the pure quartz,
By the protection of amethyst,
By the grounding force of tourmaline,
By the purification of selenite,
By the strength of hematite,
We call upon the ancient forces,
Draw out the darkness, cleanse the night,
Let this necklace be stripped of its blight.

The crystals glowed, their light pulsing in time with their chant. The necklace quivered, dark tendrils of energy unfurling like smoke, slithering toward the edges of the pentagram, only to be drawn back by the power of the crystals. Gemma's heart pounded, her gaze fixed on the dark shadows curling, writhing, fighting against the pull.

Shadow hissed, the fur along his spine standing erect as he watched from the shadows. He darted forward, his movements purposeful, as if he sensed his presence might help. He circled the perimeter, a sentry guarding their work, his bright eyes never leaving the dark tendrils that struggled to escape the pentagram's grasp.

By the power of sage, rosemary, and lavender,
By the strength of mugwort, frankincense, and thyme,
We purify and protect, We banish and bind,
Let the darkness be undone, Let the light reclaim its rightful place.

Their voices grew louder, each word imbued with raw intent resonating within the walls. The herbs crackled, the scent growing pungent, almost overwhelming, as smoke rose, mingling with the light. Gemma's pulse echoed in her ears, the tension thrumming through her veins.

The energy in the room reached a fever pitch, the dark tendrils recoiling, writhing, shrinking under the relentless pressure of their magick. Each moment that passed pushed them to the edge, like they were balancing at the precipice of something immense, a storm ready to break.

Shadow skittered closer, his tiny paws pressing into the chalk lines, his eyes wide and fixed on the dark mass. He hissed again, his small body vibrating with urgency. The tendrils had weakened, almost dissolved under the light, but then a shift.

A stillness settled into the room, an unnatural silence that cut through the chanting. Gemma's eyes widened, her gaze snapping toward the necklace. One of the dark tendrils grew denser, thicker, separating itself from the others. It pulsed, like it had found a new strength, and it shifted away from the necklace.

The ringlet moved like a serpent, an oily darkness that rippled along the floor. Shadow lunged, a blur, his paws batting at the tendril, hissing. A futile effort. The shadowy mass slid past him, slipping through a break in the salt circle.

Before Gemma could react, the wicked wisp struck, plunging into Isobel's arm.

"Isobel!" Gemma cried out, but the chanting drowned her out.

Gemma's heart seized, her words dying in her throat. Isobel's chant never wavered, her gaze fixed on the necklace, her body rigid. It happened like a whirlwind, one moment the dark tendril was there, the next it vanished, absorbed into Isobel as if it had never existed.

Panic clawed at Gemma's chest, her entire body trembling. She wanted to scream, to break the circle and pull Isobel away from the dark magick, but she knew, knew with a horrible certainty, that they could not stop now. To stop would be worse. They had to finish what they started.

Stella squeezed Gemma's hand, her eyes catching Gemma's, the intensity in her gaze saying what words could not, focus. They had to see this through.

Gemma swallowed her fear, her breath coming in quick gasps. She forced her attention back to the chant, her words quivering as they left her lips, blending with Isobel's and Stella's. Her eyes flickered between the necklace and Isobel, her stomach twisting with terror.

By the spirits of our ancestors,
By the light of the full moon,
We cleanse, we heal, we restore,
Let the darkness be no more.

Their voices wove together, stronger, determined, a desperate force against the dark magick. As the crystals pulsed, their light intensified, the air vibrated, and the malevolent power unraveled. The tendrils weakened, each one drawn into the illumination, dissolving into nothingness as it made contact.

The dark energy writhed in a final, frantic fight, but their relentless pitch pressed against it, the combined force of their will and magick pushing, burning, until like a taut rope, it broke.

A blinding light exploded from the crystals, the impact of it throwing them backward. Gemma fell onto the wooden floor, her breath knocked from her lungs, her ears ringing. The room plunged into silence, an oppressive emptiness after the cacophony of energy.

Gemma struggled to her knees, her vision blurred, her heart thundering. She crawled to Isobel, her hands trembling as she grasped her cousin's shoulders. "Isobel! Are you all right?" The sound of her words lingered like the soft rustle of leaves, barely audible, fleeting.

Isobel blinked, her eyes unfocused before they found Gemma's. She nodded, her lips parting as she whispered, "I think... we did it."

Gemma swallowed, her gaze darting to Stella, who kneeled beside the necklace, her breath labored. Stella scanned the object, her brow furrowed. She looked up, her expression softening with satisfaction. "The darkness... it's gone. We weakened it."

Gemma's chest heaved with a shaky breath, tears spilling over as she pulled Isobel into an embrace. Relief, fear, hope, they all twisted inside her, overwhelming in their intensity. Shadow, his fur still puffed up, scurried to them, nudging his way into her lap, his tiny paws pressing into her leg as he nuzzled her.

Isobel gave a tired smile, her head leaning against Gemma's. "Time to rest," she said, distant, exhaustion weighing every syllable. "Tomorrow is the full moon. We'll need our strength."

Gemma nodded, her heart still tight with fear as she looked at Isobel, the memory of that dark tendril vanishing into her arm replayed in her mind. She forced a smile, though the unease gnawed at her. "Yeah, rest," she whispered hollow.

They cleaned the space, the weight of what they had done hanging heavy in the air. Shadow scurried around, his paws patting at the charred remains of the herbs, letting out soft chitters as if expressing his own lingering worries. Gemma made a silent vow she would protect Isobel, no matter the cost. They destroyed the curse in the necklace, but the darkness dwelled in a new home.

Chapter Twenty-Eight

The last remnants of sunset disappeared, leaving only the cold silvery glow of the full moon hovering above Tin Creek. Gemma sat in the back of the creaking cart pulled by Isobel and Stella, her hands wrapped around the padded containers, her knuckles white as the wheels rumbled over the uneven path. The chill of the wind bit at her exposed skin, seeping through the thick cloak she wore. Her thoughts, however, stayed focused on what lay ahead. They neared the cemetery, a place meant for rest, but tonight, it would host a battle with something far more dangerous.

Shadow sat beside her, his tiny paws clutching the edge of the cart, his bright eyes catching glimmers of moonlight. Tension laid beneath his movements, he sensed the fear and urgency that Gemma could barely keep at bay.

At the front of the cart, Stella held her pull bar, her face carved with focus, eyes darting along the path as it wound through the darkness. On the other side of the cart, Isobel gripped the other pull bar, a lantern swinging from her free hand. The flickering light cast elongated, dancing shapes across the ground, illuminating gravestones that loomed ahead like ancient sentinels.

Gemma's gaze stayed on them, drawing strength from their calm demeanor, their sense of purpose even as her own heart pounded. Gemma pulled the containers closer, making sure nothing shifted as the cart slowed near Mary's headstone.

The cemetery stretched out before them beneath the cold moonlight, its tombstones like silent witnesses, shrouded in shadows that twisted and writhed. The air held a charged energy that thickened with each step, as though the place itself had been waiting for this moment. Gemma climbed out of the cart, her breath misting in front of her face. She cradled the fragile canisters in her hands, each carrying hope, her last chance at breaking free from the dark curse that had haunted her.

"We need to be precise with everything, like yesterday," Stella murmured, her words adding weight to the night like a steady anchor.

Gemma nodded, her hands trembling as she set the containers down, the cold sinking into her fingers. Shadow leaped from the cart, his nose twitching as he scurried along the uneven ground, pausing near Mary's grave, his ears alert for unseen dangers, wary of every whispering shift in the air.

They brushed leaves and debris from around Mary's headstone. The lantern's light danced across the headstones as it flickered. Gemma opened the containers, pulling out the crystals and bundles of dried herbs. Each object, small though it was, held enormous significance, a thread in the fabric of their ritual, each chosen to sever the dark ties of the cursed necklace.

Together, they positioned the crystals again, clear quartz, black tourmaline, amethyst, and selenite, forming a protective circle around the necklace. Its silver trinity setting gleamed under the moonlight. An invisible aura still surrounded it, a whisper not quite vanquished, echoed in Gemma's mind, watching, waiting for her next move.

Shadow prowled all over the crystals, his nose twitching as he sniffed each one, his gaze flicking back toward the necklace, his body radiating unease. He settled outside the circle, his eyes glued to the cursed object, ready to defend if need be.

Stella sprinkled herbs along the perimeter of the circle as before sage, rosemary, lavender, mugwort, all falling with precision, each herb adding its power to their ritual. The potent scent filled the night air, hanging like a thick veil around them, wrapping their spellwork in a shroud of expectation and tension.

Isobel kneeled beside the crystals, drawing sacred symbols in the frozen ground with a piece of chalk, the pentacle came first, followed by the triquetra, then ancient runes of power and protection. Each stroke of chalk reverberated through the night, the runes glowing under the moon's silvery touch. Gemma's heart matched the rhythm of each line, her anticipation mounting with every mark made.

When Isobel finished with a ring of salt, silence enveloped the cemetery. The moon hung high above them, bathing them in ethereal light, as though the world itself had gone still, waiting. The air held its breath.

Gemma stepped into her place within the circle, her throat tightening as she looked at Stella and Isobel. She drew strength from the determination etched in their faces, grim but unwavering, a shared fear pushed aside by resolve. They held hands, their palms damp with sweat, but the grip firm. A silent promise of unity hung between them, fragile but resolute.

Isobel began the incantation, and Stella followed, her tone low and certain. Gemma joined in, soft at first, but growing louder, her words rising to match theirs as they summoned ancient forces, the chant flowing from them in the language of the ancestors, woven with power.

By earth, by air, by fire, by water,
We call upon the ancient daughters.
Clear the dark, cleanse the night,
Bring forth the truth, reveal the light.
By the power of three, let it be,
As we will, so mote it be.

Their voices intertwined, the sound vibrating through the clearing, filling the night air. The crystals glowed, their light flickering like flames caught in the wind. A faint, thrumming energy moved through the circle, pressing against Gemma's skin, drawing her deeper into the ritual. The lantern flickered, casting strange, shifting shadows that danced across the gravestones. The energy in the air grew heavy, thick with intent.

Shadow hissed, his fur standing on end, his gaze locked on the necklace, watching. He darted forward, then back, his movements reflecting the collision of energies that Gemma could sense a struggle, silent but fierce, between light and darkness.

Power surged within the circle, an almost tangible force that surrounded them. The dark presence that lingered in the necklace writhed, twisted against the light, fighting the purifying power they invoked. For a heartbeat, Gemma thought they might succeed. The darkness unraveled, giving way to their combined strength.

But then, the world around them shifted.

A pulse reverberated through the space, the air thickened, and Gemma sensed a deep, unsettling force, a ripple in the balance. The ground beneath her feet trembled, the very earth responding to something ancient, something powerful pushing through.

Energy condensed, and then, with a force like a silent thunderclap, the veil between the worlds the mundane and the afterlife tore open.

The air stilled, the night falling into an unnatural silence, as if every breath had been sucked from the world. Thick and impenetrable fog rolled in, rising from the ground and swirling around the gravestones. The veil had opened, and with it came figures from beyond, shadowy forms that coalesced from the mist itself.

Gemma's heart stuttered as three distinct figures emerged, Hannah, Margaret, and Grace. They stood, their ghostly forms shimmering beneath the moonlight, their presence draining warmth from the air, chilling her to her core. Their eyes, dark and filled with an otherworldly knowing, locked onto Gemma.

Hannah stepped forward, a harsh whisper that cut through the silence, sharp as broken glass. "You thought you could rid yourself of us?" she said, her tone dripping with disdain. "You are bound to us by blood, child. There is no escape."

Gemma's stomach turned to ice. She glanced at Stella and Isobel, but they remained locked within the circle, their eyes closed, their focus unbroken. They did not see what she saw. Shadow, sensing the threat, let out an angry screech, positioning himself between Gemma and the spirits, trembling with fury.

Margaret's twisted smile stretched unnaturally, her eyes glinting with malice. "You've fought so hard, but you belong with us, Gemma. Your power, your potential lies with the darkness. You cannot change what you were born to be."

The words were an icy weight pressing down on her, the world around her dimming. The mist thickened, shadows deepening, the cold biting into her skin. Gemma shook her head, but she couldn't move, her feet feeling rooted to the ground, as if the earth itself held her captive.

Grace spoke next, soft and saccharine, dripping with mock sympathy. "Why fight it, my dear? You were born to embrace this darkness, to wield its power. It's who you are."

Hannah's nails raked across Gemma's cheek, carving a jagged line that burned as though laced with fire. The sharp sting snapped through her like a whip, forcing a gasp from her lips as blood trickled hot against her trembling fingers. She staggered, her hand instinctively pressing against the wound, the metallic tang of blood mingling with the unnatural heat radiating from the gash. The pain was visceral, a physical manifestation of Hannah's cruel intent but it wasn't enough to shatter her entirely.

Gemma's chest heaved, her heart pounding a frantic rhythm that matched the chaos in her mind. Panic surged like an unrelenting tide, drowning her in the weight of their whispered promises and accusations. The darkness pressed in from all sides, suffocating, relentless. Her limbs felt leaden, her will cracking beneath the oppressive force of their power. Their words clawed at her thoughts, feeding on her doubts, whispering truths she had feared all along, this darkness was her legacy, inescapable, binding. Who was she to resist what had shaped her from the beginning?

Out of the corner of her eye, she caught movement. A small shape, a flash of fur. Shadow.

He darted toward her, his little paws patting at her legs, his bright eyes staring into hers. He let out a chitter, sharp and insistent, a sound that pierced through the suffocating fog that surrounded her, a reminder of something more, something brighter.

Gemma closed her eyes, focusing on that sound, holding onto it like a lifeline. She thought of Isobel, her cousin, her sister in all but blood, who had never given up on her. She thought of Stella, Marisol, Jane, and all the people who had taken her in, who had shown her love when she had been lost and afraid. They had brought light into her life, the love that had carried her through even the darkest moments.

The darkness was tempting, it always had been. It promised power, control, an end to the fear and helplessness she had endured for so long. But it came at a cost. One she was no longer willing to pay.

Her eyes snapped open, her gaze locking onto Hannah. "No!" She trembled, but her strength grew within her. "I choose light. I choose love. You have no power over me."

The spirits recoiled, their forms flickered like candle flames caught in a gust of wind. The fog swirled around them, their expressions twisting with fury. Shadow let out another screech, darting toward the mist, snapping at it, unyielding.

Gemma took a step forward, the ground no longer holding her back. She could feel it, the power within her, not the dark magick of her ancestors, but a power born from love, from hope, from the people who stood by her. It was her strength, her light, and it was enough.

Gemma's eyes blazed as she took a deep breath, pulling all the power she had from deep within herself. She raised her arms, her fingers spread wide, sensing the energy that had always been hers to command. Her heartbeat slowed, her mind sharpened, no hesitation, no fear.

She focused, her lips moving in a whispered incantation, and the air responded. The wind picked up, swirling through the cemetery, sweeping away the dark fog that clung to the ground. Her hair whipped around her face, her dress flaring in the gusts that spun faster and faster. Leaves and dust lifted into the air, forming a spiral of power that radiated from her.

Above her, the sky darkened, storm clouds rolling in, pulled by the force of her magick. They churned and twisted, blotting out the full moon until only slivers of silvery light escaped through the dark mass. The wind howled through the trees, bending branches, ripping leaves free from their boughs, the air charged with a palpable, electric energy.

Gemma's cry rang out, commanding the storm, summoning its fury. The raw power of the elements pulsated through her veins. The control she had over the chaos built up inside her. A bolt of lightning cracked across the sky, illuminating the graveyard in a blinding white light, splitting the air with an ear-rupturing roar that shattered the silence of the night.

She brought her arms down with a sharp motion, and the wind obeyed. It spiraled in, tightening around the spirits of her ancestors, a whirlwind of raw power and magick. Dark clouds swirled above, flashing with the energy of lightning contained within, ready to strike at her command. The ancestors' forms shifted, their shadows bending under the force of the gale, the howling wind drowning out their voices.

Another lightning strike followed her command, searing the ground. Energy surged through Gemma, igniting her senses as if she were a conduit for something vast and untamed, a force that pulsed in time with her will, unyielding and unstoppable. She stared at the shadows, at Hannah, Margaret, and Grace, and saw their forms shudder under the relentless onslaught of wind and lightning, their dark presence fading.

"You will not control me!" Her voice rang across the graveyard, every word backed by the storm's power. "I will never be what you want me to be."

The spirits howled in protest, but their cries lost to the winds as their forms dissolved, pulled apart by the fury she commanded. One by one, they disintegrated, dark shadows unraveling into nothingness, dissolving into the mist. The wind carried their voices away, fading into silence, leaving only the storm's roar behind.

Once the storm reached its peak, Gemma flicked her wrists. The winds slowed, the storm clouds broke apart, drifting away, revealing the moonlight once more. The veil closed, the heavy pressure of the spirits' presence lifted, warmth returning as the mist dissipated, leaving the graveyard bathed in the moon's soft, pure light.

Gemma stood there, her chest heaving, the power still humming through her, though now calmer, quieter. She had done it—she had controlled her power and unleashed it with confidence. The darkness was gone, and she was still herself. A smile, small but filled with triumph, spread across her lips as she lowered her arms, the air now still around her. She had fought back against the darkness, and this time, she had won.

The spirits howled, their forms disintegrating, dissolving into the mist, their voices fading into nothingness. The veil closed, the pressure lifted, warmth returning as the fog dissipated, leaving only the moonlight, bright and pure.

Gemma stood in the circle, her breath coming in short gasps, her entire body trembling. Shadow ran to her, his little paws climbing up her skirts, his head pressing against her shoulder, a soft chitter escaping him, as though he were comforting her.

She kneeled, wrapping her arms around him, tears streaming down her face, tears of relief, of release. She held him close, whispering, "Thank you, Shadow."

Stella and Isobel stirred as the spell's energy ebbed, the cemetery settling into an uneasy calm. Their gazes shifted to Gemma, but their expressions changed the moment they saw her. Tears streaked her face, but it was the angry, jagged wound slashing across her cheek that froze them in place. The gash, still oozing blood, stood as a stark testament to the battle she had fought, though its cause remained a mystery to them.

"Gemma," Isobel gasped, rushing to her side. Her eyes brimmed with alarm and love as she reached out, her fingers hesitating before gently brushing Gemma's shoulder. "What happened? Are you hurt anywhere else?" Her voice wavered, barely above a whisper, but her concern cut through the quiet.

Stella joined them, her brow furrowed as she knelt to get a closer look at the wound. "Who did this to you?" she asked, her voice firm but trembling with restrained fury. "Gemma, what's going on? Tell us."

Their concern wrapped around Gemma like a balm, but it couldn't soothe the ache in her chest. She lowered her hand from the wound, revealing the blood smeared across her palm. "It's over," she said softly, her voice raw. "I did what I had to."

Isobel's hand tightened on Gemma's shoulder. "Whatever happened out there, we'll face it together," she said, her tone resolute, though her eyes remained locked on the wound as if it might reveal the answers Gemma couldn't yet speak.

Gemma rose, her legs shaky but her heart steady. She looked at the necklace lying in the center of the circle, now just a lifeless trinket, stripped of its power. The weight she had carried for so long, the fear of what she might become, had lifted.

She was free.

Hannah's sanctuary, buried deep within the spectral forest, quaked under the force of her fury. Shadows writhed and stretched unnaturally, dark tendrils snaking through the air as though alive, mirroring her inner turmoil. The twisted trees groaned under the weight of her anger, their claw-like branches creaking as if caught in a storm only they could feel. The clearing vibrated with oppressive energy, the ancient stones littering the ground glowing faintly with the residue of her spent magick.

She paced, her nails digging into her palms until they threatened to draw blood. Her rage was a living thing, coiling and snapping inside her. The cursed necklace, the culmination of decades of malice and planning, was destroyed. The chains she and her mother had painstakingly crafted, meant to bind Gemma to the darkness forever, had crumbled to dust.

"Gone!" she hissed, her voice venomous as it cut through the suffocating air. "All that work, all that power, wasted!" Her steps faltered as her voice cracked, and she stood motionless for a moment, her shoulders trembling.

The forest seemed to close in around her, the malevolent magick that bound this place now feeding off her despair. The gnarled roots beneath her feet churned, as though mocking her failure. She wanted to scream, to lash out, to tear this cursed sanctuary apart piece by piece, but her power, though vast, would never be enough to fix this.

"You weren't strong enough," a voice cut through the gloom, smooth and sharp as a knife.

Hannah whirled around, her eyes blazing as Margaret stepped into the clearing. Her daughter moved with the poise of someone untouchable, the flickering shadows bending as though bowing in her presence.

"Here to gloat?" Hannah spat, her voice dripping with bitterness.

Margaret's lips curled into a sly smile, her tone patronizing. "I don't need to gloat, dear mother. Your failure speaks for itself. Again." Her eyes gleamed as she gestured to the forest around them, its darkness seeming to grow heavier under her scrutiny. "First Lillian, then Mary, and now Gemma. Do you ever grow tired of losing?"

Hannah's rage boiled over. "Don't you dare," she snarled, advancing on Margaret. "You agreed to this plan, Margaret! You said she was the perfect vessel. Her bloodline, her hunger for power, it was all there. This wasn't my failure alone."

Margaret didn't flinch. If anything, her smile deepened, cutting through the oppressive air like a dagger. "Oh, I agreed because I knew you would fail. I've always trusted your ability to fall short, Hannah. But even I underestimated just how spectacularly you'd manage it this time."

The insult landed like a slap, but Hannah refused to back down. "She was ours! She had the potential to be the greatest of us, to carry our legacy to heights we could only dream of!" Her fists trembled at her sides. "If it weren't for those fools she calls family—"

"Excuses," Margaret interrupted, her voice cold. "You underestimated the light in her, just as you underestimated Lillian before her. You've always been blinded by ambition. That's your flaw, Hannah. You think raw power is enough, but you forget how much stronger people can be when they have something to fight for."

Hannah's jaw clenched, but before she could retort, the forest erupted in a cacophony of rustling and snapping. The trees themselves seemed to recoil, their groans turning into keening wails as Grace emerged from the shadows. Her presence, colder than the grave, silenced them both.

Grace's expression was etched with disdain, her ghostly form flickering as if the forest itself rejected her. "Enough bickering," she said, her voice low and commanding, reverberating with a power that silenced the other two. "Do you think your petty squabbles will change the fact that we've lost her? That our plans lie in ruins?"

Margaret, always quick to mask her emotions, inclined her head. "And yet, here you are, Grace. Come to point out the obvious?"

Grace's flickering form solidified for a moment, her piercing gaze locking on Hannah. "You failed us," she said, her words like ice. "Your reckless pursuit of Gemma cost us everything. And now, we are nothing but fading shadows."

The accusation sliced through Hannah, but her defiance flared in response. "I did what I had to do to secure our legacy!" she shot back, her voice trembling with emotion. "Don't act as though you wouldn't have done the same!"

Grace's eyes burned with fury, her ghostly form towering as the clearing darkened further. "Your arrogance has undone centuries of work!" Her voice was a gale, the force of her anger rippling through the spectral forest, bending branches and extinguishing the faint glow of the stones.

Hannah's breath hitched, the oppressive energy pressing down on her chest. For the first time, her resolve faltered under the weight of their shared rage.

Margaret stepped forward, her voice cutting through the tension like a scalpel. "And yet," she said, her tone measured, "not all is lost."

Grace turned on her, her fury unabated. "What are you talking about, Mother?"

Margaret's smile was razor-sharp, her eyes gleaming with a cruel satisfaction. "A sliver of the curse remains. Isobel carries it now."

Hannah froze, the weight of the revelation crashing down on her. "Isobel?" she whispered, the name laced with disbelief and dawning realization.

Grace's form flickered again, her expression shifting from rage to something colder, more calculating. "Explain," she demanded.

Margaret's smile widened. "When the spell broke, a fragment of the curse clung to Isobel. It's subtle, but it's there, feeding, growing. And as it grows, so will our influence."

The forest fell silent as the weight of her words settled over them. For a moment, even Grace seemed at a loss, her form wavering before she regained her composure.

Hannah's lips curled into a wicked grin, the flicker of hope in her chest igniting into something far darker. "So we haven't lost everything," she said, her voice soft but filled with new determination. "Isobel might be our key after all."

Margaret nodded. "And through her, Gemma will fall. She won't see it coming. Not until it's too late."

Grace's gaze lingered on Margaret, then shifted to Hannah. "Then we have work to do," she said, her tone cold and resolute.

Hannah's smile widened, the flickering light of the spectral forest catching in her eyes. "Let them think they've won," she purred. "Let them revel in their so-called victory. We'll remind them soon enough that darkness never truly fades."

The spectral forest seemed to shiver in agreement, the ancient stones glowing faintly once more as the witches began to plot anew. Their defeat had not broken them; it had only sharpened their resolve. And in the shadows, their vengeance waited, patient and unrelenting.

CHAPTER TWENTY-NINE

ISOBEL STEPPED ONTO THE boardwalk in front of her store where the crisp October air of Tin Creek carried a promise that whispered of change. The chill cut through her coat, and a fine wisp of fog clung to the edges of buildings, shrouding the quiet town in a soft, early-morning haze. The maple leaves, with shades of orange, yellow, and crimson, cast a vision of warmth across the chilly morning. Fall had settled over the small Montana town, wrapping it in a season of transition.

Isobel drew in a deep breath, the piney scent of the Ponderosa mingling with the earthy aroma of fallen leaves and the faint bite of wood smoke from nearby chimneys. It was a smell she'd always loved, a reminder of endings and beginnings, of seasons turning in their constant rhythm. But this October weighed heavier than any other. They had escaped a darkness that almost swallowed her cousin whole.

Her gaze drifted down Main Street, past the early fall wreaths and the scattered pumpkins that adorned storefronts. Despite the festive colors of the season, a dark shadow had loomed over them, threatening to shatter the delicate balance they had fought to maintain. The curse that almost took Gemma had drained her powers and left her a shell of the person she had been. She feared what might have happened if they failed.

But with dawn breaking through the fog, Isobel let herself breathe now that the ritual had worked. The necklace's curse had shattered, and a weight lifted from her shoulders. The secrets they kept, their magick and all that it entailed, still haunted her thoughts. But today, she sensed the town exhaling for the first time in weeks.

Leaning against the wooden railing, she watched Tin Creek as it woke up. Stores stood as silent sentinels in the mist, their windows dark, but the faint murmur of life whispered from within. Children passed on their way to school, their breaths visible in the cold air, scarves wrapped around their small faces. Dawn, the baker, swept her stoop, the soft swish of the broom adding a domestic rhythm to the waking world.

A familiar face approached, the clip-clop of hooves announcing John before she saw him. He rode up, his face bright even against the cold, his hair tousled by the wind. When their eyes met, warmth filled his gaze, and he dismounted, making his way toward her. Without a word, he wrapped his arm around her waist, pulling her close in a comforting embrace.

"It's a beautiful morning," he murmured. "Feels like I haven't seen you breathe easy in weeks."

Isobel allowed herself to smile, leaning into his warmth. His arm was a steadying presence, a reminder of everything good in the storm of her life. She rested her head on his chest, savoring the simple comfort. "I'm finally starting to believe it's over," she whispered. "It's been a nightmare. I didn't think we'd make it. We almost lost her, John."

His gaze turned serious, softening as he looked down at her. "She was so ill," he said. "I can't tell you how glad I am that she's okay now. She's like a little sister..." He trailed off, pulling her closer.

Emotion welled in her chest, tight and raw. The day would come when she'd have to tell him everything, the magick, the rituals, the hidden battles they fought, but for now, he knew only that Gemma had been ill.

"Gemma's recovery does feel like a miracle," she said, leaning back enough to meet his eyes. Shadows flickered in her mind, images of the dark tendrils, the sinister pull of the necklace. "I'm very grateful we made it through. For a while, I thought..."

Her voice broke, the memories too vivid, too near.

John cupped her cheek, his thumb brushing her skin, chasing away the shadows. "You've been so strong, Isobel," he said, his words filled with love and admiration. "You never gave up. It's one thing I love most about you."

Isobel blushed, his touch grounding her in the present, away from the fear. He had been her rock, his presence and love holding her together when everything else fell apart. The secret of her magick weighed heavy, but she pushed it aside for now, focusing on him and the promise in his eyes.

John smiled, a flicker of excitement brightening his gaze. "Speaking of...," he began, shifting the tone, "with Gemma feeling better, I was hoping we could finally start planning our wedding. What do you think?"

She blinked, surprised, her heart skipping a beat at the joy in his voice. After everything she'd been through, the idea of planning a wedding seemed almost surreal. It was exactly what she needed.

"I want to start thinking about it all, the ceremony, the flowers, your dress..." He paused, lifting her hand and pressing a soft kiss to her knuckles. "I want it to be perfect, Isobel, like you."

Her heart warmed, spreading through her chest like sunlight breaking through a fog. She could see it, their wedding, surrounded by the people they loved, laughter mingling with the crisp air. A future that once appeared out of reach, but now she let herself trust it might come true.

"I'd like that," she whispered, full of sincerity. "To finally start planning our life together. It's time to focus on something beautiful."

John's smile widened, his enthusiasm catching. He leaned down, brushing a kiss against her forehead. "How about a spring wedding? By the Bitterroot River, just us, the people we love, and nature. Like we always talked about."

Her eyes widened as a flutter started in her stomach and reached her throat. A simple wedding, outdoors, surrounded by the beauty of Montana—nothing extravagant. "That sounds perfect," she agreed, her heart swelling. "Wildflowers and greenery. Nothing more, nothing less."

John nodded, his eyes holding hers, the love there unmistakable. "Exactly. Simple, like us."

The weight that had pressed on her chest for weeks eased with each word they exchanged, replaced by something soft and hopeful. A reminder that even after the darkest nights, there was light. Life moved on, and they still had each other.

She glanced inside the store, catching sight of Gemma and Stella working over some herbal teas. She let out a deep, gratifying sigh—seeing her cousin, vibrant and alive, with no darkness marring her soul.

"Gemma's looking better already," John remarked, following her gaze.

"She is," Isobel agreed. "She's been through much, and yet, she's still here, still fighting."

Gemma looked up and waved, her smile radiant. Isobel returned the gesture, warmth flooding her chest.

Gemma's power, her magick, had faded. Isobel had watched her struggle, the quiet sorrow in her cousin's eyes when she couldn't tap into the forces that had once been hers. But for now, they had each other.

Turning back to John, Isobel got swept up into their future. "We should include Gemma in the planning," she said, her tone light. "She could help with flowers. She's good with arrangements."

John chuckled. "She'll love that. Stella, too. They both deserve some happiness after everything that's happened. My mother would love the help."

Isobel nodded, leaning into him as warmth flooded her chest. For the first time in a while, she let herself imagine the life ahead—a life filled with laughter, love, and hope.

And it was enough.

Gemma stood motionless in the center of her bedroom, her eyes closed, her breath slow and deliberate as she strained to sense the familiar hum of energy that once pulsed through the space. She came in here to reconnect, to rediscover the magick that always lived close to the surface of her skin. But since they broke the curse, the air was still. No whispers from the past, no vibrations of history or lingering emotions.

The room, which once buzzed with the weight of untold stories and secrets waiting to be uncovered, felt empty. Silent. Hollow.

Gemma opened her eyes, the reality of her situation hitting her like a punch to the gut. The abilities that once defined her, her power to read minds, her gift to glimpse the past in objects, her ability to create illusions were gone. Lost. And with them, it appeared, the very essence of who she was.

Shadow sat on her dresser, his beady eyes watching her. He sensed her distress, his small paws fidgeting as he scanned his surroundings, as if searching for something that might bring back the magick they both knew was missing.

She glanced around the room, disconnected, like a stranger in her own life. The walls, once alive with mystical layers and unseen truths, now bare and lifeless. The air was devoid of the magick that had always been her companion. Her loss swelled, a deep and suffocating ache in her chest.

Her gaze fell on the antique mirror hanging on the far wall, its surface gleaming in the fading sunlight. That mirror was once her window into the past, a portal through which she had seen forgotten moments and long-buried memories. It had shown her truths, revealed mysteries. But now, as she strolled toward it, desperation crept into her every step. All she saw was the scar, still raw and red, cut a line across her cheekbone, a mark of the battle she'd barely survived. She traced it lightly, her fingers trembling. It wasn't just a wound, it was proof that she'd faced the darkness and survived.

Gemma's fingers brushed the cool glass, her reflection staring back at her, hollow and tired. She focused hard, willing herself to connect to even the faintest thread of magick. She had done this many times before with ease. But the mirror's surface remained impenetrable, offering her no glimpse of the past, no visions, no answers. Only her own face, etched with worry and fatigue.

Shadow scurried across the dresser, chittering. He reached out with his tiny hands and tapped the mirror, tilting his head as if expecting it to react. When nothing happened, he turned his gaze back to Gemma, his curious eyes searching her face, almost as if to say, "Where did it all go?"

A sharp pang of loss gripped her heart. Part of her soul was severed, torn away in the aftermath of breaking the curse that had threatened her life. Her powers had always been more than a tool, they were her identity, her connection to the world around her. Without them, she floated adrift, unmoored in a sea of uncertainty.

She stepped back from the mirror, her body tense, her heart heavy. The weight of her lost magick pressed down on her, and for a moment, the crushing isolation came with it. How could she continue without the gifts that had defined her? How could she navigate the world when she could no longer sense its hidden layers?

Shadow hopped to the floor, approaching her feet. He pawed at her leg, making a soft noise that brought Gemma back to the present. She kneeled, scooping him into her arms, feeling his warmth against her chest. He nuzzled her, his little whiskers tickling her skin as if trying to comfort her.

The sound of the door creaking open broke through her spiraling thoughts. Gemma straightened, forcing a smile onto her lips as Isobel entered. Isobel's sharp gaze scanned the space, sensing the tension before she even spoke. Jane followed close behind, carrying a basket of freshly laundered linens.

"Hey," Gemma said, her tone overly bright, brittle as glass. She waved around the room. "Tidying up."

Isobel's eyes narrowed. "Everything okay here?" she asked.

Gemma nodded, her movements stiff, unnatural. "Yeah. Trying to stay busy." She tucked a loose strand of hair behind her ear, hoping neither of them would see through her flimsy attempt at normalcy.

Jane smiled. "That's good," she said, setting the basket on a nearby chair. "It's always nice to keep things fresh. But don't do too much yet."

Gemma's gaze snapped to the table where an old grimoire lay open, its pages alive with ancient spells, cryptic symbols, and secrets not meant for prying eyes. Panic flared in her chest, and she rushed forward to close it, but she could already see the curiosity flicker in Jane's face, her attention hooked.

"What's this?" Jane asked, her tone light but inquisitive as she reached out and brushed her fingers across the worn leather cover. She flipped through the yellowed pages, scanning the intricate drawings and strange text.

Gemma's heart pounded in her chest. Without her ability to read Jane's thoughts, the uncertainty of the moment hit her hard. She swallowed the rising panic, her throat tightening. "Just an old book," she said, her tone forced, casual. "I found it, among some other things. It's full of... interesting stories."

Jane's eyes shined with curiosity. "It looks fascinating. Where did you find it?"

Gemma's stomach twisted. The vulnerability of the moment, of being exposed without her powers to shield her, made her raw, fragile. She forced another smile, strained. "Oh, I found it tucked away in a box. I thought I'd take a look."

Isobel stepped closer, her sharp gaze moving between the book and Gemma. Her expression softened with understanding. "Old books like that can be... unpredictable. You never know what you might find inside."

Gemma nodded, her forced smile wavering as Isobel's words hung in the air. She wished she could sense what Jane was thinking, what she was feeling, but the emptiness inside her was overwhelming. It gnawed at her like a deep, unrelenting hunger—a reminder of what she had lost.

Jane, oblivious to the tension that lingered between the cousins, set the grimoire down and turned back to the basket of linens. The conversation drifted to lighter topics, but the undercurrent of anxiety and loss remained thick as the late afternoon shadows creeping across the floor.

Shadow, sensing Gemma's unease, nuzzled against her neck, his presence grounding her in the moment. Gemma sighed, holding him close, the soft weight of his body giving her a small measure of comfort.

Isobel lingered near Gemma. "If you need help," she said, low and full of care, "you know you can talk to me, right?"

Gemma swallowed hard, her throat tight as she tried to keep her emotions in check. She wanted to reach out, to tell Isobel everything, the fear, the emptiness, the loss, but the words lodged in her throat. She wasn't ready to face it. Not yet. "Thanks, Isobel. I appreciate that."

The weight of her lost magick pressed on her like a stone, heavy and unyielding. She had always read the thoughts of those around her, to see glimpses of their intentions, their fears. It had given her confidence, a sense of control. Without it, everything was chaotic and unpredictable. And the illusion-making... that had been her way of shielding herself, of creating beauty and hiding behind it when the world was too much. Now she had nothing. Except the cold, hard reality of the here and now.

The silence between them stretched for a moment before Isobel nodded and turned to join Jane in folding the linens. Their voices became a soft murmur in the background, a stark contrast to the turmoil churning inside Gemma. Like a ghost, she haunted her own life, disconnected from everything that had once made her feel alive.

Shadow jumped out of her arms, landing on the floor. He scampered over to the basket of linens, poking his nose in as if to help, his antics drawing a brief smile from Jane. Gemma watched him, the small flicker of warmth in her chest breaking through the numbness, if only for a moment.

She returned a quick glace at the mirror, hoping, praying for some sign of her old self, for some remnant of the power that once coursed through her. But her reflection offered only emptiness, her own hollow eyes staring back at her.

Losing her magick was like having the very core of her soul hollowed out, leaving behind an aching emptiness. It had been her essence, her tether to the world, the part of her that shimmered with purpose and made her whole. Now she drifted, untethered, through a life that felt foreign and barren, each day blurring into the next. How could she move forward, stripped of the gifts that once defined her?

But as she watched Isobel and Jane work, their easy companionship a comfort she couldn't quite reach, a flicker of determination sparked deep within her. Magick had saved her life. The price was her powers, but the sacrifice preserved something far more precious: her soul, her family, her future. And that was worth fighting for.

Gemma inhaled deeply, the weight on her chest loosening a little. She had a second chance. Even without her magick, she would find a way forward. She had Isobel, Stella, Marisol, and Jane by her side, and that was more powerful than any spell she could cast.

She crossed the room and joined them at the table, picking up a folded sheet and smoothing it out with her hands. The small, mundane task brought a strange sense of peace, grounding her in the moment. The world may well be muted now, but that didn't mean it was lost. She would learn to navigate this new reality, one step at a time.

As the late afternoon light faded and the room grew dim, the shadows were a little less oppressive. Gemma might have lost her magick, but she hadn't lost herself. And that, she realized, was more important.

Shadow, satisfied that his work with the linens was complete, climbed back into Gemma's lap, curling up. He looked at her with his bright eyes, and the warmth of his presence was like a promise that she wasn't alone. Not now, not ever.

CHAPTER THIRTY

GEMMA STOOD BESIDE THE makeshift arbor, her soft blue brides-maid dress fluttering in the warm breeze, as if it enjoyed the freedom of the day. The late spring sun cast a golden glow and warmth over the rolling landscape. She took in the scene as Isobel, her cousin and closest friend, stood at the altar, her face radiant with happiness as she prepared to marry the love of her life, John. The valley, dotted with wildflowers in full bloom, mirrored the joy that filled the air, the bright colors of nature blending with the vibrant emotions of the day.

Shadow, her raccoon familiar, sat beside her with his tiny blue bowtie that matched Gemma's dress perched askew. He peered at the guests gathered along the riverbank, his bright eyes flickering with curiosity and mischief. Getting that bowtie on him had been an ordeal, one filled with chittering complaints and stubborn paws. Eventually, a shiny button had served as the bribe that got him to wear it, and now, he carried himself with as much dignity as any raccoon could muster.

Gemma exhaled, the tightness in her chest a stark contrast to the laughter and cheer that surrounded her. Gemma clenched her hands in the folds of her dress, her gaze flickering to Isobel's radiant smile.

This was what Isobel and John had dreamed of for so long, a day that should have filled her heart with unshakable joy. But an emptiness gnawed at her. She stood there, smiling at her cousin, but her own sense of loss echoed beneath it all.

The world carried a muted stillness now, quieter and hollow since the day her magick slipped away. Once, she had felt the pulse of life itself, the invisible threads binding all things together. Her mind had been a doorway to thoughts, her touch a window into memories, her illusions so vivid they blurred the line between dream and reality. Magick wasn't just a skill; it had been the essence of her being, woven into the fabric of her soul. Now, stripped of it, everything seemed distant, as though she lingered on the edges of her own life, peering through a fogged pane of glass at something she could no longer reach.

She clenched her hands at her sides, trying to push away the thought, to focus on the joy radiating from Isobel and John as they stood together at the altar. The wind rustled through the branches of the cottonwood trees, sending a gentle breeze across the gathering. She wanted to absorb it all, the beauty of the day, the love that surrounded them, but it was like grasping sand in her fingers; no matter how tightly she held on, the feeling slipped away.

The soft strumming of a guitar filled the air, and Gemma watched Isobel's face light up as John took her hands in his.

Gemma pressed a hand to her chest, her breath catching as she watched Isobel's joy radiate like sunlight. Her lips curved in a small smile, but it didn't reach her eyes. An emptiness gnawed at her, a hollow place where her powers had once been. She had surrendered them to stave off the darkness she feared, to protect the people she loved, but the cost lingered. A fragment of herself had been lost in the trade, leaving her wondering if it would ever return.

Shadow waddled forward, his sights set on a shiny silver locket dangling from a guest's bag. His little paws were outstretched, eyes glinting with excitement. Gemma spotted him just in time. "Shadow!" she whispered, her eyes narrowing. He paused, looking back at her with an innocent tilt of his head, as if to say, "What? I wasn't doing anything." She let out a laugh, shaking her head. He sighed dramatically, scurrying back to her side and plopping down on the grass, sulking in exaggerated fashion.

Gemma kneeled beside him, scratching his head. "We've talked about this. No stealing today." He chittered at her, his ears twitching, and she smiled despite the ache in her chest. At least he was still here, her constant companion, reminding her of what remained.

The Bitterroot River glimmered under the afternoon sun, its waters flowing gently past the clearing where the ceremony unfolded. The river's murmurs blended with the laughter of guests and the gentle rustling of leaves, creating a symphony that should have filled her soul. But to Gemma, it all sounded hollow, as if thick wool wrapped around the world, muffling its sounds. The emotions that once pulsed around her with vivid intensity were like whispers lost in a storm, faint, distant, barely reaching her ears. It was as though someone turned down the world's volume, leaving her to navigate an echo of what used to be.

Isobel's voice broke through the fog in her mind, reciting her vows to John, her words clear. Gemma looked up, catching Isobel's gaze. There was no magick in their connection anymore, no telepathic link that allowed them to share thoughts. But the understanding between them was still there. Isobel's eyes held love and reassurance, as if she sensed the emptiness inside Gemma and wanted to tell her it was okay, that she was still loved, still important.

Tears pricked at Gemma's eyes, her emotions swirling in a complicated mix of joy for Isobel and sorrow for herself. She fought them back, focusing on her cousin's radiant smile, the love that shone between Isobel and John. This was what mattered—family, love, and the bonds that held them together. Her magick had been a part of her, but it wasn't all of her. She had to believe that.

Shadow, perhaps sensing the shift in Gemma's emotions, hopped onto a nearby stump, standing on his hind legs as he tried to get a better view of the proceedings. He let out an excited chitter, drawing laughter from a few guests nearby. Gemma's smile spread across her face. He was always there, reminding her to find joy even in the small things.

The officiant pronounced Isobel and John husband and wife, and as they kissed, the gathered crowd erupted into applause. Gemma clapped, her smile broadening, her heart swelling with pride for her cousin. Despite everything they had faced, despite the darkness that had almost torn them apart, they were here. They made it.

As the newlyweds made their way down the aisle, Gemma stepped forward, wrapping Isobel in a tight embrace. The chaos inside her stilled, and for the first time in what seemed like forever, the world settled. Isobel's arms drew her close, their warmth steadying her, the unspoken love and strength in that embrace anchoring her to something solid. The sensation was clear, undeniable, she was not alone, and she never would be.

"I'm proud of you," Isobel whispered, thick with emotion, her lips brushing Gemma's ear.

Gemma pulled back, meeting her cousin's eyes. "I'm proud of you too," she replied. "This is your day. You deserve every bit of this happiness."

Isobel smiled, her eyes glistening with unshed tears. "It's our day," she corrected. "We've been through so much together, and I wouldn't have made it here without you."

The words warmed Gemma's heart, dispelling some of the darkness that clung to her thoughts. Yes, she lost her magick, but she had the things that mattered, her family, her friends, and her place in Tin Creek. She survived what could have destroyed her, and she was still standing. That was something to be proud of.

The reception carried on into the evening, the laughter and warmth of those gathered filling the valley. Shadow, still wearing his crooked bowtie, charmed a child into giving him a piece of cake. He held it triumphantly, waddling over to Gemma with a proud chitter, his paws sticky from the frosting.

"Shadow, what have you got there?" Gemma laughed, stooping to examine his prize. He looked up at her, his eyes sparkling, and laughed. "You little rascal," she said, giving him a scratch behind the ears. He chittered again, munching on the cake, pleased with himself.

Gemma straightened, her gaze drifting over the gathering. Lanterns hung from tree branches, casting a soft golden glow over the guests. The laughter of children mixed with the soft notes of a fiddle playing in the background. She looked over to where Isobel and John were dancing, her cousin's head resting on John's shoulder, a look of pure contentment on her face. The sight brought a smile to Gemma's lips. The world might not be as vibrant as it had once been, but it was still filled with love, still full of small moments of beauty.

She turned her face up to the sky, the first stars beginning to twinkle in the dusky blue. The pain of losing her magick was still there, a dull ache that never went away. But perhaps that was okay. Perhaps wholeness wasn't the key to happiness. Maybe all she needed was to be fully present, here and now, surrounded by the people who mattered most.

As she watched the stars, a gentle breeze rustled the leaves, carrying with it the scent of the river and wildflowers. For the first time in what felt like forever, a spark of genuine hope lit within Gemma. Though a piece of her was gone, she could see the possibility of carving out a new path. A different magick, one built from love, resilience, and the people who stood by her side.

Shadow nudged at her ankle, looking at her with frosting still smeared on his nose. She laughed, bending over to scoop him into her arms. "Alright, little troublemaker," she said, pressing her face against his fur. He snuggled against her, his small body warm and comforting in her arms.

She might not have her magick, but she still had this. And for now, that was enough.

THE END

If you would like to keep up with the next release in The Frontier Witches Series and receive short stories, sign up for my newsletter at https://www.annettegrantham.com/fire-witch-newsletter/

Acknowledgements

Writing *Air Witch* required more determination than I ever anticipated. Over the course of crafting this story, I faced two surgeries, while my husband underwent one of his own. These challenges forced me to pause and reevaluate—not just the manuscript, but also myself. As much as I longed to immerse myself fully in Gemma's journey, I had to take a step back. In doing so, I began to recognize how deeply her story mirrored my own struggles.

Through Gemma, I poured out my experiences with anxiety—the way it gnaws at self-confidence and makes the simplest decisions seem insurmountable. Her growth became a reflection of my own. She wrestled with the weight of her ancestors' expectations and her fears of not being enough, much as I wrestled with my own doubts. But by the end, she found her voice. She stood tall, confronted her past, and took control of her future—a triumph that I hope inspires those who read her story.

My guiding phrase for 2024 has been "step out of your comfort zone," and this book became a testament to that promise. Like Gemma, I've been learning to embrace the unknown, to challenge myself, and to take bold steps forward. I hope you found joy in watching Gemma rise to face her ancestors, cast off their expectations, and claim her own path. In many ways, her defiance was my own, and sharing it with you has been a profound privilege.

The camaraderie and critiques from the Lewis County Writers Guild have been the whetstone for my skills, sharpening my ability to present you with a story worthy of your time. The collective wisdom of Amy Flugel, Margie Keck Smith, Wayne Wallace, Beverley Gowan, Johanna Flynn, and Kristen Franklin has been a blessing to my writer's journey. Their generosity of spirit is a debt of gratitude I carry, hoping to pay it forward with each word I write.

The vibrant community of 20Booksto50K, now Author Nation has been a beacon, illuminating the path from manuscript to marketplace. The collective knowledge shared through Facebook and Discord interactions, and annual conferences has armed me with the tools to bring this book to you, coupled with a dose of inspiration and an atlas of authorship.

Margie Keck Smith and Aimee Cardenas deserves a special mention for their roles as beta readers par excellence. Their insights have been crucial in refining the pages you hold.

To my children and stalwart cheerleaders, Rick Garza and Jennifer Swafford: their unwavering support and boundless enthusiasm have been my guiding lights. Their beliefs in my dreams fuels my courage to chase them.

At the heart of it all is Dale Grantham, my husband, who embraces my pre-dawn-bound writing rituals with love and understanding.

Last, to you, dear reader—your journey through the pages to the end fills this endeavor with meaning. Thank you for your time, your thoughts, and, if you're so inclined, your reviews. They are the lifeblood of a writer's evolution. The tale continues with a new witch and a new setting. I'm excited and I hope you are, too. Please sign up for my newletter on my website https://www.annettegran tham.com so I can keep you up-to-date.

About the Author

Annette Grantham's life reads like one of her richly imagined fantasy novels—filled with journeys, discovery, and pursuing passions. Hailing from the bustling streets of New York, Annette's early years were a nomadic odyssey from the historic Northeast to the expansive heart of Texas. Her adventurous spirit found a home in the military, where she served with dedication and honor, before she embarked on a tech odyssey as a software engineer. However, beneath the code and uniform, a storyteller's heart beat with fervent imagination.

Annette's pen has always been mightier than a sword, and her lifelong dream to weave tales has come to fruition in her writing. She now crafts enthralling fantasy novels that stitch together her fascination with bygone eras and the mystical. Her four-book series, "The Frontier Witches," is where the grit of "Deadwood" (TV series and movie) meets the enchanting allure of "Practical Magic" by Alice Hoffman. Here, readers find themselves alongside bold and spirited heroines—witches who don't just navigate but flourish in the untamed frontiers of the Old West. The prequel to the series, "Dark Witch", sets you on the journey on how Mary and Stella end up in America after their mother, Lillian, is arrested and tortured for witchcraft.

Nestled in a snug cabin in Washington, where the wild whispers of nature are but a window away, Annette lives with her high school sweetheart under the watchful eyes of a lively squirrel congregation. Her home is not just a retreat but a wellspring of inspiration where she conjures her next spellbinding adventure.

Also by

Dark Witch

https://www.amazon.com/dp/B0CCQ9W3JS

Fire Witch

https://www.amazon.com/dp/B0CR1LJ3YB

Earth Witch

https://www.amazon.com/dp/B0CZ4J5ZWG